MILES TO GO

Amy Dawson Robertson

Bella
BOOKS
2010

Printed in the United States of America on acid-free paper
First Edition

Editor: Katherine V. Forrest
Cover Designer: Linda Callaghan

ISBN 10: 1-59493-174-7
ISBN 13: 978-1-59493-174-1

Dedication

For Mom, for always believing in me and for being the best there is, ever.

For S-H, for letting go of the aliens and encouraging me to take the space and time to write.

Acknowledgments

Many people were kind enough to read *Miles to Go* in its early stages and offer valuable feedback. Heartfelt thanks to:

Brad Buehler, Mary Buonanno, Robin Eastman Caldwell, Jen Champagne, Dana B., Karen DeSantis, Amanda Farrar, Paige Forrest, Elizabeth Frengel, Soniah Kamal, Sarah Leary, Adele Levine, Mari Millard, Barb Rich, Scott Ritter, Ella Schiralli and Beck Sheehy. And to my good friends from book club, many of whom were supportive early readers.

Thanks to my favorite Canadians, Donna Malthouse and Line Parent for lighting a fire under me by wanting to read chapter by chapter as the novel was being written.

Thanks to my editor, Katherine V. Forrest—it was an honor to work with her and I learned a lot through the process. And to Karin Kallmaker and Linda Hill for making it happen.

And finally to Sally Loy Woodward, to S-H and to Alexandra Ogilvie for being there nearly every step of the way and for their encouragement, boundless patience and good judgment.

PROLOGUE

January 2001
Senate Appropriations Subcommittee on Commerce, Justice and
State
United States Capitol
Washington, D.C.
Closed Session

"May we begin, Director Wilson?" The speaker was Marcia
Joplin, senior senator from Maine, and thorn in the side of
countless administration officials.

Stephen Wilson took a long drink of ice water and winced as
the cold struck a sensitive molar. He needed to see a dentist. Just
one more thing he didn't have time for. Rubbing his jaw, the FBI
Director raised his hand in assent. He was as ready as he would
ever be. Even for Senator Joplin.

Joplin was that rare breed of Republican, liberal as only a few
senators from small Northeastern states can be. She had muscled
her way into chairing this important subcommittee through an

1

impressive series of manipulations—she was a born politician and feared by many, including Stephen Wilson.

"This is your fifth appearance, Director, and we are here to discuss your budget request for a new international counter-terrorism team. Thank you for being here today." Joplin looked as if she were on fire, her trim figure clad in an exquisitely tailored red suit.

This was the last day of the closed budget hearings and the final item on the agenda was what a few within Wilson's inner circle had come to refer to as his pet project. It was much more than that for Wilson. It was an absolutely necessary response to a growing concern that no one seemed to be heeding. An international counterterrorism tactical team was needed to tamp down extremist factions that seemed to be sprouting mushroom-like across the globe. He wasn't against taking necessary steps to protect his country even if no arrests would ever be made—the FBI had long been more than just law enforcement. But getting his funding would be difficult and Wilson wasn't hopeful. With Joplin in control, he knew he probably wouldn't have the support he needed.

Joplin began. "To get to it, there is concern that too many funds are being directed toward what many see as a largely unsubstantiated threat. Are you prepared to make an argument for it?"

Unlike the majority of her GOP cohorts, Joplin was known to be disinclined to support defense measures that she saw as little more than undisguised sabre-rattling machismo. She was on record as being a firm believer in the generous allocation of funds for the defense of country, but in one particularly vivid interview she was quoted saying that she found it frightening that so many of her colleagues, and most alarmingly her superiors in the executive branch, seemed to be overgrown children in possession of the largest, most dangerous toy box in the world, courtesy of Boeing, Lockheed Martin, Northrop Grumman and the five branches of the U.S. Armed Forces.

Wilson cleared his throat and leaned into the microphone.

"Yes, Senator. As I'm sure you know, international terrorism has been on a dramatic rise in the last ten years. It is a dire threat to the United States and it will be on our shores if we don't do something about it. In the last five years alone, there has been a fifty-three percent increase in terror-related activities across the world."

Senator Joplin pursed her lips and removed her reading glasses, laying them on the dais, her favorite emphatic gesture. "That's a dramatic number, Director, but I fail to see what it has to do with us. And as I'm sure *you* know, our role is not to police the world but to protect our own people."

Such shortsightedness had plagued Wilson his entire career. "I can tell you, Senator, many of these events should be seen as an attack on American interests."

The chairwoman replaced her reading glasses on the tip of her nose and peered at the figures just handed to her. Clearly, she didn't like what she saw. Wilson knew that they flew in the face of her vision of the world as essentially benign. She finally looked up.

"And your argument for this is?"

"You're aware of the largest events. But there are countless other smaller attacks—they are outlined in the report we prepared for the committee. Hotel bombings where Americans are known to be staying. Kidnapping and hostage-taking of Americans abroad."

"What are other countries doing about this?"

"Not enough. We don't have sufficient diplomatic relations with many of the countries where these acts are taking place. These factions are not stupid. They know to hit us where we are weakest. That's why we need to take the lead and act now."

"The FBI's Hostage Rescue Team was originally designed to attend only to domestic matters but has long taken on international missions. Why can't they continue to cover that arena?" Joplin asked.

"A team functions best when it has a clear mandate. The Cold War is over. No state will attack us openly. Terrorist organizations, loosely aligned to a state or multiple states, perhaps secretly funded by them, are willing to enact a kind of warfare that has no parameters. No Geneva Convention, no moral code enforced by the social contract that we insist upon from established governments. We must have a team devoted to confronting if not controlling these groups. And we have to show other countries in the same boat that we are doing something about it."

For a moment, Wilson believed he had gotten through to her. Her eyes finally showed some kind of understanding. Then she shook her head.

"I appreciate your concern for our national security, Director. And your forward-thinking is something that the intelligence community has sorely lacked. But we are in a serious budget crisis and quite frankly I don't think we can afford to make ideological statements to foreign countries."

Wilson felt the muscles knot in his shoulders. He forced himself to relax before he continued. "If we don't, the terrorists will make their own statement, right here in Washington, D.C."

"But that's the point. They haven't hit us and you haven't made a case that they will. And, really, your scare tactics are a little much, Director. Let's get down to the nitty-gritty. How many personnel are you asking for?"

And that was it. Her face had closed and she would hear no more. Wilson looked at the other members of the committee, but they all looked tired and resigned to let Joplin win on this issue.

Wilson sighed deeply. What he was asking for wasn't much. A small beginning that could develop into something fundamentally important, once its efficacy was proven. "Okay. We're requesting fifty special operations agents, along with the necessary support staff. The fifty agents will be divided into tactical units to be deployed on specialized missions overseas designed to prevent current and future attacks on American interests at home and abroad."

"Now, word on the street," Joplin said, "is that the formation of this team is already underway—I hear you're calling it CT3 and that a call for applicants went out months ago under the auspices of an offshoot of the Hostage Rescue Team."

Wilson nodded.

"I'll remind you, Director, that this hearing is being recorded and vocalized responses are appreciated."

"That is correct, Senator," Wilson affirmed.

"And where did you find the money for this little independent venture of yours?"

"We were able to achieve efficiencies in several areas."

"That's very convenient."

Wilson said nothing.

"Yes, it's very convenient and it puts us in a difficult position since all the resources you've already put into this are for naught if you don't receive additional funding."

Wilson knew he'd made an enormous gamble, one that would be an embarrassment if it didn't pay off and would likely damage his career.

"But," she went on, "there's no way we can authorize that much money for this. We've been very generous with the rest of your budget request." She paused, eyebrows raised, and waited for Wilson to nod, indicating his agreement.

He did.

What a consummate bitch, he thought.

"In light of your impassioned argument we will authorize funds for twelve agents for this new team as a kind of pilot project. On one condition…" She paused, removing her reading glasses again, her eyes tightening before she continued. "I have long been frustrated with what I see as the Bureau's adherence to an outmoded sexism in their hiring practices on these specialized teams. For instance, as you know, women have never been members of the Hostage Rescue Team. I want to see that change with this new team."

Wilson was expecting this, had heard through one of his friends in the Senate that Joplin planned to make it an issue. That was why when he put out the call for applicants, he allowed, even encouraged, women to apply. John MacPherson, a former

Hostage Rescue Team operator and subsequent Special Agent in Charge, would be helming CT3 and he'd make damn sure no women were ever sent on any kind of assignment they couldn't handle.

The week before, Wilson had found a few hours in his schedule to drive down to Quantico and take a look at the group of people he believed might one day thwart the kinds of threats that Americans had yet to imagine. There were fifteen women who'd made it through the application process. And there was one who stood out so starkly from the rest of the field that Wilson, against all his better instincts, wondered if she might be the exception to his hard-and-fast rule that women should never, ever, be in a position where they might have to enter into true combat.

As Wilson walked onto the maneuvers field that morning, he raised a hand to MacPherson. The applicants were practicing hand-to-hand combat. The day was crisp and clear and though they had hauled a few battered mats out from the gym, there was a lot of cold hard ground to contend with. The rules were to pin your opponent and leave no bruises—otherwise it was no holds-barred street fighting. Most of the men were paired up with other men and the same went for the women, but two of the women were assigned to fight with men. One was small and compact. Wilson couldn't place her ethnicity, but she was dark and attractive. She was paired with a stocky man who pinned her repeatedly until she finally threw up her hands in surrender.

The other woman was tall and muscular in a way that some women can be without the appearance of bulk. And there was something deeply appealing about her. Her male opponent was much larger—a tall, large-boned, barrel-chested man who should have been able to subdue her in an instant. But as Wilson watched them he saw she had three assets that the man, with all his strength, couldn't compete with. She was extremely fast with a kind of quickness that seemed to be allied with a deep instinct to survive. She was also wily and as he watched her he could see that her instincts meshed perfectly with her active mind and she was continually able to trick the man, anticipating and countering his every move. And then there was her ferocity. Wilson was sure he'd never seen it to such an extent in a woman and he didn't think he'd care to see it again. But it did give him pause. She took to heart the rule that she was to leave no bruises but she would not allow herself to be held. The man had no opportunity to pin her and Wilson could plainly see from the frustration creasing his face that he was trying with all his might.

Driving back to D.C. that afternoon, he acknowledged to himself, *Yes, there are exceptions*. He'd had a long conversation with MacPherson before he left and as he was about to get into his car he asked about the woman.

MacPherson ran his fingers through his close-cropped hair and shrugged. "What do you want me to say? She's exceptional. Like nothing I ever thought possible."

Wilson thought of his wife and daughters and decided to play devil's advocate.

"So? What's the problem?"

"You're kidding me, right? I thought we were on the same page here."

"We are, my friend. But let me ask you clearly. Is she unsuitable?"

"Depends on what you mean by unsuitable," MacPherson said too quickly. Then he drew his lips in and shook his head again before looking at Wilson. "No. She's not unsuitable."

"What's her name?"

"Rennie Vogel."

Wilson had thought a lot about Rennie Vogel since that afternoon but he would still argue for her exclusion. He saw it as a moral obligation, to keep his men as safe as he could and he believed even the most talented woman would hamstring an otherwise solid team. So with the CT3 selection period still going on as he sat in the Capitol hearing room, he continued his debate with Joplin. It was a debate he wouldn't share with his wife.

"With all due respect, Senator, our national security is at stake and this is no time for sociological experiments," Wilson said.

"Do you see women in the workforce as a sociological experiment, Director Wilson?" she said, leaning forward.

Wilson quelled a strong desire to roll his eyes. "You know as well as I do that women have been thoroughly integrated into FBI culture for years. Women have served capably as special agents, intelligence analysts and linguists. But special operations forces are a different animal. Whether you consider the Rangers, the SEALs or the Hostage Rescue Team, the men selected for these elite teams are exceptional in their physical abilities. This cannot be overlooked and I will respectfully remind the committee that the United States Armed Forces has never permitted women to serve as front-line combat soldiers on the ground. The rationale for this is well documented—"

Before Wilson could continue, Joplin said, "So, if the Armed Forces won't allow women to be grunts, how could they possibly qualify for a special operations force?"

Wilson nodded. "That's my conclusion."

Joplin passed a hand over her face.

"I hear what you are saying and I believe you believe it to be true. But we have to look at history. No one could have predicted what women have accomplished in just the last century and you know as well as I do that women have seen action on the front lines whether they were ever intended to or not." Joplin consulted her notes. "Panama. 1989. Female soldiers involved in firefights, female convoy drivers ambushed. In the Gulf War, women saw action on the front lines. What I'm suggesting to you is that just as all men aren't suitable for special operations, not all women are either. But some will be. And when you begin to sift through your applicants, qualified women will rise to the surface."

Wilson took a deep breath before he responded. "Your points are well taken, Senator, but infantry is not special operations and I believe in this one area of physical ability, by insisting upon the presence of women, you will only be putting the women and the team in danger. A special operations agent must have superior qualifications in many areas, one being physical strength and prowess. I'm sure the committee wouldn't want to be responsible for the death of an agent injured in combat because his teammate, a woman, is unable to pull him to safety."

A few senators raised their eyebrows at this, but Joplin remained expressionless, unmoved.

"And let me remind the committee," he continued, "that the Hostage Rescue Team at its inception was open to both men and women. The single female applicant excelled in most elements of the training, but she failed the exercises involving upper-body strength. And, perhaps most importantly, she was unable to perform the full-body carry that is absolutely fundamental to saving lives."

"Are you telling me, Director Wilson, that you are willing to judge every potential female applicant based on the failure of one woman?" Joplin leaned forward and held up her finger for him to see.

Wilson said nothing and thought again of Rennie Vogel.

Joplin continued, "Enough on this issue. The bottom line is that we don't have the money for this pie-in-the-sky kind of request. Another year, maybe, but this year you will have to make do with twelve agents for your new team and, Director, let's make sure two of them are women."

"Is that a stipulation, Senator?"

"Yes, it is."

CHAPTER ONE

FBI Training Academy
Quantico, Virginia

John MacPherson pushed through the doors of the Academy fitness center and drew the crisp morning air deeply into his lungs. MacPherson hated the cold and this unseasonable respite from January's usual misery made him long for home. He'd grown up in southern California and always expected to wake up to seventy degrees and a big sky full of sunshine. In recent years he almost never woke up to anything other than the moon. Today was no exception—he'd wanted to get in a good run before the meeting at eight. Working through the selection process for the new Counterterrorism Tactical Team, CT3, every day for the past two weeks, pushing them, goading them to eke out just a little bit more made him yearn for a sliver of solitude and he had finally gotten it this morning. Now he was freshly showered and ready to deliver the good news and the bad, who would step into the ranks of an exceptional few and who would pack their bags and head home.

MacPherson had played this role several times before when he led the Hostage Rescue Team, presiding over a Cut Meeting after the intense weeks of selection. He always looked forward to it as a time to separate the wheat from the chaff and finally get down to the business of building a team. But this time things were more complicated. MacPherson was rankled when the word came down about the quota stipulation. Special operations was the worst place for well-meaning people to attempt to right the wrongs of society. The world would have to balance out someplace else.

MacPherson had been an active HRT operator for seven years before "relaxing" a little and stepping back to train new operators. He knew how grueling the life was. Even more, he knew how tight the teams became and how much the members of the team relied on one another. Though intelligence and skill with the equipment was all-important, there was one thing each man had to have in no small quantity—brute strength. And a woman just didn't have it.

Rennie Vogel had come closer to it than any woman he had ever seen. One of fifteen to try out for the two spots reserved for women on the team of twelve, her performance was consistently and dramatically superior to any of the other women. MacPherson wasn't sure how to account for it. Yes, she was in peak physical condition and was a naturally talented athlete—lithe, quick, graceful—but she just wasn't very big, not nearly big enough to account for her strength. MacPherson's only theory was that adrenaline and an iron will allowed her to perform at a level far higher than her muscle mass would suggest was possible. Adrenaline was a powerful substance that had served him well in tight situations—maybe she had found a way to harness it. He just hoped she didn't lose that control when she needed it most.

There were a few other talented women as well. MacPherson had high hopes for Sonia Shah. She was strong and relentlessly positive. She could read and write classical Arabic and speak several other dialects. Perhaps most valuable, this thoroughly Americanized Arab-American could look like she was from the Middle East or South America or Italy, with a chameleon-like face that would serve the team well on undercover assignments.

Nina Bresson would have been a contender had she been stronger. She'd proven her talents in almost every category and was an especially good sharpshooter. Perhaps most importantly, all of the men seemed to get along with her well. But none of the women could touch Vogel's ability. Realizing this fact early in the program, knowing they didn't have a chance against her and would have to compete against one another for the remaining spot, they finished the try-outs because that's what you did in the FBI.

A part of MacPherson resented Vogel for challenging his assumptions and putting to the test his powerful conviction that women don't belong in special forces. But another part of him, the part that he kept hidden away because it didn't serve him well in this black-and-white world he had chosen as his work, wondered just what she was capable of. He knew they shared something in common. She didn't believe in doing anything half-assed, for good or for evil. Day in and day out he watched her push herself to the limit. The night before at the local tavern where they had all gathered for an end-of-selection celebration, she drank hard but kept herself reigned in tight, saying little and never giving away too much. This was smart. During trials, the competitive instinct is brutal and the men would use anything, fair or foul, against her in a heartbeat. It would be interesting watching her make her way. It would be even more interesting to see how she handled the pressure he was about to put on her.

MacPherson stretched out his arms—he had run too long to have time to do any lifting. Maybe tomorrow, he thought. He could already feel the morning chill beginning to break. Too bad he would be inside all day. He walked along the sidewalk toward the classroom where he would deliver the results to his nervous applicants. The Cut List, which he had printed in his office before dawn, was folded twice and sitting snugly in his front pocket. On it were the twelve names of those who'd made the team. Not reflected there was the surprise he would unleash momentarily.

He relished the thought.

Rennie Vogel learned long ago that if she could visualize something she could make it happen. Not in some self-help psychobabble sort of way, but literally. If she could see herself in her mind climbing a thirty-foot rope and pulling herself onto a training tower unassisted, then she knew she could do it. It was as simple as that. She didn't try to examine it too much—she knew she could do things other women couldn't and felt instinctively that she shouldn't overanalyze it. She knew, too, that setting herself apart too much from the other women might have a negative effect and there were times when she held herself back.

Less tangible accomplishments were something else, like the little matter of making the team. Rennie felt certain she hadn't jeopardized her chances, but at times she was plagued with an almost pathological insecurity. She never showed it and most who thought they knew her would have been surprised by her doubts. So she sat quietly in the over-warm Academy classroom waiting for MacPherson with the rest of the group—thirty-five men and fifteen women who all felt like they had traveled to hell and back every day for the past two weeks. And all for this moment.

"You're awfully quiet, Vogel. Thinking about saving the world?" Angie Carruthers said.

Angie was one of the few people Rennie knew who felt comfortable teasing her. She, Angie and Nina Bresson sat together in the front of the room away from the men, keeping their hopes and fears to themselves. Rennie smiled. "I've made no assumptions. We've all worked hard."

"Don't you love how Vogel maintains the perfect balance of incredible ego tempered by magnanimity?" Angie said to Nina.

"Come on, where's the ego in that?" Rennie said, laughing lightly and shaking her head.

"Oh, it's always there, baby."

Nina leaned in. "Is that a word? Magnanimity? Isn't it

'magnanimousness'?"

Rennie liked Angie but was wary of her. Nina, as always, tried to diffuse the tension that sometimes sprang up between them.

"The only real question is who will get the second quota spot and my money is on Nina," Angie continued, ignoring Nina's dig.

"Thanks, Ange," Nina said.

A tall brunette with patrician features, Nina was Rennie's assigned roommate and they had become close during the trials. She continued, "I actually think Shah will get the other spot, especially with her language skills."

Rennie looked at Nina. She would be disappointed if Nina didn't make the team, but she agreed that Sonia Shah was more likely to get the spot. On some level Rennie thought it was probably a good thing—Nina tended to distract her.

Rennie took a look around the room as Angie and Nina continued their nervous chatter. Shah was sitting a few rows away looking as relaxed as she always did. Sonia was into yoga and meditation, always joking that she practiced the Zen form of Islam. She was talking with Brad Baldwin. Brad was a big guy, six-foot-four and packed with muscle, but as gentle as a puppy and so far the only man on the team Rennie had become close with. He was a shoo-in for a spot on the team. Sitting near them was John Smythe, staring angrily and talking to no one. Smythe was the single applicant to come from the Hostage Rescue Team. A lot of people thought he had been coasting, just getting by doing as little as possible and thinking he would be handed a spot because of his experience. There was a lot of speculation as to why he was leaving HRT. Rennie figured he had alienated everyone with his defensiveness and unrelenting arrogance.

It was stuffy in the room. Through the window, Rennie could see the new class of agent recruits doing push-ups on the still-damp grass. She remembered her own time as a new recruit. In many ways it was the marker of the last moment when she was truly optimistic without anything to taint it. The whole world seemed to belong to her then. After her training, she was assigned

15

to the D.C. field office. A good assignment and her hometown. But excitement had quickly turned to tedium and frustration. She wanted more. When she'd read the memo announcing the new counterterrorism team and the last line that sent reverberations through the entire law enforcement community—*female agents are encouraged to apply*—she knew she had found what she wanted. And here she was.

Rennie glanced at her watch. MacPherson would be there any minute with the Cut List. Only cumulative scores would be posted, with men and women ranked separately. This was a point of bitterness for the guys. The main office decided that in order to fill the quota of two women on the team, they would have to grade the women on their own—basically an acknowledgment that the women couldn't compete with the men. Of course, the men had always believed this and some of the women did too. Rennie would have liked the chance to go head-to-head with the guys. She wasn't sure how many she could compete against, but she liked things to be fair. She was just about to double-check the time with Nina when MacPherson swept in, business as usual, without a hello to anyone, holding a single sheet of paper.

MacPherson stood at the front of the room behind a long table looking from the paper to the anxious faces of the assembled applicants. Rennie knew he was trying to build their anticipation, forcing them to understand the gravity of the moment. As if they didn't already. "Okay. Every one of you guys has worked hard and given one hundred percent. You're all well aware there are only twelve spots—two teams of five and the two alternates." MacPherson paced as he spoke. "Now, I'm not going to bullshit anybody, so here's the plan. As you know, we are required to have at least two women on the team. As you also know, the women have been ranked separately—so it is a given that the women will be two of the twelve even though their scores fall, in most cases, well below that of the men."

Rennie wouldn't take her eyes from MacPherson but she could feel Angie's and Nina's tension.

MacPherson stepped back and stroked his chin

contemplatively.

"This situation frustrates me. Once upon a time, I ruled my own little corner of the world and that world was a meritocracy. Apparently, that time is over and the boys on Ninth St. have decided political correctness is more important than keeping our men alive." MacPherson laid the paper on the table. No one could tear their eyes from it. "But since I am still the agent in charge, I will make assignments within the unit. They have left me that, so far. Thus, I have decided that the women will be the two alternates."

A groan emitted from the women across the room.

"But," MacPherson held up his index finger, "because I am a fair guy I am going to give the ladies one last chance. This obviously isn't on the protocol but I think it will prove to be an interesting exercise.

"First, I'll read the names of the team. The order is determined by your score, highest first."

The room became so still Rennie could hear the soft movement of the second hand of the clock on the wall. MacPherson finally spoke, slowly and deliberately, enunciating each syllable.

"Baldwin. Goode. Levin. Perez. Cole. Saxton. Otter. Chen. Snider. And Smythe." He paused. "And the alternates—Vogel and Shah."

Emotion played out over every face in the room, elation and disappointment.

"Now, Vogel had the highest women's score, by quite a margin I see," he said scrutinizing the paper in his hand. "Good job, Vogel. So, we're going to give Vogel a chance for a spot on the team instead of sentencing her to the life of a lowly alternate—no offense, Shah." A chuckle rippled through the classroom. "Vogel's going to run the obstacle course one last time against the man with the lowest score."

John Smythe, who already looked pissed that he barely made the team, suddenly seemed deadly serious.

MacPherson returned his gaze, coldly.

"That's right, Smythe, as the man with the lowest score, you get to race Vogel bright and early tomorrow morning." He paused before taking in the rest of the room. "For those of you who didn't make the team, this is a disappointing moment. But know this, just making it through these trials is a huge accomplishment that cannot be minimized. I hope you'll stick around for the race tomorrow."

"This is bullshit," Smythe said, his voice flat.

MacPherson stepped from behind the table and walked slowly over to him.

"You're right, it is bullshit. But it's the way it's going to be."

Smythe was gripping the edges of the desk, hard.

"Understand?" MacPherson slapped the desk, the sharp crack turning the heads of those few who were too polite to openly watch Smythe's dressing down.

Smythe could barely speak through his anger but two words somehow slipped past his lips. "Yes. Sir."

Back in her room, Rennie lay on her bed holding her shoulders. She was exhausted from day after day of pushing herself farther than she ever had. She'd hoped that after the Cut Meeting, whether the news was good or bad, she would finally have a break. Now she was presented with the most difficult challenge she had encountered. And yet she knew, at the end, if she made it, if she could just beat Smythe, she would earn a place on the team that no one could dispute, quota or no quota.

"I'm not sure I'm up for this."

Rennie hadn't meant to speak aloud. Nina sat down next to her on the bed.

"I know," Nina said, her voice full of compassion. "MacPherson just can't help making his big point. But you know, he's going to look like an ass when you beat Smythe tomorrow."

Rennie sat up and took Nina's hand.

"Oh, Nina, I'm sorry. I..." She paused. She knew she had to be cautious, couldn't say exactly what she felt. It was too dangerous. "I hoped we'd be doing this together."

Nina smiled and pushed Rennie back down on the bed.

"Relax. I went through my disappointment a long time ago. I knew the day I met you that instead of two spots available, there was only one."

Rennie shook her head.

"It's okay. It's been a great experience—albeit brutally taxing on the body—and it'll look fantastic on my résumé. And I met you."

Rennie held her gaze longer than she should have.

"Turn over," Nina said.

Rennie paused for a moment and then rolled over onto her stomach. She felt Nina's hands begin to knead the tight muscles in her shoulders. They were silent now, this first foray into the physical clearing both their minds of the potential for conversation. Nina shifted her body so that the length of her was against Rennie—just one hand was on her now, no longer massaging but tracing delicate lines over her back and neck. It felt too good.

Rennie raised up slightly. "I'd better get some rest. Morning will come quickly."

Nina turned away before Rennie could catch her eye.

"You're right. You need to be fresh."

It was still dark on the practice field. Rennie didn't take in individual faces but it seemed like the entire class had turned out to watch the competition between her and Smythe. As far as she could see Smythe wasn't there yet. The morning was sharp and fresh and the ground was still damp from the night. The tree line looked dark and ominous, a hulking mass. It was there that they would emerge for the final half-mile sprint to the finish—two orange cones brought by MacPherson. The race would be the usual one they had done in selection, a circular course that traveled a torturous path, first down through a grassy field and into the woods, eventually inclining toward a ridge, then the half-mile run back through a field to where they started.

Rennie saw Smythe emerge from a pack of men patting him on the back. He looked nervous, wound tight. She jogged in place and began to stretch out. MacPherson trotted up to her.

"You all set, Vogel? This is your big chance."

"I'm ready," Rennie said, looking him in the eye.

"Look, Vogel, don't take this personally. I think you know as well as I do that what is best for the team is more important than politically correct bullshit."

Rennie was never one to talk trash. Neither was she much of an advocate for herself. Never willing to make an argument for her abilities, she always let her actions speak for themselves. But this time, something in MacPherson's tone pushed her.

"Maybe you need to have more faith."

"What, in women?" MacPherson said.

"No, in me," Rennie said, her eyes cold.

MacPherson looked at her for a beat longer before turning away and directing everyone to clear the starting line. Smythe was bouncing up and down as he stretched out his arms. Rennie thought she should calculate her chances of winning, evaluate her strengths and weaknesses against her opponent, but she knew that, today, none of that mattered—she believed wholly and completely that she had the potential to win. This would not be a small feat. Being the guy with the worst time among this group was akin to being the guy with the worst performance on an Olympic team—Smythe was stronger and faster than your average male.

"Okay, let's line up." MacPherson was clapping his hands.

Rennie entered a place of calm in her mind as she usually did before an intense competition, anxiety ceding to a kind of placidity, where everything around her seemed surreal. Voices sounded differently, clear but as if they were coming to her from a great distance. Her vision seemed to sharpen, colors became more vivid and everything seemed to slow down. It was a strange feeling, as if she became somehow more interior, more inside herself. She placed her foot on the line.

"This will be the usual run—seven and a half miles starting right here." MacPherson stomped his foot on the concrete slab. "Down the hill and into the woods for the hellacious, obstacle-ridden trek we're all familiar with. And out of the woods there," he said, pointing north, "for the final bone-numbing half-mile run through the field to this point."

MacPherson stood between the two orange cones, his hands on his hips.

Rennie felt her pulse quicken.

"And the prize, of course…" MacPherson paused, meeting Rennie's eyes and then Smythe's. "Is a permanent position on the team."

Rennie looked over at Smythe standing next to her and caught his eye—he showed no trace of nervousness now; his eyes were narrow and hard, an unspoken threat.

"On your mark. Get set…"

Rennie looked over her shoulder at the crowd. Everyone was silent, their faces rapt with anticipation. She saw Nina and the image of the two of them lying on her bed the night before flashed through her mind. She wondered what might have happened.

"GO!"

They both had a perfect start, but Rennie quickly shot ahead as they headed down the steep hill toward the opening in the tree line. The fall of her footsteps seemed to match her ever-quickening heartbeat. She knew she could take Smythe if it were only a foot race. She was light and fast and he was too densely packed with muscle to match her pace. His strength would serve him on many of the obstacles and on the incline—after the third mile the entire course arced upward thousands of feet to a ridge.

Rennie could feel Smythe close behind and her old nemesis began to rise up inside her. A remnant of an ancient insecurity traveled up her body like a cold chill. She thought she could hear the pounding of Smythe's feet. She turned her head slightly to see how close he was, and lost her footing. She never knew if she stepped into a hole, tripped over a mound or if she just collapsed under the weight of the entire undertaking. But she fell hard and tumbled over several times, almost landing on her feet before skidding to a stop. Dazed, she looked back up the hill to see MacPherson and the rest of the class at the top of the hill pointing and yelling. She shook off the fog in her brain and turned to see Smythe at least a hundred yards ahead entering the woods.

Goddammit.

She leapt up and sprang down the hill wondering if she had injured herself, that maybe the pain just hadn't set in yet. As she entered the woods Smythe was nowhere to be seen. She could see the hurdles ahead, five log hurdles of varying height. She took the first four easily with a grab and a leap. The last one was higher and her ribs could attest to the many bruises it had given her in the past couple of weeks. She ran for it, jumped, rolled, shifted and was down. She skidded down a bank and across the few inches of creeping water in the creek bed. The other side was steep, one of the places on the course so steep that there was a thick rope to help runners make their way up. Rennie grabbed it and clambered up the bank. She hoped to see the back of Smythe when she got to the top but there was only woods and more woods and she was tearing through it too fast to hear him.

At least she didn't seem to be injured. The fall had thrown her off mentally or, more likely, was a sign that she wasn't focused to begin with. *MacPherson. Smythe. Nina.* Too much to think about. She had to get it together. She thought of Smythe so far ahead and felt a surge of frustration course through her body. She couldn't lose. She couldn't bear to go back to her dull little cubicle and her cases that never seemed to go anywhere. She had joined the FBI for a life of action, a life that had meaning and purpose. She hadn't realized in her youthful naiveté that there were never any guarantees. But as a permanent member of CT3, it was an absolute that she would be doing something that mattered. She felt her focus return and, with it, picked up her pace. She saw the simulated window just ahead, a wall erected on the path with a square cutout. Instead of crawling through it, she grabbed the top beam, tucked her legs and swung through the opening. She let go and landed perfectly in the puddle on the other side.

Ignoring the chill soaking into her socks, Rennie ran hard,

the well-worn path cutting clearly through the woods. She had always been a runner—at least ever since she had become physical. For many years she had done nothing but read and try to stay out of the way of her chaotic family. Then she had discovered motion and never looked back. Running felt so natural, she often wondered how she had done without it. Here was pure freedom, perhaps the only kind she had ever known. She leaned into it and pushed harder. Her insecurity fell away and she felt a solid rhythm settle into her limbs.

She bore down on the ravine. Traversing this deep cut always ate up a lot of time. It was fifteen feet across and angled down ten feet on each side. A rope trailed down the steep uneven descent and another snaked back up. Rennie knew she had recovered from her fall. Her body felt good and strong and she wondered if she could make up time by jumping the gap instead of shimmying down one side and up the other, as Smythe had surely done. The path was rocky at this point and she skirted the dips and bumps nimbly as she raced toward the ravine. Then she picked up speed and ran for the edge. Focusing on the strength in her legs, she leapt. For a moment it felt like she was flying, her legs still churning as she tore through the air. In that instant she wanted to stretch out her arms and turn her face to the sky, drinking in her escape from being earthbound. But not today. She came down fast, hitting hard ground on the other side of the ravine that crumbled under her feet. She felt herself fall but finally her fingers grasped the rope and finding her footing, she pulled herself to the top.

There was still no sign of Smythe but she knew she was gaining on him, she could feel it. The thought made her push herself harder. This section of the path was the last straight easy bit before turning north and climbing and curving to the ridge. The cliff face was just ahead, a sheer rock wall ten feet high. Some places were mossy and slick, but when she reached it she instinctively knew each foothold in the rock. A thick rope snaked over the edge a few feet and when she grabbed it, she took a few well-placed steps and was up and over. The incline to the ridge loomed before her. Trailing up the mountainside, it was the most difficult part of the course—except for the Wall which presented a special problem for the women. Rennie ran and climbed and ignored the pain that was settling into her legs. She put Smythe out of her mind and used the pain to fuel her. *Just take the hill. Take it as fast as you can.* Then the pain passed and she felt unstoppable, tearing up the path, taking its twists and turns, legs pumping, breath even and steady. This section ate up the most time. Glancing at her watch, she knew she was running the course faster than she ever had before. Much faster. It had never meant so much. And then the ground leveled out and she was running along the ridge. A few hundred yards ahead she could see the iconic cargo net.

She scrambled up the net, the rope thick and rough against her hands. The cargo net always made Rennie think of the countless hands and feet of those who'd struggled over it through the years, pushing themselves and asking more of their bodies than they ever had before. She paused at the top to see if there was any sign of Smythe. Then she heard a tiny splash in the distance. She knew it could only be one thing—Smythe crossing the creek where it traversed the course at the second point. She felt a huge surge of adrenaline shoot through her as she flipped over the top of the net and landed on her feet. She could do this. He was within striking distance and had no idea how close she was.

Smythe was breathing hard. He had let himself go a little soft, but it would take next to nothing to get his body back. MacPherson knew that too. Smythe didn't understand why he was giving him such a hard time, trying to humiliate him by racing a woman. He'd worked his ass off for years in HRT and looked at this selection period as a little breather. But he and MacPherson had always clashed when they were in HRT together. MacPherson had gotten leadership positions because he was willing to kiss ass and Smythe wasn't.

Smythe wondered how much distance he had on Vogel—maybe half a mile. He thought he might be able to increase it to three-quarters before it was all over. Of course, there was no use in killing himself. But MacPherson had put him into a position where he had to make a point and drive it home hard. He thought the idea of women on the team as abhorrent as MacPherson did, maybe even more. Not that he didn't love women. He had a beautiful wife he adored. He had no problem with women agents. But here, in special operations, was his world. A realm utterly devoid of anything suggestive of the female. He liked it that way. It was a place where he could join a long succession of brave men who lived purely in the world of action. Whenever he jumped from a plane or dove into the sea from a chopper or slit the throat of a drug warlord he felt like he was meeting his destiny.

And then there was Vogel. He wondered why she thought she could play at this game. Didn't she know what their enemies would do to a woman if they captured her? Smythe finally topped the ridge and his breath began to ease. He was going to have to give up his Cubans and start seriously training again. Everyone knew he could have had the number one spot if he'd given a hundred percent. He even had to wonder if he really came in tenth or if MacPherson had manipulated the scores just to fuck with his head. And what about Vogel's score? There were rumors it was high, higher than a lot of the guys', but Smythe knew that was impossible. She wasn't big enough to compete on their level. He couldn't see how some of the guys thought she was hot—not soft enough for his taste.

Smythe jogged up to the creek and splashed through it. MacPherson had put him in a bad position but at least had tried to make it okay—after the meeting he had taken him aside and assured him that it was nothing personal. Stabbing him in the back while shaking his hand—he should have been a politician.

Smythe hit the ground and scrambled through the bear pit, a low crawl through a ditch beneath crisscrossing barbed wire. Then he saw the Wall just ahead and smiled. At least by winning today he would prove that even the strongest women just couldn't make it, by far. The Wall was almost eight feet and he knew Vogel would have a hell of a time with it—all of the women did. He hopped, pulled himself up and was about to drop down to the other side when something caught his attention. He turned and saw Vogel running toward him at full speed.

By the time Rennie splashed through the creek, there was no sign of Smythe, but she knew he must be close. The course here twisted and turned, arcing up and down, which didn't give her a long view. There were only two more obstacles—the bear pit and the Wall. She could handle the bear pit but the Wall was hard. MacPherson always instructed the women to do it in tandem, giving each other a leg up. Rennie knew the men resented this. She thought she could do it alone but hadn't wanted to set herself apart from the other women any more than she already had.

Rennie took the bear pit quickly, crawling on forearms and knees, dust flying into her face and then tore off toward the Wall. The eight-foot obstacle was difficult for the men as well, she reminded herself. The boards were fitted so that it was impossible to get a foothold, which meant a well-timed jump and focused upper body strength were absolutely necessary to get you up and over.

Rennie was envisioning herself making it over when she caught a glimpse of Smythe as he reached the Wall. But his focus on it was complete and he didn't hear her. A flower of calm bloomed in her chest. Here it was. Fifty yards. She concentrated on running as fast as she could. As Smythe reached the top of the Wall he turned and spotted her coming at him. The look of alarm twisting his features was one she knew he didn't show often. Then she saw the startled look quickly turn to anger before he dropped to the other side.

This was it. Rennie knew she had to make it over in one try, no do-overs. She ran toward it headlong and everything seemed to slow. The breeze cool against her face, she felt like she filled the parameters of her being completely and when she leapt, she knew every fiber of her muscles was engaged in getting her over that damn wall. She flew at it and caught the top board under her arms, her chest and hips and knees bouncing so hard against the wooden planks she almost knocked herself off. In her mind she glimpsed herself, as if she stood off to the side—the Wall in a deep embrace, her body arcing upward, legs bent toward the sky, until gravity pulled her back down. For a moment she thought the impact had knocked the wind out of her, but she captured her breath and pulled herself up the few inches she needed to hook her knee over. She dropped off the edge, hit the ground hard, rolled and was up and running. She saw the top of Smythe's head and took off after him.

MacPherson checked his watch. It had been nearly an hour. They should be out of the woods soon. At least Smythe should be. He knew Smythe would have some good distance on Vogel. He didn't want to humiliate him. Anyone else it wouldn't have, but Smythe was thin-skinned. He just wanted to get his point across. He knew Smythe could beat Vogel, any one of the men could, but he wondered by how much.

MacPherson stood away from the rest of the team. The men were joking around, occasionally checking the line of the woods. The women stood together, close and quiet. It was always this way. Unless they were sleeping together, the sexes usually felt most comfortable separate from one another. MacPherson was glad that selection had finally come to an end and hoped that this little exercise he was putting Smythe and Vogel through would show his superiors the futility of trying to integrate women into high-level special forces teams.

"Look!" Perez pointed toward the woods. "There he is." MacPherson turned to see Smythe running toward them. He wasn't far out of the woods and he looked haggard, but the experiment was almost over. The men were yelling and high-fiving each other.

"Okay, people, back it up! Clear the finish line. Make room for the man." MacPherson waved everyone back from the two orange traffic cones. Then, suddenly, everyone's attention was riveted on Smythe. He was running hard but he kept turning his head back toward the line of the woods. Everyone followed his gaze. At that moment, Vogel burst through a mass of leaves running full tilt.

"Holy shit!"

"Here she comes," MacPherson muttered under his breath.

Rennie's feet pounded the ground so hard she thought she could feel it give way. This was the way she liked it. As the woods receded behind her, she could see Smythe wasn't too far ahead. He turned and met her eye and stumbled slightly. She could tell by the way he ran that he was struggling. She could do this. The finish line was a little less than half a mile away. As she closed the distance, she could see the crowd gaping. Some of them were clapping, some were jumping up and down, but most were just staring. She saw their mouths moving too, but no sound could penetrate her focus. She could hear her own heartbeat though, steady and even, and she used its perfect thump to concentrate everything she had on running faster than she had ever run. She felt the pain in her legs, the pain in her chest, but it was just pain. It hurt and she loved it, feeling it deeply and knowing it couldn't do anything to slow her down. And she didn't slow down. The finish line was only a couple of hundred yards away. Every second she closed in on Smythe. Poor Smythe, she thought, poor Smythe, poorsmythepoorsmythepoorsmythe, with every beat of her feet, poorsmythepoorsmythe, and she was past him. And then sensing him at her heels, she picked up the last bit of speed that was left in her and ran for the finish.

Nina caught Rennie as she tore through the cones, Rennie nearly knocking her down.

"You did it! You did it! You kicked his ass!"

Nina had her tight around the waist. They were chest to chest and it felt so good. Rennie could see MacPherson standing stiff with his hands on his hips, watching them, and saw everything she had just accomplished begin to shake under his stare.

"Oh my God, I need to sit down," she said, pushing Nina away from her. Nina would understand—she knew how things worked.

Rennie lay down flat on the cold ground and closed her eyes. The muscles in her legs were throbbing from the run. Smythe was standing at a distance, bent over and breathing hard. She wondered when he had crossed the finish line. How close had he been? She sat up and someone handed her a cup of water. Her hands shook so badly she could barely drink from it. She closed her eyes again and when she opened them she saw a large pair of boots in front of her. She squinted into MacPherson's face.

"Congratulations, Vogel. You're a full member of the team," he said, his face and voice as impassive as a stone. Then he squatted down next to her and leaned in close. "Let's hope to God you don't fuck things up."

Rennie said nothing.

And that was all. He stood and walked away.

Rennie looked around for Smythe. A few of the guys were talking to him. Chen put his hand on his shoulder, but Smythe knocked it away and walked off the field. He turned one last time and glared with undisguised hostility at Rennie.

CHAPTER TWO

CT3 Temporary Command Center
Quantico, Virginia

Rennie arrived at the conference room about twenty minutes early and sat where she could look out the window. A batch of new FBI Academy recruits were being given their tour of the grounds. Their blue polo shirts were crisp, tucked into their razor-sharp khakis and they all looked excited enough to burst out of their skin. Rennie almost felt that way today. Since the Cut, the two new teams had been training nonstop. For the last six months, they had been up at five every day running, lifting weights, shooting, going through tactical exercises and slaving away over the books in the classroom—foreign policy, geography, history, especially of the Middle East and the former Soviet republics—and everyone's favorite, the outdoor practicum on survival skills. She was stuffed with new knowledge and it felt so good. Her boredom with her previous field assignment had become mind-numbing with its attendant casework that could drag on for years and still not get anywhere. With mission work, she could look forward to intense focus followed by a quick resolution—for better or for worse.

At four months, her team began to go on assignments, all domestic. Most were hostage situations and most had been resolved through negotiation. But on the last call-out, they had dropped down onto the roof of an apartment building in Richmond and surprised a man holding his wife at gunpoint in the lobby. They disarmed him quickly and without a shot being fired. But this morning's meeting would bring something entirely different. And at 0800 it would begin. Rennie looked at her watch—five minutes to go.

Something in the doorway caught her eye and she looked up and saw Smythe. He was glaring at her from across the room and she wondered how long he had been standing there. He walked over and dropped his notebook on the table so that it made a loud crack as it hit the shiny surface. He still held her gaze as he took his seat at the far end of the table. Since winning the race, Rennie's relations with Smythe had been a little tense to say the least. But for the most part he had kept his distance. Before the race, she hadn't really noticed him but had sensed that he was short-tempered, volatile. She remembered talking to Brad about him once. He said that Smythe was the only Hostage Rescue Team member who had volunteered for the new division and he had a proven track record there. Brad figured this was probably the reason he'd come in last place—he assumed he was a shoo-in and had coasted by on his reputation.

Then Perez fell from the rappelling tower. Smythe, as the most qualified alternate, took his place and suddenly set his sights on Rennie, becoming occasionally hostile—although never when anyone was around. The rest of the time he ignored her, so she never knew what to expect from him.

"So, Vogel, you think you're ready for the big time?" Smythe's light tone belied the look in his eyes.

"As ready as the rest of the team."

"That's great—there's nothing I love more than a confidant

woman."

Smythe thought he knew how to get under her skin—but Rennie wasn't bothered by him.

"You going to bug me today, John?"

"John? That's great—we're good friends now, huh, Vogel?"

"Why not?"

Rennie had never seen Smythe this combative.

"You know, the other day I was in the tavern with a few of my buddies," he said, linking his fingers behind his head. "We were throwing back a few beers and one of my buddies said he had heard something interesting about you." Smythe rocked his chair slowly on the back legs. "You know what that might be?" His eyes were hard.

Rennie sat perfectly still. A cold chill began to crawl up her waist. If anything could fill her with fear, this was it.

No. Not now, not after making it this far.

"What do you think, Vogel? What do you think my buddy had to say?" Smythe leaned forward, suggestively stroking his chin. "I have to tell you it wasn't very nice."

Rennie's throat constricted. If she just sat quietly, maybe it would all go away. She didn't try to speak, but she held his gaze. Her expression showed no weakness, she always had a good poker face.

"My buddy heard that we're going on a suicide mission and you're our ticket to hell."

Rennie rolled her eyes as she understood that he was on the wrong track. Relief coursed through her. Could he see it?

"What's that supposed to mean?" Her voice was strong now.

"What it means is that when our mission, which Walker will be delivering to us any minute," he glanced at his watch, "when our *mission*," he said emphasizing the word, "was chosen by Assistant Director Daniels, it was chosen as a response to the quota being forced down his throat." He added with a smirk, "Or should I say up his ass?"

Rennie didn't respond.

"You don't get it, do you? It's been chosen with a view to pre-

32

determined failure, to make a point and send a clear message to those who are trying to tell him who he should hire. Or at least that's what my buddy heard."

"Suicide mission? Oh, come on, I can't possibly screw things up that bad," Rennie said lightly.

Smythe seemed to relax a little.

"Maybe. Maybe not. But from what I hear we're walking into an impossible situation."

She wondered why Smythe was wasting his breath on this nonsense.

The rest of the team filed into the room, followed by Commander Walker. Brad was pumped up and gave Rennie a big smile. She could nearly see his muscles twitching under his dress shirt. Walker closed the door and passed out a thick folder to each member of the team. He switched off the lights and positioned himself in front of his laptop. Everyone focused on the first image projected on the wall—*Operation Black Fire*.

Here we go.

Walker didn't speak, letting his silence hang like a weight. He looked at each member of the team as if to communicate the import of this moment.

"Welcome to *Operation Black Fire*."

The words on the screen were replaced by a photograph of a man with a closely clipped beard wearing a slouchy dark green Western style uniform with black epaulets.

"This is Ahmad Armin, as most of you, no doubt, are aware. He was catapulted onto the international stage a year and a half ago when he took an American woman hostage. He is an Iranian nuclear scientist who along with his brother, Nasser, also a physicist, was once courted by the CIA. Both are secular and Harvard educated. From what we can get out of the CIA, Nasser was an extremely moral man who responded to the agency's argument that Iran's political situation was so far out of control that his country's leaders couldn't be trusted with the nuclear technology he was helping them to acquire. The agency convinced him to defect. His little brother, Ahmad, revered

Nasser, and initially went along.

"Then Ahmad fell under the sway of a nationalist movement sworn to uphold the memory of the CIA's shenanigans during the time of Mossadegh. They convinced Ahmad that the Americans would imprison his brother and humiliate the Armin family and Iran."

"So, he murders his brother," Smythe spoke up, his voice laden with his usual irony. "His beloved brother."

"That's right. He kills his brother, shoots him in the head while he's sleeping, supposedly to save him from the shame he would bring upon their family and on Iran by defecting. What happens after that isn't entirely clear. From what we can gather, he snapped."

"And he finds religion," Levin offered.

"We don't think so. He's not an ideologue—he may be playing that part but we think it's a cover, an attempt to shift the blame of his brother's murder from himself to the United States."

"So, he starts a quasi-religious jihadi movement and sets up a military outpost on a piece of land in Tajikistan," Baldwin added.

"Right, setting up his brother as a martyr figure—something Nasser himself would have found abhorrent. We have intel that he's being funded by the Libyans, who love to hand out money to anyone who will stick it to the U.S. and who have pressured the ruling powers in Tajikistan to look the other way. From there, he's trained his soldiers—a ragtag group of religious nuts, teenagers and indigents who will do anything for a buck. They've launched a few small-scale attacks on U.S. targets in the Middle East, mainly in Saudi Arabia."

Walker cycled through a series of photographs of bombed cafes and an apartment building housing U.S. personnel.

"Then, quite suddenly but not unexpectedly, he kidnapped an American tourist, Reuters' reporter Hannah Marcus, who had just settled in Tajikistan on assignment and found herself in the wrong place at the wrong time hiking with some colleagues."

A photo of Hannah Marcus flashed on the screen. Rennie

remembered the photo, both from the newspapers and from FBI reports. It showed a slight woman with distinctive features and short dark hair standing in front of an unidentified building.

"Armin demanded that the United States accept responsibility for his brother's death. The U.S. declared that Ahmad had murdered him himself and demanded he release the hostage. A week passed, then two. Armin then released this photo of Marcus."

In it, Hannah Marcus sat in a folding chair looking bewildered. Her hands were bound behind her. Next to her stood an armed soldier wearing a large pair of dark glasses whose face was otherwise shrouded in a keffiyeh scarf.

"Other than this photo, we have received no other communication since February twenty-fourth, seventeen months ago. She is presumed dead."

"Wasn't she Jewish?" Rennie asked.

"Right, thanks Vogel, I was just getting to that," Walker said with a nod.

"Was she targeted as a Jew?" Rennie asked.

"We don't think so. We think it was just a bad coincidence. But it gave Armin a platform to stir up his followers by making a lot of noise about the U.S. and their support for Israel. Here's the rub. We believe that Armin has been trying to purchase materials to make a dirty bomb. We don't think he's made a connection yet, but he has a huge bankroll and he has the science to make the thing. It is only a matter of time until he finds someone unscrupulous enough to sell him the material."

Walker paused, making eye contact with each member of the team.

"Your assignment is to shut Armin down. His band of merry men, which we think number nearly a hundred, will fall apart when we take him out."

Rennie swallowed hard and glanced at Brad who looked deadly serious.

Walker changed the image to an aerial photograph. "This is a two hundred square mile image of the area." He placed his finger on a large cluster of buildings. "This is the village of Shuroabad." He moved his hand to the left corner of the screen. "You will be dropped by plane here." He indicated a field south and east of the village. The field bordered a forest on the east.

"You will be disguised as hikers, so stop going to the barber." The team looked at each other in surprise. They had trained for undercover work but hadn't expected it to come so soon.

"It is one hundred and fifty miles through the forest to Armin's camp here." Walker zoomed in on the image and what looked like a few shacks at the eastern border of the woods were revealed to be several large barracks, a barn and several other large structures.

"The anniversary of Nasser's martyrdom," he said ironically, "occurs on August eighteenth. That's four weeks and three days from today. The festivities for the day have been in the works for weeks and we've been fortunate enough to come across a very specific piece of intelligence that puts Armin right at this spot." Walker zoomed into the photograph even closer and pointed his cursor to what looked like a small stage. "At twenty-one hundred thirty hours on August eighteenth.

"Now, we haven't had any men on the ground, but the topography suggests you'll have a clear shot from the safety of the woods. If not…" He smiled wryly. "You'll have to go in and do your damnedest not to start a small war."

Walker looked around the table at the stunned expressions.

"Nothing like trial by fire, right, gentlemen?" Then Walker looked at Rennie. He hadn't forgotten her at all. "And lady."

Walker suddenly snapped his laptop shut and the screen went blank.

"You have four weeks. For the last two, in addition to your physical training, you will attend a few briefings on the history of the region, the people, the culture, but most of that material plus a detailed profile on Armin is in the folder in front of you. Read it. Memorize it. Take it into your very soul. But primarily, your preparation will involve running through your mission—again and again and again."

"So, what about the first two weeks?" Goode asked.

Walked smiled. "I thought you'd never ask. I'm sure you are all familiar with HALO." Walker looked around the table for reaction and seemed to enjoy the wide-eyed faces looking back at him.

"That's right. Instead of flying first class into Dushanbe Airport, you'll be doing a High-Altitude, Low-Opening jump from twenty-five thousand feet. A free fall. This is deadly serious, people. You are flying out tonight to Fort Bragg for two days in the Vertical Wind Tunnel and then on to Yuma Proving Grounds for a crash course." Walker paused, running his hand across his flattop. "Or perhaps I should say, an *intensive* course, in HALO jumping. The course is usually five weeks. You have two. Good luck."

Rennie had hardly been able to take in all that she had heard. She knew that life as an operator would be worlds apart from her life as a special agent, but the scope of this mission seemed wildly inappropriate for a newly formed team. She thought about her conversation with Smythe before the briefing. Looking over at him, she found him nodding slowly at her.

CHAPTER THREE

Armin Training Camp
Khatlon Province, Tajikistan

A village.

The thought of it made Hamid Abad tremble with anticipation as he walked along the dusty path to the barracks. How long had it been since he'd eaten a real meal? Or had a conversation about mundane things? Maybe he could even go to a mosque. And pray for guidance.

Six months before, when Fareed Reza had approached him as he was coming out of his own beloved mosque, the tall man had spoken of this journey as a holy mission, one Hamid was obligated to commit to, to serve Allah rightly. But now, whenever his superiors spoke of Allah or their pious obligations, it all seemed hollow.

The story of Nasser Armin had touched everyone in Hamid's own village, just outside of Tehran. His mother, his precious mother, had particularly been affected. She had listened to Ahmad Armin's hushed tone and taken his tortured face deep into her heart. Eventually his expression had become angry and his voice rose. He spoke of holy war, of vengeance.

Ahmad Armin had successfully turned Nasser, his quiet scholarly brother, into a kind of cult figure in certain parts of Iran. Ahmad was a natural orator, massaging and manipulating a crowd to a peak of frenzied excitement. After his brother's death he had traveled to mosques in and around Tehran, denouncing the Americans as murderers, a characterization easy to sell to those who remembered the past. Ahmad Armin painted Nasser as a great nationalist who had used his intellectual gifts to put Iran on an equal footing in the world. All people find comfort in a hero and they accepted Nasser as their own.

Hamid was too young and too devoted to his mother to have taken in the newfound admiration for everything American discovered by the younger generation. Hamid's mother had a picture of Nasser tacked to the wall in their cramped living room. She would say, covering her face, "The Americans again, it's always the Americans. They will not stop until they destroy us."

Fareed, Ahmad Armin's right hand-man, had told Hamid to tell no one about his offer to join in a war for the new millennium. But Hamid always told his mother everything.

"There are many evils in the world," she had said to him, holding his face between her hands. "Many misguided people killing innocent souls in the name of Allah. But this is different. Here is maybe a small chance to set right a horrible injustice." She had tears in her eyes. "It is good and right that Nasser be avenged." His mother had spoken in a measured voice, convinced that her young son could save the world.

So, Hamid left his home with nothing but the clothes on his back. To meet Fareed and climb aboard a plane. When they landed, God knows where, he was blindfolded and driven in a Jeep to this camp in the middle of nowhere, to learn all sorts of evil things. Evil things for a holy cause. This was how the world balanced out.

In the middle of nowhere.

That was what he was told that day in February, that the camp was isolated by miles and miles of wilderness. When he slipped the blindfold off his eyes, his face caked with dust, and saw it for the first time there were huge bulldozers clearing the ridge and hordes of young men completing construction on the barracks, the armory and the tiny dwellings that housed Armin and his top men. Hamid joined in the building that day, learning to use a hammer without smashing his hands and running errands for the more experienced.

Hamid learned, too, that the ridge had once been the site of a small ancient farm, a perfect spot for a long gone hermetic farmer who had wanted to escape the world. The only structure that survived the ravages of time was a small sturdily built barn with stalls running along each side of a central open passageway. This building was always under guard and it was said that if you tried to run away or turned out to be a traitor or a spy, you would be sent to the stable and horrible things would happen there.

It *had* occurred to Hamid to run away. He was ashamed to think of it, but sometimes life at the camp felt as if he had been sent to prison. He was sick with longing for home, for his mother's rough hand upon the nape of his neck. And for her cooking. He wondered if his mother had known what the camp actually was, would she have encouraged him to go?

In the middle of nowhere.

Fareed Reza had said as he rubbed Hamid's head with his hand, "Don't be a fool and try to run away. You will die of thirst and hunger and you will be eaten by tigers and bears." He took Hamid's chin in his hand. "There is nothing for a thousand miles in any direction. And if you are caught trying to run, you will be punished."

But Hamid was a good boy. Always a good boy. That was why he had been chosen out of all the new boys to go with Rashed Parto on a mission. His first mission. He was excited. Especially since it didn't involve killing anyone. Or himself.

Now Hamid pushed open the flimsy door to the barracks and was greeted by the ever-present stifling heat and a faint tinkling of music.

"Rashed?" he called out.

A burly young man with thick curly black hair popped his head up from between two iron beds. "Close the door! Do you want to get my cassette player confiscated?"

Rashed had spent a year at a university in the United States before being recruited into Nasser's Army. To Hamid's confusion, he was thoroughly trusted by Armin. He was smart and spoke English fluently, but Hamid suspected that his true use to them was that he was without fear. And willing to do anything. But he couldn't give up his pop music. He had somehow smuggled in a tape player and a cassette with ten Iranian pop songs. And one evil American song—"Like a Virgin". A song of such filth that whenever Hamid had the misfortune to hear it, filtered through his own imperfect understanding of the English language, he knew he was doing the right thing. To smite the Americans. To avenge Nasser. It all made sense.

It was Rashed who had been charged with telling Hamid he'd been chosen for the mission. He had also told him the thing that made Hamid smile secretly to himself whenever he thought of it. That they weren't in the middle of nowhere. That there was a village a little over a hundred miles to the west.

He learned that the camp was nestled on a narrow ridge against a rock cliff that climbed a hundred and fifty meters into the sky. A road south led to an isolated airstrip. A half mile north was the river. And the woods that bounded the camp on the west, dropping sharply down a steep slope, he now knew led to the village.

"So, are you ready for our field trip, little Hamid?" Rashed said loudly as he stowed the cassette player under his bed.

Hamid just nodded, looking at his boots. He never knew what to say to Rashed who spoke that strange stew, a westernized Farsi that was becoming more popular with young people. It made Hamid afraid.

41

"Come on, brother, show a little excitement," he said, hopping up and cuffing Hamid roughly on the shoulder. Rashed's violence, deeply a part of him, always seemed to be hovering, an enraged doppelganger ready to pummel the younger boy into submission at the most minor error.

"I look forward to our journey." Hamid's anxiety always made him speak his native tongue in a halting formality.

"I–look–forward–to–our–journey," Rashed mocked, moving in a jerky robotic half step, and then bursting into laughter. "Aw, come on, lighten up, we're going to have a great time, if you don't mind walking yourself to death."

Their mission was to trek the one hundred and fifty miles west through the woods to the village and deliver a package to a man in a boarding house. They were to be gone two whole weeks. They would miss the festivities being held for Nasser's martyrdom, but Hamid didn't mind. To him the trip sounded almost like a vacation, a concept he had no clear notion of. The plan was to walk about twenty miles a day and arrive in the village on the seventh day. Meet the man, deliver the package, and head back to camp. Hamid knew this was a test, a test of his loyalty and steadiness.

But something was gnawing at Hamid. Rashed had told him that they could cover much more ground than twenty miles a day. He had made the trip many times and knew they could travel at least thirty miles a day. That way, they would arrive in the village a day or two early and have time to explore and eat some decent food. Hamid wondered if this was part of the test. Was he supposed to say, *No, we must stick to our orders?* He meant to say it, even though he was afraid of Rashed's wrath. But he couldn't. Spending the last six months learning about guns and explosives, learning to act like a westernized Muslim, trying to forget who he was and where he came from, had convinced Hamid he needed this time in the village. He didn't know what to expect and he knew it wouldn't be like home, but anything was better than the camp.

CHAPTER FOUR

Shuroabad, Tajikistan

Rennie Vogel stood at the open door of the plane. This was how she always wanted life to be—every nerve alive with sensation, thrumming along at three hundred miles an hour. She looked for this in every corner of her life. She didn't always find it, but she did today. And she could hardly wait to jump into the abyss.

Goode raised a thickly gloved finger indicating the one-minute warning.

The team stood hip to hip. Lincoln Goode, Brad Baldwin, Jonah Levin, Rennie Vogel and John Smythe. Their thick helmets blocked out the deafening noise of the plane cutting through the atmosphere. Rennie could feel Levin next to her quivering slightly—from the intense cold as well as from the deep distress of a mind confronted with the idea of jumping into thin air at

25,000 feet. She gave him a thumbs-up. She knew he would get it together when he needed to. He always did.

Goode raised his hand again. *Ten seconds.* Rennie looked at Brad Baldwin who stood at her left—she could see his eyes but couldn't read his expression through his helmet. Goode gave the final signal and they stepped off the ledge. The cold hit her like a brick. This was something you never got used to. It was like a transformation, as if her skin and muscles were being forged into something stronger and harder. And it was a relief to be airborne after shouldering the weight of her equipment. Each of them was three hundred and sixty pounds of flesh and bone and gear, the maximum allowed for a jump at this height. Rennie, as the only woman and lighter than the rest of the team by at least seventy-five pounds, carried the most.

They plummeted through the frigid air at one hundred and twenty-six miles per hour, but to Rennie it always felt infinitely faster. At this rate, it took only two minutes to drop over twenty thousand feet to reach the mark where they pulled their rip cords. And that two minutes felt like a lifetime. This was when she got to enjoy herself, glancing at her altimeter periodically to make sure she didn't drown in the sensation. Her body always responded to this kind of intensity, like diving deep into a first kiss.

Rennie was thoroughly familiar with the area she was jumping into, having studied aerial photographs and terrain maps until she could have reproduced them by hand. Of course the land always took on a different hue when all of the elemental forces in the universe seemed to be bringing it to you at an ungodly rate.

Beneath her were a hundred acres of farmland—fields of cotton and potato and large tracts of pasture. To the northwest was a small Tajik village. To the east, an expanse of trees. But this, too, Rennie knew only from memory. This jump, like so many others she and her team had made back home in the past month, was a night jump. It was so dark she might as well have been flying through space. It was an uncanny experience, like a dream, falling into an endless void. But it wasn't endless. Not tonight. Rennie looked at the glowing altimeter strapped around her arm over her jump suit. *10,000 feet.*

No one on the team except Levin had any significant prior jumping experience. He had been with the paratrooper division of the Rangers before applying for CT3. The rest of them had done the standard jumps at two or three thousand feet—mostly static-line jumps where their canopies would automatically open. But this mission, their first important assignment, required a high-altitude free-fall jump and the other four members of the team had had to learn fast. That first time she had stood at the lip of a plane almost five miles above the earth, she had been almost entirely at peace and when she stepped from the edge she became something you should never become when you are plummeting toward the earth—contemplative. On that first drop, she had thought, what could come closer than this to transcending one's heavy, plodding, earth-bound humanity? Careening toward the ground she had believed, for an instant, that she didn't need to pull the cord. As in dreams, she imagined she would fly in a magnificent arc down, down, skimming the surface of the world until arcing upward again. Fortunately, that first jump had been a tandem jump and her partner had jolted her to her senses.

Rennie looked at her altimeter again—4500 feet. She began her countdown and pulled the rip cord. Her gloved fingers were still stiff from the sub-zero temperatures of the higher altitudes but she could already feel herself thawing. She tensed her body and waited for the bone-jarring jerk as the unfurling canopy snapped into place. *Thunk!* She thought she could hear her brain thud against her skull. A moment later she quick-released the rucksack that was lashed to her thighs and it dropped like a rock, still attached to her by a lanyard, a standard practice, ensuring that the bulk of the bag on the legs wouldn't interfere with the landing. The lights from the village allowed Rennie's eyes to adjust to the darkness and she was aware of her team around her, shadowy figures drifting slowly to the field below through the clear night sky.

She slammed into the uneven ground, dropped and rolled. In seconds, she was out of her rig and collapsing her canopy back into it. She pulled off her helmet and oxygen mask—her helmet now frosted badly—and breathed in the fresh night air. She never appreciated the real thing as much as after breathing pure oxygen for an hour.

Rennie quickly scanned her surroundings and accounted for all of her team within fifty yards, doing the same thing she was, dropping their packs and peeling off their jumpsuits. She knew the temperature was about seventy-five degrees—steaming, relative to what they had just come out of—and the air for a moment felt like stepping into a hot bath. Underneath her jumpsuit, she wore layers—cargo pants, shorts, jacket, long-sleeve shirt, tank top and hiking boots. She stripped off the extra layers until she felt comfortable and stowed them in her pack.

Baldwin came up to her, dragging his rucksack.

"You all right, Vogel?" He reached out his hand and they touched fists.

"Just glad to be earthbound again," Rennie said, then laughed as she got a good look at him. His hair, grown over his ears, was sticking straight up and there were red marks all over his face in the pattern of his oxygen mask.

"Hey, don't be thinking you look any better."

Rennie had become close with Brad Baldwin over the course of their training. He had come to the trials, like so many of them, right out of a field office—Philadelphia in his case, his hometown. He was a big, rangy guy with a goofy gait and an ever-present grin—he was about the least likely operator one could imagine. He had taken to Rennie immediately, hell-bent on breaking down the reserve she kept so firmly in place. She had resisted at first, but his good nature had finally broken through and now she counted him as her one true friend on the team. And best of all, he was utterly unthreatened by her.

Levin and Goode straggled up to them.

"Where's Smythe?" Baldwin asked.

"He's coming. He came down a little farther out," Levin said.

Rennie hadn't gotten to know Levin as well as she had

46

Baldwin and Goode, but she knew him well enough to realize he was about to vomit.

"Jonah, you okay?"

Levin rolled his eyes in annoyance, half-turned and retched up his dinner.

"Why don't you sit down, buddy, and have a drink of water?" Baldwin said, leaning down to him.

Levin, still hunched over, put out his hand in protest.

"I'm okay. I'm okay. Just the same old shit," he said, wiping his mouth.

Though he was the most experienced jumper among them, Levin's stomach often failed him. He was otherwise thoroughly reliable and Rennie liked him, though they hadn't become close. Maybe, like a lot of the guys, he resented her being there, taking up a spot on the team. But in all honesty, Rennie hadn't made much of an effort to get to know him either. She was never one to reach out.

Smythe joined them, laden with equipment.

"Are we ready for our nap?" He looked straight at Rennie. This was his new thing—everything seemed to be laced with some kind of sexual subtext whenever he talked to her.

"Let's get set and do our equipment check," Goode said. "We'll get into the woods and then we can see where we are."

Everyone knelt, sorting and checking their equipment. The original plan had been to fly out of the base in Germany at seven o' clock or 1900 hours on the MC-130E for the three-hour flight to their drop point in Tajikistan. After two hours of flight time, they would begin to pre-breathe one-hundred-percent oxygen to purge the nitrogen from their bloodstream and prevent decompression sickness and, finally, be ready to jump into the abyss at 2200 hours. This would have allowed them to get a couple of miles into the woods, make camp and sleep in shifts for four or five hours before sunrise. But things hadn't worked out that way. A violent thunderstorm grounded their plane and they hadn't been cleared for takeoff till midnight.

Rennie slipped her MP5—a small but powerful submachine

gun that rested under her left arm during the jump—from the sleeve on the ground. She made sure it was in proper working order before sliding it into the specially made pouch behind her backpack. They would be disguised as hikers and as such they had to have their weapons both easily available and easily concealed. This was accomplished by the large exterior pouch. So, the MP5 sat snugly between her backpack and her spine in its little nest, with sufficient padding for comfort and a side opening for easy access—just a quick reach behind the ribs and the weapon was in hand.

Baldwin as their best gun had to carry his sniper rifle in addition to his MP5. He checked each piece meticulously to make sure nothing was damaged when he hit the ground and slipped it into a long round padded pouch, lashing it under his pack.

Smythe was the team telecommunications specialist. He squatted in front of his rucksack and laid out each piece of equipment. Between them, they had one satellite phone, one GPS and a PDA loaded with a Tajik dictionary and phrase book along with information on the local flora and fauna that might prove useful. None of this, however, would be necessary unless something went wrong.

"Shit!"

Smythe kneeled in front of the equipment shaking his head.

"What's wrong?" Goode asked, jogging over to him.

"It's the GPS. It busted when I came down," Smythe said angrily.

"Don't worry about it, we're not going to need it," Goode assured him.

"We better not," Smythe said looking at Rennie.

"Those things don't work half the time anyway," Levin said.

"Of course they do. Our satellite systems ensure that," Baldwin said, looking unconcerned.

Baldwin was always the optimist. Rennie figured Goode was right, though. The satellite phone was more important. They would need it if disaster struck.

Rennie rubbed her arms. The warmth of the night had begun to seep through the chill that had sunk into her bones in the upper atmosphere—she'd be glad when they got moving.

Jonah Levin was gathering their jump equipment—the rigs, the jumpsuits, the helmets, masks, tubes, oxygen canisters and all the rest and stuffing it into the duffel bags that had held everything they would now carry with them on the hike. When Goode assigned duties before they left the U.S., Levin had joked that he was on trash duty—they had no choice but to leave the jump gear behind and it could never be tied to the FBI in any way. So, all jump-related equipment stayed and only the bare essentials for the hike and the mission would go. The farmer who owned the field would eventually stumble across it—Rennie imagined him scratching his chin and wondering where the hell it came from.

Rennie bent down and retied her boots. She wondered if anyone had ever made a HALO jump wearing Timberlands—hers had been modified to meet the stability standards required for the jump. The idea that the team would perform this, their first important mission, undercover, had come as a not entirely welcome surprise. The mountains of Tajikistan had drawn adventuresome hikers from around the world for years. Most knew to stay clear of the trouble spots. Occasionally, though, one would find himself someplace he shouldn't be. And this was their cover—just a bunch of stupid hikers who didn't have a clue they were edging up on a terrorist training camp. The essence of their cover was twofold—first, to draw as little attention as possible and secondly, and most importantly, to get themselves out. This was not going to be a scenario where they ran out of the woods and a chopper would be waiting for them. No, the U.S. didn't have a friendly base near enough to launch an extraction operation. They would have to walk out.

Goode was staring at his maps, looking thoughtful. Rennie wondered what was on his mind. She knew he was stressed that they had lost so much time. Goode was the oldest and most experienced special agent. He had spent ten years in the New York

City office—maybe the toughest assignment in the country—and had seen everything there was to be seen. When he was assigned the leadership position, right after Smythe replaced Perez, he had immediately taken the reins of the young team firmly in hand. He made a point of getting to know each of them and had done his best to cool the tension between Rennie and Smythe.

Everyone had their packs on now and stood waiting for orders, looking as much like ordinary hikers as such a group could. Goode finally put his map away and joined them. He looked at his watch and took a deep breath.

"It's nearly zero three thirty now. We lost a lot of time due to the storm."

Rennie knew what was coming.

"By the time we get deep enough into the woods to bed down, we'll only have about two hours of sleep before sunrise. I think that's a waste of time. So, let's push through tonight and we'll all have a good sleep tomorrow night."

Rennie knew Goode wasn't happy to be delivering this news and from their stony expressions, the team wasn't too glad to receive it either. But they accepted it.

"Hooah, boss," Levin said quietly and without enthusiasm, but with a big grin. It was an old, ironic joke between them, an allusion to the pumped-up enthusiasm so often stereotyped in movie portrayals of special forces or the military. Their team had a reputation for being unusually laid-back.

"Okay, let's move out," Goode said.

Rennie shifted her pack on her shoulders until it was in a comfortable position. She felt good. The field was damp from the night but it hadn't rained in at least a couple of days, so it wasn't mucky and walking was easy. She loved night work, she always seemed to be at her best after the sun set, but she was worried about Goode's decision not to take any rest. This was no training mission. This was the real deal and they all had to be in top form.

Ending a man's life on orders was not the most comforting proposition Rennie had ever encountered and she wasn't certain how to feel about it. She knew that on some level she hadn't taken it in entirely, hadn't allowed it to absorb into that part of herself that mattered, the part that made choices about how to live a good life in the world. Of course she'd considered when she decided to try out for CT3 that she might have to end a life. That it was even a likelihood. But assassination left a bad taste in her mouth. It was an acknowledgment that her country had exhausted all other possibilities and could no longer afford to play fair.

They were almost at the edge of the woods. Goode stopped and waited for the team to gather around.

"Okay, we go in single file, people. Keep your wits about you. We don't expect to have any company this far out, but you never know. Godspeed."

They all touched fists and filed into the coal black forest.

The woods were dense and the lights from the village were immediately snuffed out. Goode and Smythe led. Rennie fell into rhythm behind Levin. Baldwin brought up the rear. They were keeping a good pace. Rennie took a deep breath. The woods smelled organic and lush. The temperature was just right for a hike. It was fortunate that the terrain was mostly level, because it was very dark, the moonlight barely penetrating the thick canopy of leaves. Her senses were on full alert as she concentrated on each step. Every twig that snapped beneath their feet reverberated through the forest and through her nerves as they made their way through the black night ever closer to Armin and the mission they came so far to complete.

CHAPTER FIVE

They weren't making good time. Goode knew his decision to push through the night without rest was the right one. The woods were more dense than he had hoped. They needed to find one of the many paths he knew inevitably existed and would ease their way. At least the ground was mostly flat. It was the final few miles that would be the worst. From that point—as the aerial photographs showed—the mountain arced upward, at first gently and then, for the final half-mile, a forty-five degree incline up to the camp on the ridge.

But here and now, they struggled, picking their way over vines and rocks and fallen trees, through seemingly virgin woods. It would be dawn in an hour or so. Then they would stop, eat breakfast and rest for a few minutes.

Goode felt a little weary already. As the old man of the group, he had more than his share of aches and pains, but he wasn't about to let them slow him down.

He wondered how Vogel was doing and felt guilty for it. He never treated her differently from the others and believed she had rightly earned her place on the team. But a part of him looked out for her with more care than for the men. He turned his head and caught her eye. She looked strong and focused.

He thought of his wife then, alone in their apartment near Central Park. At least he hoped she was alone. She hadn't made the move with him to Virginia, kept saying she was looking for a job in D.C. But she hadn't done anything about it. During their last conversation before he flew to Germany, he wanted to ask whether all of this added up to a kind of unspoken separation. But he knew he couldn't handle the answer if it didn't turn out to be the one he wanted. Not now. He would confront it when he got back.

Struggling through the dark woods made him think too much. He missed New York. He hadn't grown up there, but it had come to feel like his hometown. He and his wife always went out for sushi every Friday. A Midwestern boy, eating raw fish—he had to shake his head. He'd changed a lot since leaving Indiana. The FBI had changed him. Growing up he had wanted nothing more than to get out of Muncie. As far away as he could. And now here he was, picking his way through the woods in a country he had never even heard of before switching majors from psychology to international politics in college.

It was finally getting light. The warmth of the night was already passing into the heat of the day. Goode wiped a thin sheen of sweat from his upper lip. Just ahead was a turbid streambed, almost completely dried up—they wouldn't be getting any water from there.

"Let's break after we cross here."

"Sounds good to me," Smythe said.

"We can have a bite to eat and rest our weary bones for a half an hour," Goode said as he slowed and stepped carefully from rock to rock. "Careful here, people, a few of these are slimy," he called out in a low voice.

"Aren't you going to lay out the red carpet for us, boss?" Levin said.

"Sure thing, I'll get right on it." Goode liked to keep things easy, it kept the team on an even keel.

As Levin was about midway across the streambed, he slipped and one foot went deep into the sludge to the ankle.

"Shit!" he said, almost falling in completely as he tried to shake the slime from his boot.

"See what you get for being such a smart-ass, Jonah," Baldwin said from behind.

Goode patted Levin on the shoulder when he finally stepped onto solid ground. "Poor Jonah. It's always something, isn't it?"

Levin had no luck. Baldwin always said he was being punished for denying his ancestry. Levin had been adopted by an older Jewish couple from a Jewish orphanage, but he liked to relate an odd fantasy of his parentage. He speculated that a couple of WASPy kids got themselves into trouble and decided to leave the baby on the doorstep of the Jewish orphanage.

"So Levin, why would a couple of rich Protestants want their kid to be raised by Jews?" Smythe asked as he plopped down on the ground.

"Because like all good WASPs, they believe in the Jewish elite, and they thought, at least their boy will have a good education."

"You went to Harvard didn't you, Jonah?" Rennie asked, ripping open her MRE and digging into it hungrily.

"Indeed I did," Levin said, smiling broadly.

"You're so full of shit, Levin. You came up with this nonsense just so you can brag about going to Harvard," Smythe interjected.

"You know, Jonah, my parents are WASPs and I never heard such vicious stereotypes from them," Baldwin said.

"Your parents aren't WASPs. You're Catholic," Levin said arching his eyebrows dramatically. Levin could find the drama in any situation.

"Okay, well then, I went to school with a lot of WASPs,"

Baldwin said.

"Right. At Catholic school. Lots of WASPs at Catholic school in Philly, huh?" Levin said, looking disgusted with Baldwin.

Goode laughed as he took a small sip from his water bladder, swallowing the last of his chipped beef and gravy. It was always rough going down cold.

"Be careful with your water. We have to have enough till we make it to the river," Goode said. "We can't count on these streams. It's been too dry."

"This is what it's all about isn't it, boss? Pain and suffering," Levin said.

"That's right. Pain and suffering and death and taxes. They all get you in the end."

Rennie was thirsty. Everyone had been rationing their water carefully and had about a liter left. Rennie had a little less. It was her weakness. She was always thirsty. A certain amount of dehydration was a certainty on a hike of this length. You just couldn't carry enough water, it would weigh you down too much. The team had trained for this, hiking for days through the Virginia woods with minimal water supplies. She could handle it better than your average person, but the body just doesn't function right without enough hydration. She capped her water bladder before she was tempted to have one more gulp.

She stood, stretching out her arms and back before she strapped on her pack. She could feel the first trace of fatigue settle into her shoulders. The woods took on a different aspect now that it was light. It made her feel exposed. The day ahead of them was daunting. Goode wanted them to cover thirty-five miles. It was doable. Especially if the land stayed level. They only needed to cover a little over two miles an hour, which under normal circumstances would be easy. But they had all gone without a night's sleep and by day's end would have hiked twenty hours straight. And they would move slower and slower as the day crept on.

Ahead of her, Levin was constantly fiddling with his pack, as if he couldn't get comfortable. She wanted to say to him, *Forget about it, comfort is not an option*. But the less conversation the better. They needed to stay as quiet as they could.

She had always been good at being quiet. *Quiet as a mouse*, her father would say to her when she was young. *What kind of a mouse?* she'd ask. *Why, a church mouse, of course.* They were Catholic. She was never one to make the ex-Catholic jokes, but she had gotten out as soon as she'd had the chance. She had known even as a small girl that the faith didn't speak to her. Her loss of faith—though in reality she never had it—had been a tragedy to her father. That, and other things.

She fingered the St. Catherine's medallion that hung on a link chain around her neck. Her father, dead of a sudden and massive heart attack ten years now, had given it to her on their one and only family vacation. To Montreal. A great city for Catholic tourists. She would never forget when he pressed it firmly into her palm. *Carry this with you always, Renée. It will keep you safe.* Her father was often a silly man, but occasionally, when he felt a particular kind of reverence, he spoke like a priest. She had kept it with her, not to keep her safe, but as a memory of her father who had loved her even through his disappointment.

The sun was shining bright and hot now, the morning almost gone. Her tank was damp below her breasts. *The river.* Already it was all she could think about. She would treat the water and drink her fill. Eating only made her thirst worse without anything to wash it down, but she had to keep up her strength.

Rennie unclipped her water bladder from her pack and took just enough to wet her lips. Then, glimpsing a movement out of the corner of her eye, she brought the muzzle of her weapon instantly toward it.

"A deer. Fifty yards to the right," she said and the message was passed up the line to Goode who raised a hand in acknowledgment. Smythe reached out his hand toward the creature, pointing it like a gun, dropping his thumb.

Rennie thought of Smythe's dog, a big old yellow lab that he brought once to a cookout at Brad's place in Alexandria. She had watched him with the dog, playing with it, feeding it little scraps of food. She wondered at the time how she could reconcile that image of Smythe with the one that sometimes reared its ugly head in her direction. Life was full of conundrums. Shoot the deer, love the dog, harass the woman.

Rennie ducked to avoid a branch.

"Here we go," Goode said, consulting the compass that hung from his belt loop.

Finally, they had stumbled onto a path and it was headed in the right direction—east and slightly north.

Hot damn! The expression was one her wild Aunt Laurel often used and it occasionally came to Rennie unbidden. Her spirits lifted, knowing their way to the water would be a little easier—unless the path veered off course. If they were lucky, it would lead them right to the river.

CHAPTER SIX

Rashed loved his gun. His weapon. Sometimes he would pose with it in front of a mirror. Like Travis Bickle. *You talkin' to me?* Here in the woods he stroked it lovingly, cradling it as he lounged at the river's edge. It was an old Russian submachine gun that he revered in a way he knew was impious. But Islam had not spoken to him in a long time. Not since America. Just another reason to crush them, for poisoning his soul against his own religion. Rashed took off his cap and wiped his brow.

Hamid reclined next to him, his feet trailing into the water.

"You know, Hamid, there are fish in that river with razor sharp teeth that could reduce your feet to a pile of bones in an instant."

Hamid pulled his feet out of the water in a flash and crab walked backward up the bank.

Rashed doubled over in laughter. "You're so gullible, Hamid. Why are you such a fool?"

Hamid drew his knees under his chin. "I don't know."

Rashed shook his head. The boy *was* a fool, but he wasn't stupid. He would require manipulating if Rashed was to get what he wanted in the village. But he was in charge this trip and he *would* get what he wanted. He almost always did. From the moment he was informed that he and Hamid would be making the delivery on their own, he knew that he would buy a woman in the village. He continued stroking the sub-gun. Pulling a clip out of his pocket, he slipped it into place, relishing the sound. Rashed hadn't killed yet, but he would. He anticipated the moment with the patience of a man waiting in the night for his tardy lover. He glanced over and saw Hamid watching him warily.

"Don't look at me, asshole."

Hamid was unarmed—he was too young and too much a fool to be trusted with a loaded weapon.

"Fill your bottle. We will walk tonight and be nearly halfway by morning."

Rashed loved the woods at night. *The woods are lovely, dark and deep.* The phrase slipped into his mind—something from a literature class he had taken at the American university. Hamid knelt at the river's edge filling his bottle. Rashed stood, feeling the strength in his legs. They had probably walked twenty miles that day and he wasn't at all tired. He popped the clip out of the machine gun and slipped it back into his pocket. He would have preferred to keep it loaded but the twenty-five-year-old weapon had its quirks and one was firing without the trigger being pulled. He turned and looked up the slope toward the line of trees. The river, open and shimmering, still held the last light of the day, but darkness hovered over the woods, a black depth he could hardly wait to pick his way through. If only he had a Walkman, so he could be joined by a thumping bass beat.

Rashed turned to see if Hamid was finished. He flinched visibly as he realized the boy was standing directly behind him, waiting, his face open and sad. Rashed threw a punch, catching him hard on the shoulder with his fist.

"Let's go."

Baldwin paused to scrape the mud off his boot onto a rock. The team had been following the path since morning with a brief break for lunch. They had made good time even though each and every one of them was thoroughly exhausted. He had begun to fantasize—not about sleep—but just laying his body down.

"Hey Vogel, you wanna take the first guard shift tonight?"

"Uh, no thanks, Brad*ley*," she said, emphasizing the last syllable of his given name. "I think I'll take my chances on the draw."

Goode told them midday, as they sat gnawing on their hateful plastic-encased meals and nursing their water, that they would stop at midnight for five hours, each taking an hour of guard duty. Four hours sleep for everyone. It seemed unfathomable.

Actually the first shift wasn't a bad deal. It meant you would have to figure out how to stay awake and alert for an hour, but after that you were rewarded with four hours of blissful uninterrupted sleep.

Baldwin's boots began to muck up again. He reached back to adjust his sniper rifle where it had shifted under his pack. Some sharpshooters he knew described their relationship with their weapon as symbiotic. They saw it as an extension of themselves and when they fired, it was like reaching out and laying a finger on the temple of their target. But to Baldwin it was just a tool, albeit one he treated with great respect. He had to see it in the bigger scope of things. Yes, he was traipsing through the woods because at the end he would line up his sights, squeeze the trigger and a man would fall. Most guys saw this kind of act as a battle between two men, a cord drawing them closer and closer together until the fatal moment. But Baldwin saw the cord branching off, from himself as well as the target, into a vast network of connections that was encompassed by two contradictory ideologies—good and evil, justice and injustice—though he never used such words. He wasn't naive, he knew that all that seemed right in the world sometimes mingled with all that seemed wrong, and he never knew with certainty that he was doing the right thing. Only the stupid and the fanatic are afforded the gift of unambiguity.

Baldwin never imagined he would wind up in the FBI. Especially on a special forces unit. His great love was the history of politics and he had planned on entering a master's program out of college. But his interest in foreign policy and his high scores on the GRE had drawn the notice of an FBI recruiter and he couldn't refuse their offer to actually affect the outcome of events in the world. And here he was, strapped with weapons instead of a book satchel.

Vogel stumbled in front of him and he stepped forward quickly and grabbed the back of her pack before she went down.

"Hey, girl, you okay?" he said quietly. The rest of the team hadn't noticed her misstep.

"Yeah, yeah. I'm fine," she said, her breath shallow. But he could see that she wasn't. She was pale and he had seen her drain her water a half mile back.

"Here. Take a big swig of this," he said, handing her his water bladder.

"No, really, Brad, I'm fine."

Baldwin grabbed her by the elbow and swung her around to him. "Take it," he said, his eyes communicating to her that no was not an option.

"Hey, would you two quit flirting and come on," Levin called out, craning his neck behind him.

"Okay," she said, taking it from him. "Thanks." She put her hand on his arm and gave it a light squeeze.

Levin always teased that Baldwin and Vogel had something going on. Levin was too self-involved to have noticed what seemed clear to Baldwin soon after he met her—that Rennie would never have any interest in him or any of the other men on the team. Baldwin found Rennie to be one of the most physically arresting women he had ever known, but he had never allowed himself to feel anything for her other than a deep friendship. She hadn't opened up to him about her personal life much, but he knew she would eventually. It was dangerous for her to reveal the intimate details of her life to anyone. Bureau culture was still such that if your personal relationships were anything other than the norm, you had to be careful. But he had encouraged his friend Marta, who briefly dated his sister in college, to quietly ask Rennie out. Later, he wondered if this had been a mistake, if he should have just minded his own business.

Marta Waugh was the house physician for the training academy at Quantico. She also performed testing and took care of anything else that might come up for the special forces teams, HRT and now CT3, that were based there. Baldwin had known Marta since their days at UPenn. He was still an undergrad and she was finishing up her course work in med school. And when he had heard about the opening at Quantico when he was still a special agent, he'd let Marta know.

A few days before the team left for Germany, he pulled her aside and asked her how things were going with Rennie, but she stonewalled, wouldn't give him any hint of what had happened. He figured Rennie, ever cautious, must have declined.

Baldwin raised his water bladder to drink, but paused before it touched his lips. Rennie might need it more than he would before they reached the river. Her step seemed more sure now that she had a little water in her. He reclipped the bladder to his belt without drinking, just in case.

What the fuck was going on?
Rennie felt like every ounce of strength had just drained out of her. She looked at her watch. It was already past midnight and they would have to stop soon. She wondered how much she was slowing down their progress and how much the rest of the team had noticed. This shouldn't be happening. She had trained for this. Water had always been a weakness, but never like this. Her pack felt like a boulder strapped to her shoulders and she could feel the outline of her sub-gun through its pouch, wearing a hole in her back. She hated to think it might be hormonal. She would *not* allow the fact of her being a woman to do anything to bring

the team down. She shook her head. It was still unbearably hot. The humidity was like D.C. in August—so thick she felt like she was crawling through it.

She had fantasized that they would reach the river tonight before they settled down to camp. And she would drink. But it wasn't going to happen.

The guys in front of her suddenly stopped. Goode had his hand raised. Holding her breath, she reached back and slipped her sub-gun from its pouch.

"Okay, this looks like a good place to stop," Goode said.

Thank God. Rennie stuffed her weapon back into its home, eased the pack off her shoulders and set it on the ground. Everything hurt. She squatted where she was and wiped her forehead with the back of her hand—cold sweat. She was going to be sick. *Don't pull a Levin.* She leaned forward, feeling the gorge rise in her throat, when a bottle seemed to appear out of a fog.

Brad.

"Here, drink. I have plenty."

She looked up at him. He wavered in her vision, her eyes unfocused. She nodded and laughed weakly, suddenly delirious with the thought of it.

"Thanks. Thanks. I owe you one."

"Sure you do."

She drank deeply and her stomach almost rejected it.

"Gather 'round, people. Let's draw straws for guard duty," Goode said motioning the team to him.

Goode stood in a small clearing. The foliage was mashed down and it looked like deer might have used it for their own camp. Surrounded by evenly spaced tall, thick poplars, it looked like a place for some kind of ritual. She thought of that old Hawthorne story where a coven of witches meet in the woods outside a tiny New England village, and a shiver ran up her spine.

Goode clutched five twigs in his fist. "Everybody grab one."

"Aw, Christ," Levin said, holding up the shortest twig.

Baldwin put his arm around Levin's shoulders in consolation. "You just need to accept who you are, Jonah, and maybe you'll have better luck," he said, laughing.

"Fuck off, Baldwin."

"Okay, here's the lineup—Levin, Vogel, me, Baldwin and Smythe. We'll start timing as soon as everyone settles in."

"Looks like you won the lottery, Smythe," Levin said.

"Whatever, I could take it or leave it."

"Oh, yeah? Want to switch?"

"Nah, you look like you could use the discipline," Smythe said, giving him a two-fingered salute.

Levin held out his arms. "Why is everybody giving me a hard time today?"

"You bring it on yourself, Jonah," Baldwin said, kneeling to unhook his bedroll.

Rennie spread her sleeping bag on the ground at the base of a tree. Her stomach was still churning from the water, but she began to feel the beginnings of hunger. Maybe she could shake this thing off. It was very dark, with only a sliver of moon not obscured by angry-looking clouds. Sleep would be a boon and she hoped her body would experience a resurrection by morning. Rennie tossed her MRE on her sleeping bag and stood up to stretch. Goode ambled over to her.

"You doing okay? You were looking a little worse for wear there for a while."

"I'm fine. The lack of water was getting to me but Baldwin gave me some of his and I'm a lot better now." She nodded. "Really."

"Are you out of water?"

"Yeah." Rennie knew what was coming.

"You know you're supposed to report that to me. We're a team out here, you know, so don't pull any heroics—we all have to get through this."

Goode turned and walked back to where he made camp. He pulled a half-full bladder of water from his pack and tossed it to Rennie. "I'm like a camel, remember that. I always have extra water."

Rennie took a big drink from the bag and noticed Smythe

looking at her and shaking his head.

Bastard, she thought.

"What is your meal du jour, Vogel?" Levin asked.

"Tonight I'm having the ever-popular beef enchilada with refried beans."

"Mmm. Does that come with the cookie or the brownie?"

"The cookie, unfortunately." Everyone loved the brownie.

"Okay, people, eat up. We need to hit the sack pronto," Goode said.

Levin rolled his eyes. "Why does he always call us 'people'?"

"He has a Chairman Mao complex," Baldwin said.

The team chuckled, unified, thankful for a light moment and for rest.

Rennie swallowed the last of her meal and took a big drink of water. She lay on top of her sleeping bag and felt her body conform to the uneven ground. She had an hour to sleep before Levin woke her. Then she would wake Goode and sleep for three more hours. It felt too good to lie down and her breathing immediately became deep.

Rashed was tired. His legs finally ached from walking for so long, but he would never admit that to Hamid. They would push on until morning when they would have a much deserved sleep. Then in a day and a half—or two days at the most—they would arrive in the village and he would find a woman.

A woman who would do whatever he wanted.

Rashed had just about had his fill of the dark woods—he always grew tired of everything he claimed to love. It would be light soon. He and Hamid had spent the last five hours picking their way through the pitch-black forest. They had a flashlight but Rashed had decided that they weren't to use it. He had no fear of stumbling across anyone in these woods. Local people far and wide knew to steer clear of all routes to Armin's camp. But Rashed wanted this trip to be a kind of initiation for Hamid—he would come out of it tougher. Maybe he would even come out of it a man. He could already feel a kernel of hatred growing in the boy. Hate for Rashed, for his hardness and his cruelty. Rashed loved seeing that hate sprout. He fed off of it.

Hamid stepped on a dry branch and a loud crack sounded through the forest. Rashed was on him in a moment, his face an inch from Hamid's. He wanted to play with him, knowing the horror his angered face would present to the boy.

"Do not make a sound!" he seethed and looking around said, "Don't you know anyone might be in these woods and you and your big clumsy feet could get our heads blown off."

Rashed released him roughly and Hamid fell to the ground, his face filled with terror. Then Rashed spoke again in a barely audible voice.

"I won't die because of you. Though you might," he said, his teeth glinting in the pale moonlight, "because of me."

Rashed's face was wicked in its anger as Hamid looked up at it from the ground. A sliver of moon framed the larger man's head like a halo. The effect was disconcerting.

Rashed was enraged and Hamid couldn't puzzle out why. He seemed to have become angrier the farther they got from camp. And then, making them walk all day and into the night—Hamid felt like he might collapse. He didn't even know what he was doing. He and Rashed were to deliver a package—Hamid had yet to see it—that Rashed carried in the pack on his back. He couldn't imagine what was in it. Guns, perhaps. All business in the camp seemed to have something to do with guns. Hamid was glad he hadn't been allowed to carry one on this trip. He hadn't proved very proficient with them yet. Fareed Reza had taken him aside one day during target practice when his recoiling weapon had actually flown out of his hands and nearly killed the boy shooting next to him. Fareed, at least two heads taller, had put his arm around his shoulders and told him not to worry, there were other things he would be useful for, he would find his place in the organization. That was the last time Hamid had any hope that everything would be all right. Here in the dark of the blackest night he had ever seen, with Rashed acting like a madman, life did not seem in any way all right.

Hamid heard a loud snap. Rashed was in his face again, his lips against his ear.

"I said, do-not-make-a-sound."

"It wasn't me. I swear on the Holy Koran."

Rashed became alert. He handed Hamid his pack before slipping the clip of bullets from his pocket.

Hearing a rustling, Hamid caught Rashed's eye and pointed to the left. With the clip still in his hand, Rashed edged toward the direction of the noise. The woods were dense here. Each step was carefully chosen. Hamid placed his own foot in the slight indentation in the ground left by Rashed's boot prints.

And then Rashed stopped. He was utterly still.

Suddenly, Hamid heard voices. His heart leapt into his throat and he pressed his feet into the ground so he wouldn't run away as fast as he could. Then he was able to discern the words or at least the language—English.

Rashed turned to him, his eyes aflame, his lips twisted into an unholy grin. He mouthed one word—*Americans*.

CHAPTER SEVEN

Rashed felt gleeful, joyous, rapturous. The bloodlust that had throbbed within him, simmering just under the surface for as long as he could remember, boiled in his brain. And now he could indulge in it, luxuriate in it. And best of all, they were Americans. He looked at Hamid, standing perfectly still with a frozen look of terror on his face. Here was his chance, the offering he had been waiting for. He wouldn't have to wait any longer for the call to arms that never seemed to come. After all the endless drills and tedious speeches that never led to anything—at least not since he had joined up—he would put Armin's supposed ideology into action. In an instant, he had thrown the magazine into place and his finger depressed the trigger.

Smythe roused slightly. Goode was waking Baldwin for the

change of guard and had made some remark. Baldwin laughed quietly. Then Smythe heard the unmistakable sound of a magazine being snapped into place. Before he could even raise his weapon, the first volley of bullets had made a pattern across his chest. He could hear more bullets biting into the ground to his left and finding their home in flesh. He looked over to see Goode lying next to Baldwin. Goode was already dead. Smythe saw Baldwin unload his MP5 in the direction of the enemy fire and then his body jerked as he was hit in the neck and chest.

Smythe could feel himself dying. Where were Levin and Vogel? His vision was beginning to blur, but he was able to make out a crumpled mass that used to be Levin. Even in the darkness, he could see red everywhere amongst the silvery greens of the forest. Then silence. Smythe lay very still. His sub-gun was lying next to him but he couldn't seem to reach for it. He caught movement out of the corner of his eye. A man leaned over a young boy who was obviously dead. Baldwin must have hit him before he was shot. *Is it possible there were only two of them?* The man rolled the dead boy over roughly with his boot. He was searching the boy's pack. He was looking for more ammunition. He needed another clip. Smythe gazed longingly at his MP5, but no amount of desire could induce his useless limbs to move. *It's over*, he thought. Just then, from somewhere behind him, a figure flashed by.

Vogel.

He saw a look of anger and surprise in the man's eyes as she charged at him. But he was fast and swung the butt of his weapon up quickly and smashed it against her head. Smythe wondered where the hell her weapon was. Vogel dropped fast, holding the side of her head which was covered in blood. Then the man threw down his useless gun and was on top of her in an instant. Vogel opened her eyes and seemed to come to as soon as he was on her. They struggled, a mass of flailing arms and legs. Smythe could hear the man repeating over and over again, his voice gravelly, in lightly accented English, "I'm going to fuck you, I'm going to fuck you."

Smythe smiled to himself. So, Vogel was going to get it in the end after all. He would have laughed if he had the strength. The man seemed to have her where he wanted her—she was neatly pinned and unable to move. She looked stoic, her eyes closed, her face set. Then she turned her head and looked at Smythe. She locked eyes with him and shook her head. Her eyes were black with rage.

This is not happening, this is not happening.
He was strong, so strong. Rennie knew his lust made him even stronger. She could smell it on him, his breath peppered with it. How had they gotten to this point? Why hadn't she taken her weapon with her when she went behind the tree? This was her fault. But what happened to Goode? When she'd stepped away from their camp, he had been awake and alert.

Rennie lay still. She and the man had reached an impasse. They breathed heavily, almost in unison. Any moment, he would make his move. He had already wedged his body between her legs. Did she have the strength to resist him? But then, Rennie felt something hard strapped to his outer thigh against her knee.

A knife.
She turned her head and saw Smythe covered in blood laying at the base of a tree. He wasn't dead, but he was close. He was watching her. And he was smiling. The man put his mouth against her ear again and said, "I'm going to fuck you." He let go of his tight grip on her wrist to reach for the fastening of his pants. That was enough. Rennie wrenched her arm down to the knife and slammed her head into his nose. Blood gushed over her chest. She pulled the knife from its sheath and plunged it into his back. He arched upward, his face a mask of terror and astonishment. Driving the knife deeper into his back, she gritted her teeth and twisted it, feeling its resistance against his muscle and bone. He released his grip on her and she grabbed the back of his head with her other hand, forcing him to look at her before the light in his eyes faded.

"Who's fucked now?" she said and rolled the man's body off

hers with a violent shove.

She shook her head, still dazed from the blow of the gun. Then she saw movement to her left and drew her legs up, ready to move. *Smythe*. His eyes were heavy-lidded but there was life in them. She scooted toward him. The ground around him was saturated with his blood. *You're dead*. His lips trembled. It wouldn't be long now. Then she realized he was speaking and she leaned down to him and put her ear to his mouth.

"You?" He spoke in a whisper. "You get to be the hero? Goddamn."

She felt tiny puffs of air against her cheek as he attempted to laugh. She drew back from him. His eyes were unseeing but his lips continued to move. And then they stilled.

Rennie tried to stand quickly, to right herself and regain what little control she had, but the blood pounded painfully at the wound on her head and she sat back down hard. Tremors shaking her body, she sat hugging her knees to her chest and reluctantly surveyed the scene. Five men—*no, six*—another lay a few feet into the woods—dead around her, some staring the unmistakable glare of death. And Brad. Rennie covered her mouth as a sob caught in her throat. She forced herself onto her knees and crawled slowly toward him. Tears now blurred her vision as he wavered and danced through the distortion. She stopped short of where he lay slumped against a tree. She rested her hand on his leg and cried quietly, mouth wide as if a scream might emerge, but only a few choked noises slipped from her throat.

Get it together, Rennie. Get it fucking together.

She passed her hand over her face as if to clear away all the pain and confusion that had burrowed into her mind. She had to think.

The satellite phone.

She needed to try to make contact. She stood slowly and made her way to Smythe's pack. She glanced at him, his eyes still gaping, and thought of the moment that had passed between them as the man was on top of her. He had seemed so satisfied. *Bastard.*

Hero. Could he possibly see the world that way? Heroes and villains. She reached into his pack and found the phone. The number she needed to call was committed to memory. She powered on the phone and raised the antenna. The signal was weak but it might be possible to make a successful call. She stared at the signal indicator. She could imagine Brian Ryder's voice at the end of the line. He manned communications at CT3's Central Command at Quantico. And then what? What would she say? That the team had been ambushed and she was the only one alive? It would only confirm to every naysayer who had been against a woman's inclusion on the team that it was a disastrous experiment. And she would be the scapegoat.

Was she responsible? How could she be? The only reason she wasn't dead, too, was that she had stepped away from camp to relieve herself and was returning when she had heard the first burst of gunfire. But she hadn't taken her weapon with her. A fatal error. One that shouldn't have happened. It was against every protocol that she would have left her weapon. And now everyone was dead. She looked again at the signal indicator. This could be the FBI's only chance to take Armin out without the assassination being tied to the United States. She stepped away from the camp and the signal grew stronger. She stared at the satellite phone, considering her options. Then she glanced over her shoulder at the brutal scene behind her and powered down the phone.

Rennie went back to Brad, remnants of sobs still catching her breath, and arranged his body so that he lay flat, his arms crossed over his chest. Then she turned to Goode and did the same. The condition of his head showed that his death had been mercifully brief. Levin was a mess, riddled with bullets. She hooked her arms under his shoulders and dragged him so that he lay next to Baldwin and Goode, leaving a trail of blood. Then Smythe. She hated to touch him, but arranged his body next to the others. She laid their weapons and their packs alongside of them and then took their sleeping bags and covered them.

Her strength had returned now that she knew what she had to do. First she went for Baldwin's sniper rifle. It almost seemed like a sacred thing to her, because Brad had treated it that way. A deadly thing of power that could snuff out a life in a second. Rennie had some training on the weapon, maybe even more than most. After the initial team training she had gone out with Brad a few times to shoot, with this very rifle. So it was familiar, but she knew she wasn't an expert. She lashed the gun under her own pack and stowed the ammunition in a pocket. Then she went back to Goode to get the maps and the medical kit. Leaving her bedroll where it lay, she dumped most of her extra clothing and began filling the space it left with as many MREs as could fit. Finally, she bent to Goode's pack, pulling from it the M2 mini-bomb and storing it in the cargo pocket of her pants.

Water. Her weakness. Rennie collected three extra bladders, mostly empty. Once she got to the river, she could fill them. Now she turned her attention to the man she had killed. She didn't want to get near him after all that had passed between them, but she had to investigate his body. Even if she couldn't use anything she found, she would need it for her report. Stilted sentences began to compose themselves in her mind, but she put a stop to it. There would be time to worry about salvaging her career—later. She hoped.

Rennie stood above the dead man. He had to be from Armin's camp. There were no other outposts in this remote part of the country. She put her boot on his hip and shoved, but he was too heavy. Steeling herself, she sank down on her knees, grabbed his trousers and shirt and rolled him over. She looked at him coldly. His eyes were wide and he still had a look of surprise on his features, mouth agape.

Rennie had never encountered death in this form, in the field, from combat. And by her own hand. She couldn't analyze what she was feeling. It was a kind of pure rage, one that had passed from the sort of madness that confounds the mind to one that offers a cold, raw clarity she didn't know was in her. Her tremors had long ceased and she was, for the moment, as calm as if she had just woken from a long and deeply restful sleep.

She suddenly grasped his shirt again, with both hands, and

heaved him up to her, her strength returned, and stared intently at his features.

This is the man I killed.

Just as suddenly, she dropped him back to the ground, his head lolling, and began rifling through his pockets. She found a small penknife, a handkerchief and a pouch with a few Iranian coins, confirming he was likely one of Armin's men.

Rennie moved to the boy next. He seemed impossibly young for a soldier, almost a child. She felt a rush of reverence for her country well up inside her—they didn't employ boys to fight their wars. Young men, yes. But not boys. She hesitated before touching him. His neck and torso had been destroyed by gunfire and were nothing but a pulpy mass. One leg was twisted at an odd angle. He was already down before she had darted from behind the tree and run at the man. Rennie wondered who shot him.

She could see a rectangular outline in one of the pockets of his pants. She knelt and discovered a little book of Koranic sayings. She shook her head and laid the book on his chest, covering it with his hand. The rest of his pockets yielded nothing, but his pack was another matter. In it were the usual items needed for a long hike and, at the bottom, a thick envelope. It wasn't very heavy and certainly wasn't a bomb. Rennie pried it open and slipped out the cache of papers. It was a short document, maybe ten pages, handwritten in Farsi. Rennie could recognize a few words but not enough to interpret it. The final page was a hand-drawn map, showing a network of buildings in a few blocks radius—Rennie recognized it as the nearby village.

Again she thought of calling in, felt the weight of the satellite phone in her pocket. But what good would it do? She had no way of interpreting the document. She returned it to the envelope and slipped it into her pack. Safe and sound.

Rennie stood and took a deep breath. It was only seven in the morning and she was already sweating heavily. She stripped off the long-sleeved blood-soaked shirt, rolled it and tied it around her hips. Her tank top wasn't nearly as bloodied and the air felt good on her shoulders. She surveyed the scene again through the thin morning light. There was nothing else she could do. She slipped on her pack, heavier now from the added equipment, and set out in the direction of the river.

CHAPTER EIGHT

Armin Training Camp

Fareed Reza was growing tired of his life.

"You make an unlikely terrorist," he spoke to his reflection, the razor pausing on his chin. He shook his head and laughed derisively under his breath. It was perhaps the first time he had ever used the word in relation to himself and the work he did for Ahmad Armin. *Terrorist.* He laid the razor on the table next to the basin of water and stared into his dark eyes, his expression one of blank horror.

What have I done?

He'd come down a long strange path after he left London. He loved London, its intensity, its diversity, as one good neighborhood yielded to another not quite as good and then that yielded to something raw and buzzing with every sordid permutation of life one could imagine. It always suited him more than the city of his birth, New Delhi, with its stifling heat and open sewers and where his family endured in the small Muslim minority. And it certainly suited him more than Ahmad Armin's camp clinging to its little mountain ridge.

Fareed had been a good student and had gone up to Oxford to read history, a discipline he had little passion for, but he was a good son and it was what his father wanted. Finishing his degree, he entered a graduate studies program in London. It was a time of intense political activism in the city's Muslim community and Fareed had begun to become interested in politics. He even imagined he might run for office one day, but his father had quashed the idea with a dismissive wave of the hand. "Politics is a dirty business, my son will not soil the name of his family."

It was finally the complicated stew of East and West that had brought him to where he stood, shaving his face in a makeshift house on a dusty cliff. In a replaying of one of the oldest conflicts known to man—the old country against the new, tradition against progress, father against son—his father's dismissive gesture had roused a rebellious instinct, one that in a moment of uncharacteristic anger sent him walking London's poorer neighborhoods in search of something, anything, his father would revile. He'd found it on the doorstep of the city's most controversial mosque where he met a man who would introduce him to Ahmad Armin. He had enough of the West in him that he was unable to swallow his father's wave of the hand like a good Indian boy would and, in truth, he was instantly fascinated by the politics of the mosque. But he was soon to learn that activism tainted with violence went far beyond the inevitable corruption in politics. And though his mind was nimble enough that he was able to construct elaborate justifications for what he considered to be a purely intellectual antagonism toward the West, he knew that there was only rot at the core of it. Now, that hard vein of defiance, born out of his father's fateful gesture, had finally begun to crack with age.

Fareed picked up the razor again, recalling the summer after his first year at Oxford. He had taken a month in the States with his father's money—they were still on good terms then. He'd stood in the West Wing of the National Gallery transfixed by a portrait of a woman. Da Vinci's *Ginevra D'Benci*. Feeling a presence behind him, he turned, taking in a woman who had such a striking resemblance to the portrait that it took his breath away. She, too, was consumed by the painting and turned her wide dark eyes upon him when she heard him gasp.

"Someone said I look like her."

She was simple and direct and an American—American to the core, unthinking in the way that most cannot afford—and he fell in love with her in an instant. They spent three weeks together. Fareed had not yet developed any firm ideology, but he had been long certain that American influence around the globe was a dangerous entity. To love this woman seemed like the ultimate betrayal of his principles, something he couldn't stomach. So, one morning, like a coward, he left her before dawn, without a word, hiding himself away from her until his return to England. Her image had come to him at unexpected moments in the last weeks, sometimes superimposed with the image of Da Vinci's great portrait. Lately he had begun to believe that this cowardly act defined him. He had never confronted anything directly—his father, the woman and, perhaps that of most consequence, his ideology. He had always taken the route of the snake.

Fareed wiped his face with a towel. He had aged, these past few years. At forty, he was no longer boyish. He folded the towel and hung it neatly on the rack. He moved to the roughly cut window of his hastily constructed house and pulled the curtain aside. Looking onto the maneuvers field, he watched the young men going through their drill. He thought of Hamid. Nice boy. He had tried to prevent Armin from sending him with Rashed to the village. But perhaps it would make him feel useful and ease some of his homesickness. Fareed regretted recruiting him. A nasty business—recruiting young boys.

He sometimes felt that he and Armin were playing a child's game of war and he suspected the game was about to become more serious. Armin had begun to talk more frequently about doing something on a larger scale, an event creating an impact that would put them on the run for the rest of their lives.

He heard a soft tap at the door and walked through the spare front room to answer it. A boy stood before him squinting in the harsh morning sun.

"General Armin has requested your presence."

"Tell him I'll be right there."

General Armin. Fareed shook his head. How absurd. Armin's mental state seemed to be deteriorating. It was bad enough when he put on a uniform, but this recent development of titling himself seemed beyond reason. Always mindful of his appearance, Fareed smoothed his shirt front before stepping into the blinding sunlight and heading for Armin's quarters.

Rennie had been walking all day. She was soaked in sweat, her tank top clinging to her. At least the heat was finally beginning to break. She had about an hour before she would need to make camp. She would certainly reach the river the next day. It had been sweltering since the sun came up and she had already gone through most of her water. She had to stay hydrated or she knew she would get sick again. At least the hiking was helping to alleviate some of the stress. At times she wished she could just break into a run. She had always been a great runner. It was one of the things that set her apart from the others in her class—no one could outrun her, not even the men. But she had to save energy and pace herself.

Running sometimes made her think of Brad's friend, Marta. Brad's friend. She still thought of her that way, but Marta was her friend, too. Friends of a sort. Rennie had tried to steer clear of Marta. She had picked up on a flicker of attraction when she went in for one of her physical checks. MacPherson would send her in to run on the treadmill a couple of times a month and Marta would measure her heart rate, her blood pressure, her lung capacity, all in search of the key to her uncommon physical abilities.

One day, after a test late in the afternoon, Marta had asked

Rennie to have a drink. Rennie caught the subtlety in her voice and the pointed expression on her face that suggested a drink might not be all she had in mind. Rennie hesitated. She had experienced this kind of overture before and always declined. She had never been willing to risk anyone finding out—it would have been career suicide. But now, after working sixteen-hour days, seven days a week for months, she finally had a weekend off. A night out with an interesting woman seemed too comforting to pass up.

They had agreed to meet at a restaurant near Marta's apartment in Adams Morgan. Driving up I-95 back to the city, Rennie breathed deeply, feeling a fraction of the strain she had accumulated over the past few months begin to slip away. She thought of her little apartment on Capitol Hill, an English basement, only a few blocks from where she grew up. She hadn't been there in weeks, hadn't slept in her own bed in months—not since the team had received their orders for the mission. She missed it. It was her sanctuary, a place of safety and a place of isolation—something she never had growing up in her busy household. She kept it her own, rarely had anyone over and never invited anyone to stay the night.

Driving down Independence Avenue, just past the Capitol, she swung a left onto Second Street. A few more turns and she was parked in the graveled courtyard behind her apartment. Living in the shadow of the Capitol, Rennie never took its grandeur or what it represented for granted. She loved her country, though not blindly like so many of her colleagues. Sometimes, when she was tired and came home from a day studying the not always rosy consequences of American influence, the thought of so much concentrated power filled her with dread.

Opening her apartment door, Rennie breathed in the familiar musty odor. It was an old building and her basement had doubtlessly flooded countless times and would forever carry the feeling of damp. She tossed her suitcase on the bed, poorly made from her last too-short stay.

She sat down heavily on the edge of the bed and caught

her reflection in the mirror of her old dresser. The mirror was mottled and warped with age. She stood and leaned toward the spotted glass. How long had it been since she had really looked at herself? With her routine at Quantico, she was out of bed, in the shower and out the door in fifteen minutes or less. She would be gone before the steam on the tiny bathroom mirror had dried.

Now, she saw that she looked very tired. And she needed a haircut. She ran her hands through her thick, dark hair, tucking a few strands behind her ears. She wore a tight black short-sleeved shirt. She had always been thin, but the incessant training had made her very lean. She could see her collarbones clearly beneath the stretchy material of her shirt and her arms seemed little more than muscle and bone.

She shouldn't have made the date with Marta. She was exhausted. And she was taking a huge risk. Marta was Brad's friend, but she had no idea whether she could be trusted. It was too late to cancel. She wouldn't stand her up. She wasn't like that.

The restaurant was very dark. Rennie was late and apparently so was Marta, unless she had already left. Rennie sat down at the bar and ordered a drink.

"Hey! Sorry I'm late." Marta slipped onto the stool next to Rennie and laid her hand on her arm. "I had a few things I had to wrap up at the office."

"Don't worry about it," Rennie said, moving her arm from under Marta's hand with a glance at the bartender. "I've only been here a few minutes."

They moved to a table, ordered their food and made the usual small talk about work. Rennie felt awkward, unable to find her natural composure. She drank her wine quickly and poured another, feeling it settle into her limbs and slow the panic in her brain.

After the waiter cleared their plates, they sat slowly sipping the last of their bottle of wine. There was a lull in the conversation. Marta, her elbows on the table, was fingering the rim of her wineglass. Rennie felt more relaxed than she had in months and for the moment didn't worry about who might see her. She watched Marta's finger on the glass. When she looked up, Marta was watching her intently. It was an unmistakable look of attraction, a look that could mean only one thing, but somehow mixed in with it was a trace of sadness too. When they stepped onto the sidewalk, leaving the warm intimacy of the restaurant, and Marta said, "Would you like to see my place?" the look was gone and the question sounded almost innocent.

But it hadn't been of course. Stepping into Marta's apartment, Rennie could see the clean outlines of her furniture in the mix of moonlight and citylight coming through the open windows. Then Marta's hands encircled her waist and she felt her mouth on her neck. A sharp bolt of desire coursed through her body and settled between her legs. Rennie lifted Marta's head and their mouths met impatiently.

They kissed just inside the door, in the dark. They didn't pause to speak a word of meaningless endearment or to look into each other's eyes. All they wanted was to be mouth and hand and flesh, understanding the need for efficiency. Somehow they made it to the bedroom.

Afterward, they lay atop the duvet on the bed where they had fallen, hungry for each other. Marta lay with her head on Rennie's breast, an arm across her body tightly gripping her hip. Then she seemed to doze for a moment. Rennie looked down at her, Marta's expression one of slumber, and felt her throat constrict. She couldn't allow herself to dwell on the fineness of the moment. She didn't have space for such things in her life now and knew she shouldn't imbue it with meaning that wasn't there. She bent and lightly kissed the woman on the forehead, lingering a moment. Then Rennie shifted and slipped from underneath her.

"Marta, I need to go."

Quickly awake and shaking off her drowsiness, Marta said, "Oh, okay, sure, yeah, I need to get up early myself."

Rennie dressed quickly, an emptiness replacing the afterglow of their lovemaking. Marta was in the kitchen drinking a glass of water when Rennie came out of the bedroom.

"Would you like a cup of coffee or something before you

go?" she asked distractedly.

"No. Busy day tomorrow, you know. Thanks, though." She paused. "It was a nice evening."

Closing the door and running down the stairs to the street, Rennie wanted to get as far from Marta and her spare, dark apartment as she could. It wasn't as if she hadn't done this kind of thing before, it was just that she had always allowed herself to forget what it felt like afterward.

Letting go of the memory, Rennie threw her pack against the base of a tree where she would camp for the night. The thought of Marta always carried a twinge of desire and a slight queasiness. They had been together a few times after that first night. Marta had an edge to her, moments when a sharp nastiness would emerge, but she grew tender in bed. After that first time, they skipped dinner, neither willing to develop a fiction that they were actually dating. Such relationships were bred by Bureau culture. Rennie wasn't surprised by this, she knew how things worked, but she had hoped after signing up and getting a feel for the lay of the land that she would be able meet someone on the outside and do the normal things people do who are interested in one another, instead of succumbing to the easy lure of furtive couplings with other desperate colleagues.

She shook her head wondering why she was thinking about Marta. She felt a deep twinge of guilt, manifesting itself in a sharp pain across her brow, for allowing herself to focus on something so mundane when her team lay dead miles behind her. But she couldn't allow herself to think of them. Not yet. Any thought of them took her mind to places she couldn't handle right now— to intimately physical images of their bodies cold, their blood congealed, night creatures that prey on the weak and helpless drawn to their inert vulnerability. She knew that allowing such images to form completely would bring her down. And she couldn't be brought down.

Rennie was exhausted from the day's hike and from smothering crippling thoughts. She had made good time, a little over forty miles, she calculated. *Forty miles*. There was a time when covering

83

that much distance in a day with a heavy pack strapped to her back would have been inconceivable.

She had never been much of an outdoors person, growing up in the city. Games of competition would occasionally draw her out of her room, her cloister, her father had called it. She was always there, reading a book, usually sitting on the floor leaning against her bed where she couldn't be seen if someone opened her door. There in the world of books, she wasn't anyone's daughter, anyone's sister, just herself, imagining what it might be like to live a different life.

But after she left for college, she suddenly began to get a sense of herself and her place in the world. Her first dose of reality. She began to think of herself for the first time as a woman. Before that, she imagined that when womanhood was conferred upon her (it was never clear how this would happen) it would bring with it certain privileges that she had missed as a girl, privileges not given to children. She learned, and perhaps she had always known it, that the absence she felt was not a condition of childhood but a condition of femaleness. This was a kind of revelation. She felt she had to do something, anything to remedy her sense of powerlessness.

Her first instinct was to move her body. She took herself to the gym and began running around the ancient indoor track overlooking the pool. She started with just a few miles. Years of inactivity made her lungs strain for each breath and her legs were shot through with pain from her first experience with lactic acid. But her body quickly acclimated to motion and she could hardly believe she had lived so long without it. Soon she was running for hours, ignoring the pain which began to seem meaningless to her, something not quite real that she could compartmentalize as something not part of her, something one chose to feel or not to feel. She chose not to. She had yet to reach her limit, that point where she couldn't take another step or couldn't perform whatever was required of her. She only knew how good it felt to run and reach the place where she could go on forever, where she felt strong, and no one could stop her. Eventually after much hesitation she ventured into the weight room and saw to her surprise that she wasn't the only woman. Her physical conditioning became a kind of obsession and eventually she almost forgot why she had begun it all.

Rennie stretched out on the ground at the base of a tree that would be her home for the night. She had eaten about an hour before as she walked. Estimating that the river was probably only about thirty miles away, she wanted nothing more than to drink every drop of her dwindling water supply. She had considered pushing on, but knew she needed to treat herself with great care at this stage.

She was beginning to grow accustomed to the woods. She felt her body conform to the hard ground. The trees above her were still, the leaves and limbs silhouetted against the sky. The moon was large and low and just out of view but its light illuminated the black sky, revealing ghostly churning clouds. Rennie's mood shifted as she took it all in. The clouds, moving and swirling, seemed violent and stood in counterpoint to the stillness where she was. She, too, was still, lying silent. But inside violence reigned—the violence of the previous night, the violence she herself would commit two nights hence for the sake of the mission, and the violence of her thoughts and emotions, shifting and colliding deep under her false calm. She pushed it all away and tried to rest.

She had no way of knowing if Armin had these woods patrolled. The absurdity of sleeping with no protection fell over her like a pall. She must rest, but to do so was to put herself at incredible risk. If she was discovered, she only hoped that death would come quickly. She had no choice and it felt like a sacrifice. At least the two dead men supposed to be en route to the village wouldn't be soon missed.

When she woke to her watch alarm vibrating gently on her wrist, Rennie felt like someone was holding a warm hand over her mouth and nose. She couldn't breathe. The night had become oppressively hot. She kicked her legs trying to throw off an imagined blanket, but found she was without cover. She stood slowly, her limbs stiff from the night on the hard ground. It was barely light. She stripped off her tank and cargo pants and stood beneath the canopy of trees trying to get air to her limbs. But the air had no freshness to it. It was close and perfectly still, like the last breath of someone in the grip of a fever.

Dressed again, she grabbed her water bladder and took a big drink. She only had about two cups left, not nearly enough to sustain her for what she had to do. Knowing it would take her most of the day to hike to the river filled her with dread. This thought got her moving.

She packed up and ate as she walked. The MRE this morning was hard going down, the heat destroying her appetite. She found a good trail, likely made by the local red deer, a variety larger and wilder in appearance than anything she had seen in the States. Would the trail lead her straight to the river? Her compass indicated she was heading in the right direction. She was already covered in perspiration, sweat stinging her eyes. She stopped, pulled a T-shirt from her pack, wiped her face and tucked it in the waistband of her cargo pants.

Around noon the ground began to get damp and then so soft her boots were sinking into it. She had to be close to the river now, but had to veer away trying to escape the muck. The area clearly flooded regularly and she wondered if she'd have to traverse what might turn into a swamp in order to get to the river. The farther she walked, the deeper the mud seemed to get. She kept moving farther south and farther from the river. She thought that it must start to solidify soon and then she could cut back northeast. Her boots were already caked with the muck and in some spots she sank to the ankle.

Finally free of it and back on solid ground, she stopped to drink one of her last sips of water. The trees here were farther apart and the sun shone bright and hot on her head and shoulders. The moisture in the air had increased as the sun moved to its highest point and she began to worry about becoming dehydrated again. She felt lightheaded and took off her pack and sat at the base of a slim tree. She was already completely drained. She wished she could just close her eyes until the hottest part of the day had passed, but she knew she needed to stem her dehydration before she became ill.

She stood and struggled back into her pack. She hadn't felt the weight of it earlier in the day, but now she could feel the muscles in her back and shoulders straining against it. She decided to head northeast again to see if she could skirt the bog. Maybe it wouldn't be too bad. She tried not to think of what prehistoric life might be lurking there.

The ground looked entirely normal in some spots, until she stepped on it and heard the sucking sound against her boot. Thick viscous mud oozed from under whatever greenery and dead leaves were on top, hiding the soft ground underneath. A light suction formed and she had to pull her foot out of the mess with each step, as if forces deep within the earth were trying to pull her in. She paused against a tree to shift the weight of her pack. She felt very weak.

A large log lay across her path. She stepped over it and her foot plunged into the sludgy earth on the other side up to her knee. The weight of her pack pushed her down hard, deep into it, scraping her back leg against the log. Trying to steady herself, one arm went into the mud and the other grabbed hold of the log before the weight of the pack forced her headfirst into the mess.

She pulled herself back onto the somewhat more solid ground on the other side of the log. One leg felt heavy, coated with mud and grime, the other was bleeding through her pants from a long gash where her shin scraped the log. *This is bad*, she thought, *really bad. Here I am dying of thirst and there's a swamp between me and the only water source I know of.*

She sat down heavily on the log. It shifted and sank a little underneath her. She scraped the mud off her leg and hand. The cut on her leg was still bleeding. She couldn't deal with that right now, she had to get to water or she would pass out. Her vision was beginning to cloud and she figured she wouldn't have misjudged the solidity of the ground if she were at full capacity. She looked at her watch. *Two o'clock*. She tried to survey the ground to determine where it was soft and how deep it was. Looking over the log to where she plunged in, she should have realized that the area was impassable. *Okay, concentrate*. It didn't seem as bad farther along. She began walking east and couldn't see any place that looked as soft as where she'd fallen. She turned and headed northeast again. The cut on her leg was beginning to sting, but it wasn't bleeding anymore.

The ground was more solid now, but Rennie realized she wasn't walking steadily. She couldn't seem to put one foot in front of the other in a straight line. And she was moving very slowly. She could barely pull her T-shirt from her belt to wipe her face and when she did she realized she was no longer sweating and she began to shake. Every modicum of moisture left in her was going to support her organs. She raised her hand to her face and felt herself crumple in a rush of emotion. She sank to her knees as the ground danced and wavered in front of her.

I'm going to die here.

She knew it. Her skin felt ice cold and she shook violently from head to toe. And then her nose picked up something in the air.

She smelled it before she saw it. And the temperature felt just a touch, the merest shade, cooler. The air had a moist, organic smell. Then she saw the water and wondered if her eyes were playing a trick on her.

She struggled to her feet, falling before she regained her height. She drew in a deep breath and felt an almost religious ecstasy course through her body. She threw off her pack and rushed to the muddy edge of the river. She plunged her arms into it to the elbow and rejoiced in its coolness. She brought her cupped hands to her mouth, but stopped as her lower lip touched the small pool of water. She violently shook out her hands and wiped the trickle from her lip.

"Shit! Shit! Shit! Get it together!" She turned and grabbed for her pack, ripping it open and searching its pockets for her iodine tablets. Her hands couldn't stop jumping as she twisted off the cap of her water bladder and knelt again to the water to fill it. She felt her sub-gun swing around from her back and caught it just as the tip of its muzzle slipped into the river. *Goddammit, goddammit, it wasn't supposed to be like this.* She was falling apart and everything was going wrong.

No, you're okay, you're okay.

She just needed to drink and eat and gather her strength again. She dipped her water bladder into the water and filled it, dropping in two of the tablets and tightening the cap. Now, she had to wait at least ten minutes while the tablets did their work. She crawled back from the river into the shade, dragging her pack with her.

Leaning against a tree, she stared at the water bladder, her face slack. Her skin felt clammy and she was covered in grime. She knew she was sick but accepted the knowledge dumbly, ignorant for the moment of the possible consequences. She looked at her watch and realized she hadn't noted what time she put the tablets in. She raised her hand to her mouth as her face twisted into a picture of grief. "I can't do this," she said quietly as her body kicked lightly with the emotion. And then she knew that she would die, right there on that spot, unless she did something. She looked at her watch again. She knew she couldn't risk a guess. She turned the bezel to the current time to clock the ten minutes and resumed her dead stare at the water bladder.

She would try to eat something while the iodine tablets killed any lurking bacteria in the water. She hadn't eaten since morning and this accounted in part for her condition. She looked through her MREs, chose a beef stew and ripped open the package. The sight of the brown glop made her stomach shudder and she tasted acid in her throat. Her stomach leapt a few times as she put the first spoonful in her mouth. She put the odor and taste out of her mind by concentrating on the second hand moving around the dial on her watch. She forced down several bites and then finally, the time elapsed, she uncapped the water bladder and drank the entire liter in almost one gulp. The water tasted horrible, but it didn't matter. She felt better just knowing she had water in her system. She scooted back to the edge of the river, refilled her water bladder, added another two tablets and then reset the bezel on her watch.

She crawled back to her tree and checked out her surroundings. She could see several hundred yards down the bank of the river until it turned slightly. The river's edge was sandy for part of the way and then ceded again to woods. A slim path cut through the woods, keeping along the river. She hoped the path had been made by animals and not by roving bands of mujahedeen.

It was late afternoon and she only had a few hours before she lost her light completely. She could make good progress in that amount of time if she weren't so thoroughly wiped out from dehydration. She'd camp here for the night and try to repair whatever damage she had done to herself. She needed to drink as much water as she could before setting out again the next morning.

After a few moments of rest, she filled the three bladders she had brought with her from the ambush site. She added the tablets and then, after ten minutes, she slowly drank another liter of water. Before that first taste she had felt like a dry hard husk, so empty of moisture that she might never soften again. Now she intended to saturate herself. She ate another MRE—her appetite had returned—drank the foul water and leaned against her tree, feeling her body come alive.

She knew she would be able to reach Armin's encampment the next day in good time. She would take the shot at night, as planned, as Armin presided over his brother's memorial festivities and then run like hell.

She pulled her pack to her and unlashed Brad's sniper gun. She remembered her training as a shooter. Snipers usually worked in teams of two—shooter and observer. She wasn't very proficient at either and now she was on her own. She assembled the two pieces of the weapon and peered through its scope. She flinched as she caught a glimpse of an animal on the other side of the river. The scope was equipped with night vision and that was what she would likely use for the shoot. She broke the gun down and laid it at her side.

The sun was nearly down, staining the sky a streaked mass of orange and pink. The river had taken on a glassy mirrored quality that made it look as if you could walk on its moving surface. Rennie looked around carefully and started pulling off her clothes. She was covered with grit and grime. Her legs were still streaked with mud. She laid her clothes over the unloaded sniper gun and slipped the sub-gun across her naked chest and back. The strap was rough against her skin.

She stepped gingerly into the water, her feet sinking deeply into the soft, slippery mud. Once she was a few steps from the bank, the mud ceded to sharp rocks but she still wore her hiking boots—she couldn't risk a foot injury—and they would dry quickly as she slept. When the water was up to her knees, she squatted, immersing herself, and rubbed at the grime coating her body with her hands as best as she could. The water was gloriously cool to her skin and if she weren't naked she would have enjoyed her dip in the river. But she couldn't help but continually scan the banks for movement. Sloshing back through the mud, she climbed up the bank, her sub-gun in her hands as she emerged from the water.

Rennie dressed quickly, feeling vulnerable, the water on her skin dampening her shirt and pants. She had fresh clothes in her pack but would need them when she reached the village after the shoot—a woman covered in blood and dirt would arouse attention she couldn't afford. It had been a harrowing day and she had lost some time, but the water and food and even the bath seemed to have taken effect. She felt almost born anew or at least how she imagined that might feel. A little tired and weak but somehow energized. A slight breeze came off the river and floated across her still moist skin.

She lay her head back and looked at the sky. It was still hazy—this was humid country—and the haze patterned the sky and danced across the surface of the water. When she fell asleep she was almost relaxed.

CHAPTER NINE

Fareed Reza woke early. He had slept badly, suffering in the heat and consumed with the memory of his conversation with Armin the day before. It brought to mind the time when he was first introduced to Armin, a few years ago, in London, when Armin was scouting around for help in building his movement. Fareed had been attending the Masjid Ibrahim in East London for about a year. He had been turned off by the religious hysteria of so many young, poor Muslims, brought to a frenzy by the political speeches that took place there after worship. But he soon came to realize that here lay power, right before him, like an offering. Here he could affect things, directly skirting the difficulties of legislative politics. He never thought of it as terrorism, even as he'd watched the reports of that first explosion.

Abdul-Haafiz al-Katib was not the spiritual leader of the

mosque, but he wielded great power there. It was he who brought in the speakers who incited the young worshippers to leave their new country, travel to their ancestral homes and take up arms against the West. And it was he to whom Ahmad Armin appealed for help in setting up his camp.

Fareed had never felt comfortable with al-Katib. He was a rough man with rough manners and the snob in Fareed found him distasteful. But then al-Katib approached him, with deference as he always did—a nod to Fareed's wealth—saying, "I think I have found a calling for you, brother." Fareed was intrigued, more so when he discovered that al-Katib wanted him to meet Ahmad Armin.

Everyone in the Muslim community was well familiar with Ahmad Armin. His story had struck a chord with many, resounding throughout mosques all over the Muslim world and in Europe. It fueled the anti-Americanism that filled the hearts of extremists, young and old. No one believed that Ahmad Armin had murdered his brother. In the beginning, Fareed wasn't certain. He was a man devoted to reason and without more evidence he withheld his judgment. Until he met Armin. Sitting in an outdoor café in SoHo, listening to the man's story, he was convinced that the Americans killed Nasser Armin when he changed his mind about defecting. The CIA, fools that they were, had once again interfered with Iran's right to manage itself, and once again, it would come back to haunt them.

That meeting had been the tipping point for Fareed. Before, he had been a detached observer, waiting for the right opportunity to make his mark in the world. With Armin, he had found his cause. Like many, he was powerfully affected by the man's personality. Fareed hadn't seen the instability in Armin then, perhaps it hadn't yet emerged. He was carried along by the man until he was so deeply involved that he didn't know how to extricate himself. Their original intent had been to assemble an army and make threats. All Armin wanted was for the United States to admit that he hadn't killed his brother—he wasn't so naive to believe that they would accept responsibility, but he knew it was within their power to clear his name without admitting any American involvement. But he badly misjudged the extent of the Americans' stubbornness. After Armin sent out his demands and then his threats and was ignored, he changed. Prone to fits of anger, he ramped up the religious element in his speeches. Before he had used just enough of it to keep the attention of their little army of young fanatics. Now, he constantly invoked the call for jihad, citing the more violent passages of the Koran.

Then came the kidnapping of the female American journalist. It had seemed eminently reasonable at the time, but had turned out all wrong. And then they had begun the bombings. Fareed knew he had crossed a line and could never turn back. Or could he?

When he had stepped through the door of Armin's office the day before, Armin was in a state, flushed and perspiring and frantically shuffling papers on his desk.

He finally noticed Fareed standing before him. "Sit, sit," he said, motioning toward the cushioned chair in front of his desk. "Why aren't you wearing the uniform?"

Fareed sat and crossed his legs without answering.

"Why aren't you wearing the uniform?" Armin's eyes glittered with something Fareed had recently begun to see in him. He suspected it was madness.

"I told you I think it's absurd. I agreed to wear it tomorrow for the festival. But not until then."

"You must not be so difficult. We must be together in this if we are to further our cause."

This is what their relationship had evolved to. Since their crimes had become more deadly, Armin had relaxed his psychological hold over Fareed and treated him like a partner. Fareed would wear the uniform at the festival to appease Armin, to stop his badgering, but the event loomed large in his mind as a spectacle he wanted no part of. It was to be a display of over-the-top propaganda, punctuated by fevered, hysterical speeches and gunfire. It rubbed roughly against the last shreds of his dignity.

"When will Rashed reach the village?" Armin asked.

"In a day or two." Fareed shook his head. "I think you have too much faith in him. I should have gone myself. This thing is too important."

Armin moved from around his desk and laid a hand on Fareed's shoulder. "You must trust my instincts. The young man has abilities. Someday he will be a great leader in our movement."

Movement. Cause. Holy mission. They had always used such rhetoric for recruiting purposes, but for many months now such language had begun to leech into Armin's private conversations. Fareed never responded to it and didn't now, only cocked an eyebrow to show his dissent.

He had argued with Armin for hours about his decision to send Rashed and Hamid, a mere boy, on such an important errand. But Armin was resolute and could not be swayed.

"If and when he returns with the photographs, we will have the Americans in a place they cannot worm their way out of," Fareed said.

"Yes, if the photographs really exist and are authentic, we will be in a very good position. But in case they aren't, I have contacted our old friend al-Katib. We will be able to take things to the next level if the photographs don't pan out."

"What are you talking about?" Fareed stood, unable to remain seated at the thought of his old contact. Al-Katib had gotten himself into some very dirty business since he had introduced Fareed to Armin.

"Al-Katib can get us material. For a price, of course."

At that, Fareed placed his hands on Armin's desk and leaned forward, staring deeply into his eyes. He searched and failed to find any trace of sanity. Fareed turned and walked from the room without a word.

There is always a price, he thought, remembering the scene from the comfort of his bed. Armin's "material" meant nuclear material. For years, Fareed's judgment had been clouded by the force of Armin's will. But now he saw things clearly. He would get out, as soon as he had the chance. Go back to London maybe. Restore relations with his family. But first there was the matter of the stable.

Waking before her alarm vibrated, Rennie could hear her blood pulsing in her ears. Now, for the third time since she had dropped through the frigid night air into an unsuspecting farmer's pasture, she woke to a world seemingly created anew. For the third time, the world she knew, or thought she knew, had been dismantled and built again in the night as she slept. After the ambush, the dawn had brought with it a world transformed, a world where life could be snuffed out in an instant in a rush of inconceivable violence. No amount of training could have prepared her for that moment. She would never be the same woman again. In that moment, the animal in her had come alive and the ultimate desire to survive sent a panic coursing through her veins that made her just want to run, far, far away from the chaos she had woken to. The second time, struggling awake the following morning, alone and fighting desperately against her body's need for hydration, she knew all her training, all her hard work had come down to making it through the woods in one piece.

And now. When Rennie opened her eyes, she knew that *this* was the day. Her body knew this was the day. When she looked around her campsite, at the river and woods beyond it, she saw it all with new eyes. Everything was crisp and sharply outlined. Her nerve endings seemed to have stretched, reaching for the surface of her skin, and she felt the fabric against it suddenly keener than before. The air, too, seemed to have rarified. Or, maybe, it was just her, a new her, able to extract from it just what she needed. Today was the day of all days that would determine the course of her life. On this day, she would live or die. She would succeed or fail. Nothing else would ever matter so much.

Rennie filled the pockets of her cargo pants with everything she might need for the shoot. She packed her bag, eating an MRE and drinking water as she did so. She had maybe half an hour before the pall of night lifted. She sat down next to her pack and unlashed the sniper gun. She snapped the two halves together and flipped the bipod into position. Lying on her belly, legs spread, she switched on the scope's night vision. The world turned a sickly green and she saw a large buck on the other side of the river turn his head as if he were suddenly aware that a large deadly eye had opened upon him. She only hoped she had his instincts.

Rennie felt the ground lumpy under her as she stretched over it, fingering the trigger guard of the gun, peering through the scope into an unfamiliar world. She imagined Armin in the cross-hairs of the scope and knew she would pull the trigger when the time came. Pull the trigger and then go, as fast as she could, running back through the woods to the village where she would arrange transport to the capital city of Dushanbe. And fly home.

Home. She couldn't think of it now. Here, at this moment, it had no meaning; it couldn't penetrate through the layers of defenses she had built up over the past few days. No such place of safety and comfort could exist, not when she lay on the hard ground preparing herself to bore a bullet deep into a man's brain. But she could imagine running. The man would fall and she would run, harder and faster than she ever had, and she wouldn't stop, until she was safe. Adrenaline ramped up her energy at the thought of that run.

When the sky began to lighten she got up, lashed Brad's gun back onto the pack and hoisted it over her shoulders, heavier now that she had filled all of her water bladders. She carried her sub-gun in her hand and began walking.

Every sense that Rennie possessed was on high alert. She couldn't afford to miss anything at this stage. She continually swept her gaze from left to right and then turned a hundred and eighty degrees to look behind her every twenty or thirty paces. The morning passed quickly, becoming hot. Her shirt became sticky and damp and then so wet that she had to stop and wring it out. She left it off, tucking it in her belt, and just wore the tank top. She ate at ten and again at one. She was in such a high state of adrenaline that her body was rapidly burning up whatever food she put into it. She had a fleeting thought that she was low on MREs, but it passed just as quickly. The matter at hand edged it and everything else out of her mind.

She was making good time. She hated to do this last stage of the hike without the GPS. It was so easy to become reliant on the technology, but she was familiar with the topographical maps and the aerial photographs and had a good sense of where she was.

About mid-afternoon she began looking for a place where she could hide her pack so that she could scale the steep incline up to the ridge unencumbered. The ridge was a natural formation several hundred yards up that had provided a kind of terrace, long ago, for a British colonialist who gave up on politics to pick up the plow. He had engaged in little more than subsistence farming, but the few square miles of cleared land had offered Armin a small haven ideal for his camp. One or two sturdily built farm buildings remained which he'd put to use.

It wasn't long before she saw a recently fallen tree, a victim of a lightning strike. Ideally for Rennie, it had fallen across an old log, with its tallest boughs brushing the trunk of a tree a few yards from it, giving her a small leafy cave to hide the gear she wouldn't need for the shoot.

Rennie threw down her pack and stretched out her shoulders. Her tank was so wet with perspiration that every bone and curve of muscle was clearly outlined through the thin material. She unlashed the sniper gun from her pack and slung it across her shoulders so that it rested on her back. She pulled out one of her water bladders, made sure it was full, and slipped its clasp over her belt. Then she shoved her pack deep into the mass of foliage.

Suddenly the scene became a kind of tableau and she saw it as if from a great distance: the tree, the hidden pack, a young heavily armed woman standing alone. She might never return to this spot in the woods. She would take this mission through to its completion. If she didn't make it, she knew it would be said, speculated upon, whispered around the halls of the Bureau, that they would have succeeded if there hadn't been a woman on the team. But if she were to go back alone now, without trying, it would be the same deal. She would play the sacrificial lamb in every scenario but one: to push on and to shoot Ahmad Armin. She understood the risk, even the insanity of considering it—she was alone and virtually inexperienced with the gun—but this was the only option. The only option for her.

She turned and continued walking east. She knew she was close, maybe five miles from the encampment, and she walked as carefully as if the area were covered in land mines. She held her sub-gun in both hands, safety off. The woods again took on a new aspect. She imagined the trees harboring Armin's men. Stray branches and fallen leaves cried out to expose her with every step. The forest seemed her enemy, in collusion with Armin.

Time, too, seemed to enter a new dimension, passing rapidly as she crept along. And then she was at the bottom of the incline. It wasn't as steep as she had feared, but she couldn't see the crest. It was the twilight hour and the woods were permeated by that strange hue when the light begins to fail. A shiver ran down her spine and the fine hairs stood up on the back of her neck as fear tried to trap her. She shook it off as fast as it came upon her. Unhooking her water bladder, she drank the last few cups. Then she folded it and slipped it in the pocket of her cargo pants.

Here we go.

She started up, at first crouched low, but soon flattening herself as close to the ground as she could. The slope was dense, with tall, thin, evenly spaced trees interspersed with the occasional jutting rock. Vines covered the ground in tight knots of confusion that gave her sure footing. She needed to be as close to invisible as possible. She moved slowly and soundlessly, the sniper gun secure at her back and the MP5 tight in her hand. It was almost completely dark now and she was thankful for this. From the light above her, she could tell she was very close to the top of the slope. She paused to wipe her hands on her pants. Then she heard the voices.

CHAPTER TEN

August 18, 2001
Armin Training Camp

Rennie heard them before she saw them. She was thirty feet from the crest of the ridge. She couldn't tell if they were close or if the slight breeze had carried their voices from farther away and she couldn't see anything over the slope, the angle was too steep. She drew herself into a low crouch so she could move quickly if need be, bracing her foot against a tree to keep her balance. Every sense seemed to open and expand to its fullest capacity. She thought she could even smell them. Then, just as quickly, the voices retreated. It was completely dark now, but she could see a halo of muted light at the crest of the ridge coming from the lights of the camp.

She lay perfectly still, well camouflaged by the dense vegetation, but in an uncomfortable position, a kind of half-crouch, half-sprawl. Her muscles were bunching up and she forced herself to ease her body flatter to the ground. She looked at her watch. Almost 2100 hours. If all was on schedule, the festivities were due to begin in half an hour.

The men so close to the edge of the woods had surprised her. She thought of the plan of the camp she had studied until she knew it like she knew the layout of her own apartment. The Bureau's intelligence had obviously erred in estimating the distance between the forest and the nearest buildings. She would have to top the slope to get her bearings anyway.

She hated to leave her spot. She felt safe there, hidden in the brush. She moved out slowly, still on her belly, and inched her way up the steep incline. The ground was more viny here and she used the tangles to stay her footing and still allow her to keep the sub-gun in her hand, with the safety on to avoid any chance of an accidental firing. Nearing the top, she heard more noises—wheels on an unpaved road, and faint music. She had no idea what sort of security they would have at this time of night. It was believed that they were more concerned with the road. They would never suspect an attack from the woods. Still, Rennie paused before lifting her head. She feared the split second it would take to raise her head over the edge of the slope. She might rise up only to hear the retort of a weapon and know that she was dead. This night, though, was tied to a schedule and the thought of time slipping away from her pushed away whatever fear remained and she looked over the bank's edge.

The two-dimensional picture imprinted in her mind suddenly sprang to life. Buildings rose from black lines on a white page, taking on form and texture. There were the barracks, a series of huts sharing a common roof. And there was the old stable. What was it used for now? Perhaps more barracks. Or storage. North and to her left was the activity she had heard. There was light and smoke and the forms of soldiers walking from the barracks toward the maneuvers field. Intelligence had posited accurately that this was where Armin's speech would take place.

It was almost a quarter after nine and Rennie needed to be in position by the time Armin stepped up to the podium.

Fortunately, he was known to be verbose. The plan of the camp the FBI had was very close to what she was actually seeing and she knew she needed to move farther north in order to get a view of the maneuvers field. She shifted her position carefully, ducking her head out of view and crawling awkwardly along the steep, vined edge, occasionally peeking over to check her line of sight.

It was completely dark, the only light coming from the field where a bonfire raged and spotlights were trained on the makeshift stage that came into view. Rennie's adrenaline shifted up a notch. As long as Armin took the stage, and everything pointed to that notion, she would have what appeared to be a clear shot. She settled into the brush, pulling some of it around her, camouflaging herself as much as she could. She swung Brad's already assembled sniper gun off her back and snapped the bipod into position.

Hunkering down, she peered through the scope. The scene suddenly leapt to life before her eyes. The clarity the scope brought, in addition to the strong light source, was astounding. Rennie could see the splintering planks of the stage smeared with mud. The grass around it looked bitten up by too many heavy boots. She raised the barrel of the gun slightly and flinched as the head of one of the men moved through her crosshairs. Soldiers were bustling around everywhere. They didn't look like a band of ruthless terrorists, at least not most of them. A lot of them were young boys who looked like they were playing dress-up. Rennie wasn't surprised at this—she had read the profiles. What surprised her was how much they looked like any group of boys, joking and making rude gestures to one another, filled with the excitement brought about by the break in their routine.

The conditions for the shoot were almost perfect. The light wind had died down and the night was still very hot which was ideal, since colder, denser air would create more drag on the bullet. Rennie estimated she was about a half-mile from the stage. It was far, but she had shot accurately at that range before.

It was hard to tear her eyes away from the stage. She didn't want to miss the moment Armin stepped into her line of fire, but she needed to scan the area and get her bearings. About two hundred yards directly in front of her was the stable. She was in line with the wide center aisle that cut through the middle of the ancient structure. She flicked on the night vision on the scope and the world again changed to radioactive green. She swung the barrel of the gun past the stable across a few hundred yards of dirt and gravel to the barracks. There was a road that ran behind these buildings, parallel to the line of the woods. She could see a few men walking toward the maneuvers field. She scanned past the barracks until her line of vision was even with the crest of the bank where she hid and then moved the scope left. Again she swept slowly past the barracks, the stable and then to the mess hall and what they thought was Armin's house. She lingered there, moving along every inch of the building. Dim light shone weakly through the small covered windows. Then she heard commotion from the stage area. She moved her sight left and switched off the night vision.

Men were packed around the stage, pressing up against it. She could feel their excitement and it affected her, elevating her adrenaline and setting her even more on edge. Everyone seemed to have their weapons in hand and Rennie longed for the familiar feel of her sub-gun. With her face against the cheek pad, she could smell Brad's musky scent caught in the fibers of the leather and took a small comfort in it. Armin was nearby. She knew it. The crowd was beginning to take on the aspect of a large group of people caught up in the same all-consuming emotion. It was an arena where that emotion would rule the day. She hoped Armin didn't fire them up any more than they already were. A loud roar rose from the field and the crowd began to press forward, focusing their attention.

And then he was on the stage, stepping up to a tall crate that the soldiers must have moved there to act as a podium while Rennie was doing her scan. Rennie held his face in the scope and watched him smiling, his gun raised in triumph. *Ahmad Armin.* She needed to let the crowd settle in a little before she took her shot. She concentrated on controlling her breathing, keeping her breaths slow and shallow. She could feel her adrenaline jumping wildly, pulling at its leash, begging her to just squeeze off a few rounds and watch his head explode, but she kept a tight hold on it. No mistakes now. She needed to wait for the right moment, keeping him in her sights. Then make the shot and run like hell.

Through her scope, she watched him as he calmed the crowd so he could begin speaking. He looked smaller than he had seemed in the many photos she had seen. Dumpier. He didn't look particularly dangerous, but if Rennie had learned anything during her time at the Bureau, it was that murderous instinct can come in any form.

Armin began to speak, raising a bullhorn to his mouth. She trained the crosshairs at the spot on his head just behind his right ear. Her index finger was on the trigger guard where it was supposed to be until she decided to make her shot. She scanned over the crowd at the edge of the stage. Everyone was listening intently and occasionally roaring their agreement. She moved the barrel of the gun back to Armin. He was becoming emphatic, gesticulating with his gun and punching the air with the hand holding the bullhorn. The crowd grew louder. To Rennie, they sounded almost panic-stricken, fueled by his rhetoric. Then Armin began to fire his gun in the air. The crowd joined in. *Now is the time.* Rennie flipped off the safety and put her finger on the trigger. Armin was moving back and forth, rocking against the crate as he leaned into it. She just needed him to pause. Just for an instant. Then a light flickered out of the corner of her eye. She jerked her head to the right, waiting for the sensation of hot metal passing through her brain. She saw a red glowing point at the entrance of the stable passageway. Someone had just lit a cigarette.

Rennie swung the barrel of the gun toward the point of light and flicked on the scope's night vision. A soldier stood with a hand in his pocket, leisurely smoking a cigarette. Why wasn't he pressing up against the stage with everyone else? Then he turned and looked down the passageway to his left. Rennie followed his line of vision with her scope. Leaning over the top of one of the stable's Dutch doors was a woman. She was very thin and had short dark hair. She was motioning to the soldier for something. A small woman, something feline about her, with distinctive features.

Hannah Marcus.

The American woman kidnapped by Armin almost two years before and believed to be dead stood very much alive in the crosshairs of Rennie's scope.

Fareed Reza unbuttoned the high collar of his uniform. It was too bloody hot to be wearing the god-awful thing and he had never felt more like a man playing a part. But perhaps it had always been this way. He hardly knew who he was anymore. He lit a cigarette and drew in deeply on the bitter smoke. He had stepped away from Hannah Marcus's stall to give her a moment of privacy as she ravenously ate the food he brought her from Armin's celebration. She wasn't starving but it was the first thing approximating decent food she'd had since beginning her captivity. None of them ate well in the camp, but her diet was particularly paltry.

Standing at the opening of the stable, Fareed turned his face to the sky. It was a clear night, a beautiful night. If only he were anywhere but here.

He heard Hannah set her plate down.

"How about a smoke, Fareed?"

He stepped back from the opening of the stable and knocked a cigarette out of his pack. "They aren't very good. Just cheap Indian cigarettes. I haven't been able to get anything better."

"I guess I'll have to take what I can get then. You have a beer in any of those pockets?"

He smiled at her jab at his uniform. He always admired her ability to maintain her sense of humor in the face of everything she had endured. He found he was attracted to her and felt like a fool for it.

Fareed stepped back to the opening of the stable; he wasn't in the mood to talk tonight. He had grown tired of Armin's festivities for his brother before they had even begun. Disgusted by the impending pomp and Armin's inevitably bombastic speech, he had slipped away to relieve Hannah's guard and to give himself a moment of peace. The absurdity of the evening, Armin firing his weapon into the air like a maniac, only confirmed that he had to leave this place, resume a life of some kind of normalcy, a life without guns and bombs and the death of innocents. But then there was Hannah. Armin had long accepted that she was just a casualty in this mess she had stumbled into, but lately he had taken to calling Hannah The Jewess. It was unlike Armin, and Fareed feared for her.

That morning when he had awakened, knowing he had to get out before his collusion with Armin caused him to step even further into the abyss, he thought of Hannah alone in her stall. He wanted to go to her, to tell her he would make her safe. Still in the flush of sleep, still in that place of dreams where anything seems possible, he imagined himself slipping away in the night and spiriting Hannah away with him. Now he saw how preposterous it all was, a foolish romantic notion born out of desperation. He would leave—Armin couldn't stop him—but he would have to leave Hannah behind. If he left like a thief in the night, taking their hostage, he would spend the rest of his life looking over his shoulder. But if he left without her, he thought—he had to believe—that Armin would let him be.

He could make an argument to Armin for setting Hannah free, but he knew it wouldn't be heeded. No one even suspected she was still alive. In many ways she wasn't, living like an animal, eating scraps and sleeping in a stall. And she knew too much. Fareed had told her too much, in moments of weakness, when she seemed to be the only thing in his life that was civilized. She was unlike any woman he had ever met, hard and soft, full of an aggressive cynicism tempered by an expansive heart she almost never showed. And she was beautiful in a way that made him ache.

When she was taken she had only been in Tajikistan a week,

covering a story for one of the wire services on the country's transition to a market-based economy. A group of colleagues had planned a day hike in the mountains and asked her to join them. She was the only American. Hikers who did their homework knew better now, but then the area was still considered safe. He thought of the photograph taken of her soon after her abduction, the one they issued to the press. Hannah had been a difficult prisoner, never showing the fear they wanted to capture on film. She only gave them anger, never the weakness they needed to broadcast to the world to show their power and make every American traveling abroad feel vulnerable. So they drugged her and the picture was snapped, Hannah looking like she was in shock, wide-eyed and confused. Long after she was taken, she'd begun to trust him—at least a little. He suspected she wasn't one to ever trust completely no matter what her circumstances.

Fareed dropped his cigarette to the ground and crushed it with his boot. He could hear Armin bellowing to the crowd as he walked back to Hannah's door.

"You okay? You seem a million miles away tonight," Hannah said.

Fareed thought of London. "Not quite that many," he said as he took a key and unlocked the stall door.

"What are you doing?" she asked, suspicion suddenly in her eyes.

"It's okay. I want to talk to you about something."

He stepped inside, leaving the door partly open.

"Let's sit," he said.

The guard tossed down his cigarette, opened the door where Hannah stood and went into the stall. Rennie didn't think, she just acted. Climbing over the edge of the bank, submachine gun in hand, she ran for the stable. The moment she leapt from the cover of the woods, she knew how vulnerable she was but also knew that she had to reach the doorway to the stable before the soldier came back out. She didn't allow herself to think what he might be doing there. She knew better than anyone that these people, those who transformed their religion into something murderous, were capable of every form of brutality.

Rennie covered the two hundred yards in about thirty seconds, her feet pounding a rhythm into the hard ground. She crouched low, just out of sight, beside the opening of the wide center aisle of the stable. She had thumbed off the safety of her sub-gun the moment she left her sniping position. She'd rather not shoot the soldier, for though the sub-gun was silenced, it still made an audible retort. She reached down and unsnapped the hold on the knife at her thigh.

She could hear the crowd growing louder under Armin's influence. Nocturnal insects chittered all around. Crouching lower, she peeked into the stable. The passageway was clear and low voices came from inside the woman's stall. Her boots silent on the dirt floor, she crept slowly to the door. The stall, like many, was equipped with Dutch doors. The top half was fully open and hooked to the wall. The lower half was open a few inches. A light flickered, probably from a candle. Their voices were louder now but she couldn't discern the words. She peeked through the opening in the lower door, ready to fire if necessary.

The next few moments blurred together as she acted even as her brain assimilated the information her eyes offered her. Seeing the guard standing over the woman, obscuring her from seeing Rennie, she bolted from her cover and silently crossed the few steps between them. She let go of her sub-gun, its strap keeping it handy, and slipped the knife from its sheath. In an instant, one arm encircled the guard's chest while the other passed the blade under his jaw. She could see Hannah Marcus over his shoulder scrambling backward on her cot, her face in shock. The guard's body kicked, struggling for what seemed like an eternity, not so much against her, but against the life rushing out of him. She held him tight, feeling his terror until he finally sank, slipping motionless from her grasp. Later, much later, Rennie would remember the pressure of the knife and the way the skin gave under it, unresisting, making the man seem so pliant, so weak. But then, she dropped him to the floor of the stall, bare and clean, feeling nothing.

Hannah Marcus was pressed as tightly into the corner of the stall as she could be, her arms wide, her palms flat against the wall. Her mouth was set and she looked at Rennie with wide dark eyes. Her gaze was impenetrable and for a moment Rennie was transfixed by it.

"My name is Rennie Vogel. I'm with the FBI. We've got to get out of here." Rennie put out her hand to the woman.

Ignoring Rennie's proffered hand, Hannah moved to the edge of the cot and put her feet gingerly on the floor. She moved as slowly as if she were wading through mud. She stood unsteadily and reached down to the guard, placing a hand on his shoulder, her expression unchanged.

Rennie knew at once that getting the woman out of the stall and into the woods was not going to be a simple task.

"We've got to hurry," Rennie said.

Hannah still said nothing. Rennie could see that she couldn't get her body to move.

"I'm going to help you." Rennie slipped her arm around Hannah's waist and moved her to the door. She was very petite, with a small frame. And thin, very thin. Rennie edged them into the passageway, sub-gun in hand. She closed the door behind her and fastened the padlock with one hand. She hurried them both toward the exit of the stable. At the doorway, she carefully looked around the corner.

All was clear. Hannah still seemed weak and unable to walk on her own. Rennie threw one of Hannah's arms around her shoulder and put the arm with her weapon around the woman's waist. And then she was off, half-carrying, half-dragging her as they ran the two hundred yards to the woods. Out in the open she could hear Armin more clearly. The crowd was clapping and yelling.

This was madness, almost suicidal. Armin and his soldiers were only a half-mile away. If they were seen at this point, they would be caught. Rennie stumbled as Hannah's legs buckled. They both went down, hitting the ground hard. Only Hannah had a free arm to break their fall and their knees took the worst of it.

"Up, up!" Rennie pulled Hannah to her feet roughly. They had to get to the woods.

Rennie was nearly frantic as they struggled across the last twenty yards. Hannah was moving more easily now. The shock of the fall seemed to restore some of her strength. Crashing through the thick foliage, Rennie eased her down onto the vine-covered slope. She looked exhausted just from their short run. How would they ever make it through the forest?

Crouched low, Rennie scanned the woods and then turned back to the encampment. Everything seemed quiet except where Armin was still giving his speech. She checked her watch: 9:45. She wondered how much longer he would speak, if she had time to take a shot. The sniper gun was still in position where she had left it. From the way he fell, the soldiers would know the direction of the shot and quickly figure out it had come from the line of the woods. She knew it would be risky. The whole area would be swarming in seconds with the armed soldiers, pumped-up and bloodthirsty from Armin's speech.

It was too uncertain. She would be risking more than her own life. She looked down at Hannah lying next to her. She was gazing up at Rennie with a slack, unreadable expression. Rennie knew when she left her team dead where they camped that it was unlikely she could make it through the woods, take the shot and get out on her own. But now this. They had never imagined that Armin still had Hannah Marcus. It had been a year and a half since he had released her photograph and made his demands. The FBI assumed she was dead. But she wasn't. Rennie had to decide. *What was this woman capable of?*

CHAPTER ELEVEN

Hannah Marcus couldn't think. Her body was slack on the slope, her feet braced against a tree so she wouldn't tumble down the steep incline, her fingers gripping a tangle of vines. Her ability to reason seemed to have shut down—and her emotion with it. She knew things—that Fareed was dead, that she was no longer locked in her stall, and that this woman claiming to be FBI was squatting next to her, peering through the scope of a gun—but she couldn't assimilate any of it into anything meaningful. Each stood in isolation, somehow bearing no relation to the other. She had never experienced this kind of disconnection and she didn't even have the energy to be worried about it.

She usually kept it all together. She had not fallen apart during her abduction or her long captivity. She had allowed herself once, and only once, to sob in despair, face down, on her uncomfortable cot. But that was unlike her. She was never one to feel sorry for herself, had never felt privileged enough to allow herself that luxury. She tried to force herself to understand her situation.

My name is Hannah Marcus. I am a journalist. I was kidnapped by a group of Islamic fundamentalists.

Wait. That wasn't entirely right. Fareed was about as religious as she was. *Again.*

My name is Hannah Marcus. I am a journalist. I was kidnapped by a group using the cloak of Islamic fundamentalism to further their agenda.

Whatever that was. Fareed had only told her so much. *Fareed.* She never even knew his last name. He had been good to her. Maybe even kept her alive.

I lived in an old stable for eighteen months, just biding my time, never holding out hope of being rescued.

That wasn't entirely right either. She knew that the United States never negotiated with terrorists, but she had indulged in fantasy, on occasion. A helicopter, the beating of blades in the night—descending in a rush and disgorging a clot of men, black-suited, faces covered, to rush her into the monstrous aircraft and fly away.

I was rescued by a woman, an FBI agent. Rennie Vogel.

A woman. She had never imagined this scenario and she had imagined many. A lone woman.

The engines of her mind began to rumble to life. How likely was it that her government, which was not in the business of rescuing their abducted citizens, would send a single female to rescue her? Not likely. Not likely at all.

Hannah heard the scrape of metal against metal and looked over at Rennie who was still fiddling with the long gun. She could see her almost clearly in the moonlight, accentuated by the lights from the stage. Tall, her body very defined, she looked like she'd been through hell getting to this point. Her clothes were filthy and she was covered in scratches and her head had a huge bump, still slightly bloody. But underneath it all, she was striking.

Hannah turned her head further to see where Rennie had the gun trained. Sounds began to filter into her consciousness as she saw a man standing in front of an excited crowd speaking into a bullhorn. It must be Armin. Hannah spoke Farsi, had spent most of her career in Iran, and was able to pick out a few phrases. A shiver went down her spine. Armin spoke of jihad and the killing of infidels. Her mind seemed to finally be clearing. She glanced at Rennie again. She had her eye pressed tightly against the scope which seemed to be aimed directly at Ahmad Armin.

"Oh," Hannah said aloud. All of her mental functioning seemed to return to her in a rush of clarity. Rennie turned to her, her face tight with anger.

She spoke quietly, punctuating each word. "Do not make a sound. Sit there and pull yourself together. As soon as I fire this weapon, we will run as far and fast as we can." Her face softened. "You have to find the strength. If you don't, we're both going to die, because I won't allow us to be captured. Find the strength. It's there. Just draw on it."

She thought then that Rennie would reach out to her, a reassuring hand on her shoulder. It was something in her expression. But then the look passed and she turned away. Hannah drew herself up on her knees to be ready to scramble down the steep hill. So, this was it all along.

An American agent sent to assassinate Ahmad Armin accidentally discovered I was alive.

She rescued me anyway.

Rennie turned back to the scope. She could only hope Hannah would be ready when the time came. After she fired the sniper gun, she calculated they would have three-and-a-half minutes to get ahead of the men. Four minutes, tops. Thirty seconds for the men to react to the shooting and three-to-three-and-a-half minutes for them to run the half mile to the line of the woods. That's if they assumed the shot came from the woods. Rennie wondered if she could divert their attention to the road.

She scanned the camp with the scope. It was split by the road.

On the side that ran parallel to the wood line was the staging area where Armin spoke at the far left. Then a large barracks. Next was the little stable where Hannah Marcus had been kept captive. Then another smaller barracks. Beyond that, the road curved sharply out of sight. On the other side of the road were the residences of the leadership and the eating quarters. And directly across from the stable—Rennie could see it through the center passage which ran the length of the small structure—was the armory.

Rennie reached down and gingerly ran her fingers over the outline of the device in her cargo pocket. It was an M2 SLAM mini-bomb.

She positioned the crosshairs of the scope back on Armin's head as she unbuttoned the pocket of her cargo pants and removed the bomb. It would be risky, insanely risky. She would have to expose herself again out in the open. Plus, the bomb was equipped with a timer and the shortest setting was fifteen minutes. She had no idea how much longer Armin would speak. She paused, flashing on an image of Hannah's intelligence profile. It wasn't very thick and she had wondered at the time why there wasn't more. Just the two photographs everyone had seen on the evening news, a couple of sheets of background information and the summary of what was known about the kidnapping. But she was able to recall a particular piece of information. She could see the page in her mind as if she were holding it in her hand.

Languages spoken: English, German, Farsi.

"You speak Farsi," Rennie whispered.

"Yes."

"Do you have any indication how much longer he will continue speaking?"

"It's hard to say. It's too far to hear much, but he seems to be on a roll."

Rennie held Hannah's gaze for a long moment as she thought.

"Okay. Here's what's going to happen." Rennie outlined her plan.

Hannah seemed to be looking at Rennie as if she were taking

114

her in for the first time. A wave of guilt washed over Rennie as she saw herself through Hannah's eyes. She had never imagined she would be compelled to take a man's life in front of a civilian. Hannah finally spoke, interrupting the moment of understanding that had passed between them.

"Why don't you set it for less time?" Hannah asked. "He could finish soon."

"I can't set it for any less time."

Hannah shook her head. "That's brilliant."

"If anything goes wrong before I get back, run. As fast as you can," Rennie said taking her compass from her belt loop. "Just keep going west and you'll eventually reach a village."

Hannah looked skeptical as she slipped it into her pocket.

Rennie didn't say what she thought, that the likelihood of her making it with no supplies was slim to none. She looked at the woman for a long moment. She looked wasted, her arms thin and reedy.

"What do I do when I make it to the village?"

"Just use your wits. Try to find someone you think you can trust. And contact the FBI or the American embassy as soon as you can."

"Okay." Hannah smiled weakly in resignation.

Rennie could see that she knew she would be in disastrous trouble if Rennie didn't make it back. She picked up the M2, set the timer and synchronized her watch with it to the second. She carefully put it back in her cargo pocket.

"I'm going," she said, taking a last look at Armin, who was still speaking.

Hannah put her hand on Rennie's arm. "Be careful."

Rennie nodded and was off and running the two hundred yards to the stable, sub-gun in hand. She ran fast, feeling her adrenaline ramping higher. Moving through the passageway of the stable, she crouched at the far opening. The road, dusty and deeply rutted in places, was about ten feet from the stable door. All was clear. As she crossed the road, the mass of men at the staging area to her left came into view. She couldn't see Armin, but could hear him. She knew he could stop at any moment.

The door to the armory was padlocked. The building was about thirty-six feet square and she fleetingly wondered what was in it. Hopefully only light bombs, grenades, IEDs—the usual. What sort of hell would she unleash by blowing it up? The armory was raised about two feet on wooden stilts, the best way to keep water out of a poorly constructed building.

Rennie dropped to the ground and scooted under the structure. Gingerly, she pulled the M2 from her pocket and placed it about ten feet in. Crawling back to the edge, she flinched as she heard a volley of gunfire. She hunkered down and peered out, ready to fire, but the men were only firing their weapons into the air, consumed by Armin.

Darting from beneath the armory, she crossed the road and pounded through the short passageway of the stable. At its opening on the other side she stopped and checked the wood line. She couldn't see Hannah and hoped she hadn't panicked and run already. All clear, she ran for the woods. *This is it.* If she could make it to the woods, they just might have a chance. She reduced her pace as she came into view of the staging area, figuring a slowly moving figure wouldn't be as noticeable. Passing through the green curtain of the wood line, she found Hannah no longer prone, but up on her hands and knees, alert and waiting for her.

"It's done."

Relief passed over Hannah's features. Rennie looked at her watch. She held up four fingers to Hannah. Four minutes until detonation. Rennie handed the sub-gun to her and crouched to the sniper rifle. Looking through the scope, she could see Armin still in position. She lay flat, her legs spread wide. The weather hadn't changed, the conditions were still perfect. She wanted to wait until the last possible second before making her shot. That would give them their best chance. Could she do this? Complete the mission and bring Hannah Marcus home? It seemed almost absurd.

Two minutes.

Rennie lay perfectly still, her finger on the trigger, ready for

116

the pull the moment the M2 detonated. Not a sliver of doubt crept into her brain which was jumping on adrenaline. That would come later. Now she was ready.

Thirty seconds.

Her mind cleared. So intent, she was almost completely unaware of her body in its uncomfortable position, tenuously gripping the incline. Her breath was shallow, just enough to sustain her without affecting her position. She was aware only of the crosshatch at the end of the scope and that tender, vulnerable spot on Armin's head. Then she heard the explosion. In the first instant, in that first fraction of a second, before Armin had time to react, she pulled the trigger. She never heard the bullet leave the muzzle, but she saw his head snap violently before he dropped to the ground. Lifting her head from the scope, Rennie saw a few men rush to Armin's inert body, but most had already turned away from him, focused on the blast in the armory.

Before the second explosion erupted, the domino effect from the munitions in the building, Rennie turned to tell Hannah to run but she had already started down the steep slope, arms akimbo, the MP5 in one hand. Rennie scrambled after her, tearing down the slope, dancing over jutting rocks. It felt good to move, to break the deep tension of the last few hours. Rennie quickly gained on Hannah. Then she was by her, snagging the sub-gun and taking her hand.

Careening down the slope, Hannah Marcus found herself falling. Not to the ground—Rennie Vogel had too firm a grip on her to allow that to happen—no, she was falling into a place in her mind she couldn't seem to extricate herself from, mired in a swamp of quashed emotions. How could she have kept it together so long through her captivity, only to fall apart now, when it mattered so much? The survivor in her struggled against it. She thought she had managed it, she had always managed everything, but it all came back—her parents, her capture, Fareed. She put her hand to her mouth, feeling her face transform into a mask of pain. The trees and rocks and vines, flying past her, grew cloudy and then drowned under the salty wave of her tears. Throughout her entire life, from the beginning, to this which felt like the end, she had kept the pain compartmentalized, shelved where it belonged, and now it all came crashing down.

She remembered Fareed unlocking the padlock on the Dutch door of her stable. She had had a moment of fear, having spent a lifetime learning from her parents to never trust anyone. But then she saw his face reading her ambivalence and she relaxed. Only in her world could the most interesting man she had met in years be her captor. And an Islamic militant. Just her luck.

Hannah's tears felt warm on her cheeks. For a moment this woman who held her hand, nearly dragging her down the hillside, seemed the enemy. Fareed, however much goodness and refinement was in him, had made a terrible mistake. And he had paid for it. She would mourn him someday when she could make sense of it all, mourn him and absolve him of his sin of only being a man and not a hero. The tumultuous emotion gripping her began to subside. It had to. She had to forgive this woman, this Rennie Vogel, for killing what felt like her only friend in the world. Hannah squeezed Rennie's hand then, in a need to reach out to her, to let go of the hatred that had bubbled up inside her since Rennie came through the door of her stall like a dark apparition. It was a strange moment for such an intimate gesture as they raced for their lives, and she figured it would go unnoticed, but she had to offer it for her own sake. Then she felt the pressure returned.

Her eyes clear of tears now, she looked at Rennie and wondered if she had noticed her breakdown. Rennie returned her gaze, eyebrows raised, questioning, and squeezed her hand again. Hannah nodded, indicating she was okay, not realizing until then that they had slowed their pace. Rennie, seeing she had pulled herself together, kicked it into gear, peeling forward. Hannah willed herself to keep up.

Then she felt Rennie's arm around her waist, holding her tight, she looked over and saw the woman caught up in the deep concentration of keeping them both aloft. The ground seemed to be skittering under their feet, a kaleidoscopic blur of green and brown in the moonlight. Hannah could hear gunfire in the distance. Were the soldiers shooting at them as they ran away? She looked at Rennie again and caught her eye. Rennie, who seemed to realize that Hannah was coherent and running better on her own, let go of her waist and just held her by the hand. Hannah could feel Rennie wanting to go faster and tried to increase her pace. The first inklings of freedom began to course through her, sending a sharp chill up her back and along her arms. Could they actually make it and escape the hell they had found themselves in?

Then Hannah noticed a massive log crossing their path about twenty yards away. They would need to slow considerably to scurry over it. She was exhausted and anticipated the break in their demanding pace. But as the distance diminished, Rennie hadn't slowed at all and then they were upon it and Rennie had Hannah around the waist again. She leapt as they reached the log, lifting Hannah with her. For a moment Hannah felt like they were flying, that they had somehow just taken off and would keep going higher and higher. A second later she felt her feet clip the log and they both fell hard to the ground, rolling over one another, their limbs in a tangle.

Hannah had a moment's respite where the pain made her feel more alive than she had in years, but only a moment. In a second Rennie was up and pulling Hannah to her feet.

"Are you all right?" Rennie bent to examine Hannah's legs, scraped but not bleeding. She looked upset with herself, perhaps for miscalculating Hannah's abilities.

"I'm fine. Don't worry."

Rennie nodded as she popped the magazine out of her sub-gun and then reinserted it to make sure it wasn't damaged in the fall, scanning the woods at the same time, searching for any sign that soldiers had followed them.

Hannah leaned against the log, smooth and clean from enduring years in the elements. Rennie studied their surroundings.

"I'm trying to get my bearings. I hid a pack of supplies in a fallen tree. It should be somewhere close by. I think."

"You don't have GPS?"

"It was damaged..." Rennie hesitated before completing her thought. "Before."

Hannah accepted this, but knew there was something else she wasn't saying.

"We're going to need to move more slowly for the time being, until we can find the tree. We'll need the supplies. There's water. Food. Ammunition."

"Do you think they're coming after us?"

"I don't know. Hopefully they are focusing on the road."

They walked quickly. Slow for Rennie seemed to be a little less than a run. But Hannah was thankful for any break in their pace. In her former life she had always been fit, but the year and a half in the stable had left her muscles weak and stringy. She had tried to exercise in her stall, doing push-ups and sit-ups, but her guard would come to the door and stare at her with a mixture of lust and loathing until she finally gave up.

Rennie stopped and pointed to a huge fallen tree, still covered in leaves. It was massive and lay perpendicular to the direction they were traveling. Handing Hannah her sub-gun again, she crawled into it, disappearing into a dense mass of leaves and branches as tall as Hannah.

Hannah looked at the sky, so clear and dark against the moon, and thought this was the first good day she could remember in a long, long time. Good in that she had a small hope that she would live a normal life once again. Then she heard the sharp crack of a branch breaking at a distance. Her head snapped up as she ducked behind the tree. Peeking over a thick branch, she saw a flash of red cloth about a hundred yards away in the direction of the camp. *Not now, not when we've made it this far.* Hannah squeezed through the leaves and branches, following Rennie into the lush green bower.

CHAPTER TWELVE

Rennie found the pack still in its hiding place. It hadn't been disturbed. The way the tree had fallen, branches splayed, it had created a niche within, large enough for two or three people to lay comfortably. A perfect place to camp for the night. She and Hannah could sleep there completely hidden from sight. But they were too close to Armin's outpost. She heard a rustle of leaves and saw Hannah crawling into the space. She looked frightened and Rennie knew something was wrong.

"They're here." She was pointing back toward the camp.

"How many?"

Hannah shook her head. "Maybe five or six, I don't know."

Rennie shoved the pack to her. "Inside is extra ammunition, clips. And a 9mm pistol. Look for a silencer and screw it onto the pistol. Bring them to me after I get into position."

She took the sub-gun from Hannah, moving the selector to

full-automatic mode, and crawled on her belly until she could see through the foliage. They had good cover, branches tight around them, but little means of escape if they weren't able to maintain the upper hand. She couldn't see them yet, but she could hear them. They were talking, seemed to be arguing. And getting closer every second.

Rennie considered her options. Five or six men if Hannah was right. She hoped to God there weren't more. The sub-gun held thirty rounds. She was in good position and would be able to take the first shots unnoticed. The gun was silenced but would make some sound. Depending on when they came into view, she would either take precision shots in bursts of two or just unload on them.

Then Hannah was next to her, crawling in close at her right side. Rennie felt the warmth of her body and was glad she wasn't alone. Hannah placed three fresh magazines next to Rennie at her elbow. She held the 9mm, silencer in place. Rennie took it from her, checked the assembly, switched off the safety and handed it back. She leaned into her, her lips grazing the lobe of Hannah's ear.

"Seventeen shots. Wait until they are all in view and I begin firing before you even think about pulling the trigger. If they are spread out, shoot from the right. I'll take the left."

Rennie drew away from her. Hannah nodded her assent. She looked frightened but together.

Rennie leaned against her again. "You can do this." A stray thought flitted through her brain, an inappropriate thought. With the heat from Hannah's body soaking into her own, the soft, delicate skin under her lips, and the thought of death permeating every pore of her body, Rennie thought of kissing Hannah Marcus, then and there, as they lay on the ground, ready to engage in battle.

But she turned away quickly, her body attuned to the matter at hand. The men's voices were very near. Though it was almost pitch-dark within their leafy nest, the bright moon overhead gave her uncanny visibility. The woods had taken on a ghostly hue, the leaves and rocks seemed to glow in the moonlight. Then she saw the first glimpse of them. A head there, and then an arm, moving through the trees. The voices were louder and they were arguing with more vehemence. This was good. Anything that distracted them as they came into view would be to her benefit.

Even though her body cried out to pull the trigger and feel the gun engage, she waited. She needed to see them, all of them. To know how many there were.

Suddenly, they were all in view. Six men, all in uniform, all carrying Kalashnikovs, that sturdy old Russian machine gun. One—he looked the oldest and was probably the leader of the group—had a shiny medal pinned to his chest. He was arguing with a man who looked to be about twenty. She could see their faces and except for the two engaged in discussion, the rest were young, certainly teenagers. One, at the far right, looked to be no more than thirteen. He had an alertness about him the others lacked, caught up in the conversation of the two men. The boy continually scanned his surroundings, his small features molded into a mask of adult concentration. Then his gaze locked onto the tree, his eyes seeming to look straight into Rennie's own. He couldn't have possibly identified their position, but it unnerved Rennie. She nodded at Hannah and prayed the woman was a good shot.

With the selector of the sub-gun set for two bullets to fly with each trigger pull, she put her bead on the men at the left. She was so ready. Her finger on the trigger, the retractable stock tight against her shoulder, she leaned in, allowing the weight of the weapon to sit comfortably in her left hand. As soon as she pulled the trigger and heard the familiar *ffft, ffft* of the MP5 and felt its slight buck, Rennie settled into the moment. In controlled bursts she hit the two men at the far left. They went down fast, clutching at their wounds, dark stains spreading on their uniforms. The rest of the party looked confused at first, not having heard the shots. Then the realization of what they had stumbled into fell over their features and the silence of the night exploded into chaos as the men dove to the ground and began shooting.

Hannah was firing next to her. She could feel Hannah's thigh, hard with tension and pressing against her own. Rennie saw her hit a man at the right. Hannah had passed over the young boy. The remaining men—three down, three to go—were all returning fire, but wildly, still unsure exactly where the shots were coming from. One unloaded his clip in auto-mode in a few seconds and was frantically searching his pockets for more ammunition, rolling from side to side as he lay on the ground. The other two, the leader and the small boy, were more conservative, firing single shots and trying to get some cover. Rennie knew a few bullets had come near, maybe even so near that they were lucky to be alive. She took aim at the leader and fired, hitting him in the hand. He screamed and dropped his weapon. Rennie moved to fire on him again and felt the horrible vacant pull of her trigger. Empty.

Drop the magazine. Reload.

The leader recovered his weapon and was taking shots again. He and the boy had located their position and bullets were suddenly everywhere around them. They bit into the ground in front of them throwing up sprays of dirt. They slammed into the thick limbs, leaves raining down on them. The man, who finally found a full magazine, rolled over in pain. Hannah had caught him in the shoulder. He tried to move back, using his dead comrades for cover, firing all the while. Rennie swung the muzzle of the sub-gun to the right, fired and caught him just below the eye, quickly finishing Hannah's work.

Two of the men, the first two Rennie had hit, had fallen on top of one another, creating a small barrier that the leader was using for cover. Rennie was having trouble hitting him. Then he surprised her. Standing, exposed, the man yelled to the small boy, waving his hand and telling him to run. He had just stepped over the bodies of the men he was hiding behind when Rennie's bullets found their home in his chest. He lived long enough to know the boy had not heeded him.

The boy, who Hannah had spared, continued firing on them, his shots amazingly accurate. Rennie could see his small face

124

behind the huge weapon and it gave her pause. Then, she felt a sharp sting on her left arm. Before she could think, before she could take stock of the damage he had inflicted, blind rage seared through her brain. She flipped the selector on the sub-gun all the way down to full-auto mode as she arced the barrel to the right. She squeezed the trigger even before she reached him. The full force of the bullets caught him in a terrible line along his torso, lifting his small frame off his feet and throwing him violently backward. Rennie saw the familiar Nike logo on the bottom of his shoes as he hit the ground.

Silence.

God help me.

Rennie fired a few more rounds into the motionless bodies. They didn't flinch. All dead. She turned to Hannah whose face was set and dripping with perspiration. The woman set her weapon on the ground and her hand began to shake wildly.

"Is it over?"

"Yes." Rennie suddenly felt buoyant, surging with the knowledge that they were still alive. She put her hand on the back of Hannah's neck. "You were amazing."

"Oh my God! You're bleeding!"

Rennie looked down at her arm as the pain reached her brain. An intense burning traveled down her arm and up to her neck. Blood was seeping slowly from the wound.

"Shit."

Okay. The blood has already slowed. That's good. It can't be very deep.

"Do you have a first-aid kit?" Hannah looked panicked.

"The pack." A lump had lodged in Rennie's throat. Anxiety. It made it difficult to talk. "Lower pocket. And there should be a flashlight."

Hannah opened the kit and laid it in front of Rennie, looking at her helplessly. This brought Rennie back. *You can't rely on this woman—she's been through too much.*

"There should be a sterile cleaning pad. Find that and then look for a pressure bandage. Also, water. I'll need water."

Rennie hated to use their small supply of water, but she had to clean her wound. Infection would be the end of her.

With Hannah holding the flashlight, Rennie poured water over the red gash. The blood, dark and glossy, thinned under the water and became pink as it cleared the cut and she could see that the wound wasn't very deep, only a few millimeters. Nothing important had been compromised.

Thank God.

Rennie applied the cleaning pad, the antiseptic ramping up the pain. She wanted to scream and pound her fists against the ground, furious at being injured. But it could have been much, much worse. Though the wound was still bleeding, it continued to slow. The pressure bandage would take care of the rest.

"How's the pain?" Hannah said, calmer now.

"Could be worse."

"Are any of these pills for pain?" Hannah said, searching through the medical kit.

"Yes, but I want to keep my wits about me."

Hannah nodded.

"I heard them talking," she said as Rennie dealt with the pack, stowing the medical kit and the extra ammunition.

"Did you pick up anything?" she asked, focusing on her intently.

"A little. They were arguing about whether they should have concentrated on the woods or the road."

"And?"

Hannah smiled. "Apparently everyone else is on a wild-goose chase."

"Finally, something has gone right," Rennie said.

Hannah looked at Rennie quizzically.

"Let's get moving. They will send another team out when they don't find any trace of us on the road."

Rennie sat up and brushed the dirt from her forearms. She had two more clips in the pack and switched out the partially empty one for a full one. She reloaded the pistol Hannah had emptied. Climbing out from the niche in the tree, she was careful not to bump the wound on her arm. She held the branches so

126

Hannah could crawl through.

"Stay here. I want to check out the bodies before we move on. It will only take a minute."

She opened the pack again and tossed Hannah an MRE. "I don't know if you have the stomach to eat right now, but it would probably be a good idea. We have a long way to go."

Hannah stared at the package for a long moment. "This can't be worse than the stuff I've been forcing down for the last two years, can it?"

"You might be surprised."

Rennie left her and went to the bodies. It was all too familiar. A scene of death. Men sprawled, contorted on the ground. In the moonlight, it was almost picturesque. The darkness of their blood against the silvery leaves. The contrast of their weapons against the rocks and trees. A tiny theater of war playing out in the endless drama of nature. And most importantly, the thing that made such perceptions at all possible—they weren't her friends.

Rennie swallowed hard. Too familiar. But different enough that she would be okay. She would have to be. She picked up one of the Kalashnikovs. Hannah should have a weapon more powerful than the pistol she used so effectively. She ejected the empty magazine and collected a handful of replacements from the pockets of the dead men.

Rennie found Hannah sitting on the ground behind the fallen tree scooping the contents of the MRE into her mouth with her hand. Somehow she hadn't noticed the plastic utensils included in every package. Standing over her, Rennie saw her as impossibly small, a small ravenous animal. Even though she had eaten only a few hours before, Hannah consumed the MRE as if she were starving. You never knew how a body would react to killing—hunger or retching. She leaned down to Hannah and rested her hand lightly on her shoulder.

"We have to move."

She checked her watch. Almost midnight. If all went well, they would reach the river by morning. She wondered how much stamina Hannah had, if she could push on, running on adrenaline.

They walked quickly side by side, each hyperaware, listening for any sign that another band of men had followed them into the woods. Rennie's arm burned with pain, but she separated herself from it. Knowing it wouldn't kill her, she wouldn't let it slow her down.

The night was warm, close. Rennie's bloodied shirt was sticking to her. She would change before they got to the village. *The village.* It seemed fantastically remote, like a pipe dream. The team's original plan had been to check in at a rooming house in the village. It wouldn't be unusual—they were posing as hikers after all. Then, after a night of rest, they were to hire a car to Dushanbe and fly back to Germany on a commercial airliner. There would have been nothing to connect them or their actions to the U.S. government. Rennie would follow the same plan, but it would be a bitter pill with her team lying dead in the woods. She thought of the satellite phone then, snug in a pocket of her pack. She would call in when they got to the river. The idea filled her with the deepest dread she had ever known. She wondered when the families of her team would be notified and she was unable to stop herself from imagining the funerals, accusing eyes everywhere.

Rennie heard movement behind her and spun around, MP5 at the ready. She scanned the woods, crouching to the ground and slipping her pack off her shoulders. Hannah was already in position and looked as if she were about to fire her weapon. Rennie followed the direction of her barrel.

"Deer. It's just a deer," she said quietly.

Hannah exhaled forcefully.

"Good response time."

Hannah shook her head. "I guess you never know what you're good at until you do it."

Rennie realized then that they were a team and had to rely on one another. And though Hannah might slow them down, Rennie was glad she was there, thankful not to be alone.

A deer.

Hannah wondered what else was lurking in these woods. She didn't care as long as they didn't run across any more of Armin's men. A true city girl, she had an elemental discomfort with nature. She saw it for what it was—raw, brutal, unforgiving. Sometimes, finding herself in it, she became jumpy, succumbing to ancient fears, images of spiders and snakes creeping into her consciousness. And on certain moonless nights, there was that inky, infinite darkness that seemed to have no depth, so dark it obliterated perception, like trying to move through a void.

And here she was, stuck in the woods. She didn't want to believe in luck, chance, destiny—whatever you wanted to call it—but she had to, especially now, even though it chafed against her adherence to reason. Always, her parents' story and the stories of countless others who lived and died without rhyme or reason ate at her precious seat of rationality. She knew she couldn't accept living in a world of such randomness. Both of her parents had made it through Ravensbrück as children, had clung to one another in the chaos, and emerged with the blackest humor known to man. For them, everything in life was filtered through the prism of that time when the world teetered dangerously on its axis. They saw America as a paradise but they retained an intense skepticism of any government, including that of their beloved adopted country.

She whispered a prayer—something she never did—that they were still on this earth, still puttering around the apartment in Baltimore where she grew up. She thought of her own beautiful, tiny apartment in Dupont Circle. She knew her apartment was a contradiction, a minimalist paradox that defined her. Spare pieces with clean lines that expressed her ultimate conundrum— a desire for beauty and a desire to have nothing. If you have nothing, nothing can be taken from you. But then there was her art. The paintings on her walls were a slap in the face of what she supposedly was trying to accomplish with her furniture—no crisp lines, no muted blocks of color, no simple constructions, but a riotous, swirling chaos of color and texture, images—sometimes violent—that never failed to evoke a response. Buying them never felt like commerce, but like a tithe. Hannah wondered if this experience would change her taste, transform it into something darker, more violent—if that were possible.

She took in her surroundings. The forest was drenched in moonlight releasing them from its interminable depth. Rennie strode ahead. She always seemed to be moving forward, strong and resolute. Hannah wondered how the woman had gotten to this point, in a position where she took men's lives and could rest assured that she had done the right thing. *Rennie.* An odd name. Hannah wasn't sure it suited her. She thought of Camilla—a minor figure in Virgil's great epic poem. A woman of battle who was devoted to Diana, the goddess of the moon. She had captured Hannah's imagination as a teenager. Here, as Rennie waded through the moonlight, gun in hand, covered in blood, she seemed to embody her.

Hannah mused how unlike Rennie she herself was. She was never one to take action. She was an observer. Always seeking out the truth, it was what had drawn her to journalism. But she knew that the truth was slippery. She knew about hidden agendas, secret plans and how in a moment the world could explode into chaos. Just as her own little world had. How can you ever know that what you are doing isn't actually carrying out a plan of evil you are unaware of? Hannah had a million questions for Rennie. Her reporter's instincts had finally kicked in now that she had a moment of quiet.

At first she had assumed Rennie was a lone assassin, but who would send a woman for such a job? The FBI may have changed a little over the years, but not that much. It was still an old boys' club. An assassin wouldn't come out of the FBI anyway. At least she didn't think so. For years, the FBI had been a purely domestic operation, but as the world became smaller and the United States found itself with more and more enemies, the Bureau had begun opening offices in foreign countries. Besides, Rennie had said that she was associated with a special forces team. Hannah had done a piece once on U.S. special forces years ago before she began covering Iran. She knew then that women weren't accepted by any of the units. She supposed things could have changed. Caught up in her new assignment, she hadn't done any research on the issue for a year or so before she was captured. But the question remained: why was she working alone? It didn't make sense.

Hannah's muscles were already aching from the exertion. But it felt good to be outside. Her first taste of freedom. Hannah glanced over at Rennie. She looked tense and Hannah wondered if she was in pain. She knew almost nothing about this woman. She did know that her very life depended on her.

"How much farther to the village?" Hannah asked quietly.

"It's a ways. We'll stop at the river first. To stock up on water."

Then Hannah remembered the remark Rennie had made: *Finally, something has gone right.*

Hannah was ambivalent, but decided to risk the question. "What happened to the rest of your team?"

Rennie jerked her head toward her, thrown off guard. So, that was it. Hannah immediately regretted asking it the way she did.

"I'm sorry—"

"They're dead." Rennie turned away. "They're all dead."

They didn't say more. Hannah knew to let it be. They walked on in silence.

At first, little changes in the terrain, a slight incline or a dip, a fallen tree to step over or a large rock to skirt, kept the long walk interesting. Hannah appreciated almost any variation, to keep her mind occupied. But as the hours wore on and her legs felt heavier and heavier, she began to make mistakes, stumbling and slipping from fatigue. Just when she thought she couldn't take another step, Rennie spoke.

"We're here."

Hannah looked up, tearing her concentration away from the ground, from her focus on each step. She was surprised to see that the night had almost passed. Light had begun to seep into the darkness. She saw the river snaking between its banks and realized she was holding herself—the temperature had dropped and she was cold. Reaching the river felt like a milestone. Hannah didn't know how long their journey would take and part of her didn't want to know, but she knew that getting to the river meant that they were making progress and were that much farther away from her life in captivity.

CHAPTER THIRTEEN

Rennie felt a combination of relief and fear as they reached the river. She hated to stop walking but Hannah needed a rest. She seemed to have burrowed deep into herself to a place where Rennie couldn't count on her to help keep watch. She looked as if she could do little more than put one foot in front of the other.

"We'll stop here for a bit."

Hannah nodded. She looked cold and exhausted. The breeze coming off the river was a welcome change from the stifling heat they had endured through most of the trip.

Rennie slipped off her pack and fished a small pair of binoculars from a pocket. It was just getting light. She was at a different spot on the river from her trek in, hopefully a little closer to the village, but it was hard to tell. It was rockier here and sandier too. As she scanned the river line, she saw a spot a couple of hundred yards down where a large rock hung over the bank. Over many years, the river had carved away a niche, a small shelter, and the water was low enough that it looked dry. Rennie pointed it out to Hannah who looked so weary that Rennie thought she might balk at going the short distance.

They walked on the higher ground to avoid leaving their trail in the sand. When they reached the rock, Rennie leaned over and saw that the drop down to the sandy spot was a little over six feet. The hollow area where they would stay was deep enough to hide them from view if someone were to come along the bank. It wasn't quite a cave, but it was as close to real shelter as they were going to get. They climbed down alongside the rock. Rennie snapped a small branch from a tree as they went.

"I want to leave as little sign of us as possible," she said when they reached the bottom, using the branch to smooth their footprints in the sand.

Hannah sat down in the hollow of the rock and leaned back against it.

"Mmm, comfy."

"I know you need sleep, but I need you to do something for me first."

Hannah raised her eyebrows in a question.

"I intercepted a document from Armin's men on my way in. It's written in Farsi. I need you to tell me what it is."

"Okay." Hannah looked interested.

"It's maybe ten pages. You don't need to read it word for word. Just enough to give me a sense of its importance."

"No problem."

Rennie handed Hannah the envelope. While she was reading with a pen-sized Maglite, Rennie set to work filling their water bladders. At least with the extra bladders she wouldn't have to worry about becoming dehydrated again. The water was cold and her hands chilled quickly. She would like to bathe—she was as grimy as a human being could be—but it would be too much of a risk. If all went well, they would be at the boarding house in two days and hopefully they would have hot water. A hot shower, a soft bed, a meal on a plate, all the little comforts she had always taken for granted seemed fantastically distant now. She promised herself that if she made it back alive, she would always value the small things.

Rennie felt the toll the last few days had taken on her body. Blood throbbed in the wound on her arm and pain shot through her back and shoulders as she bent over the river. The bruise on her head from the stock of the gun was still sore to the touch but healing well. She needed rest, maybe as much as Hannah needed it, but it would have to wait. She knew she could push herself when she needed to and now was the time.

The water bladders filled, Rennie washed her arms and face and neck, shivering at the touch of the cold water. That would have to do. Hannah was still intently reading as Rennie made her way back to her. Leaning against the rock, Rennie added the iodine tablets to the water. Her pack was next to her. In a padded pocket was the satellite phone, like an accusation, snug and waiting in its bed. She should have called in long ago. At least now she could say she had done what they had come to do. And had rescued an American hostage. It wouldn't mitigate the horror of the awful report she had to make, but it was something.

Rennie felt Hannah's eyes on her.

"Do you have any idea what's in this?" Hannah asked, holding the document.

"No."

"It's a list of names. Of men, and a few women, and their affiliations with various terrorist organizations, along with detailed information of completed crimes. Most of the network leads back to a mosque in London."

Rennie frowned. "Is there any data regarding future events?"

"No. Whoever compiled the list appears to have had only rudimentary intelligence. But there is a map."

"Yes. It's of the village."

Rennie had noticed the hand-drawn map on the last page of

the document.

"What does this say?" Rennie asked, pointing to a mark on the page.

Hannah squinted at the map. The writing was a little smudged. "I think it's some kind of boarding house."

Their meeting place. "Any notation about the time?"

"No." Hannah turned to Rennie and smiled. "But there is a room number."

Rennie thought. "This had to have come from Armin. The thugs I took this off of—well one was just a boy—they couldn't have had this kind of information. This implies connections. It must be from Armin. But why would Armin be passing this to someone?"

"Someone must have something Armin wanted."

"Yes, but this looks like the type of information that would be turned over to the intelligence agency of a state, a state that fights terrorism."

"There's one more thing." Hannah paused. "One name on the list seems to be highlighted, to have more details than the rest."

"And?"

"He's an American."

Rennie closed her eyes. She could never understand how anyone could turn against their country. She could see that her country, her government rather, had made mistakes, many mistakes over the years. But a country is not its government. A country is its people. Who could turn against their own flesh and blood? And then she thought of Armin and his brother.

"What's the name?"

"Someone called Jon Harrison."

Rennie couldn't think. The name sounded familiar, but she couldn't put her finger on it.

"I'm not sure how this relates to anything, but I need to call in and make a report."

Hannah looked like she was about to say more. Rennie knew she shouldn't be having this conversation with her, but Hannah was in it as much as she was.

"Is that all?"

"I think so, but I only scanned it."

Rennie took a deep breath and retrieved the sat-com from her pack. The signal was strong here by the river away from the forest's canopy. She punched in the numbers from memory. She only heard a partial ring before a male voice on the other end said, "Yes." A pause and then, "We're secure." She thought it was Brian Ryder, who ran night communications at CT3's central command, but couldn't be sure from the gaps in the connection.

"This is Agent Rennie Vogel." She could hear a shaky panic in her voice and tried to tamp it down.

"Yes. Go ahead, Agent Vogel."

"Armin is dead."

"Why isn't Agent Smythe making the call?"

This wasn't going to be easy.

"He's dead." She paused. "They're all dead. We were ambushed the first night as we slept."

She knew he wouldn't ask why she hadn't called in then, that wasn't his role. He said, "You made the kill?"

"Yes."

"Where are the bodies?"

"I can't say precisely. GPS was destroyed during the jump."

"We'll have to facilitate withdrawal after you are out then. Where are you now?"

"I'm at the river."

"Are you safe?"

"I don't know. We saw action several hours ago from a group of soldiers who came after us. There were six enemy casualties. We think the rest are focusing on the road as the likely route the shooter took to escape."

"We? You're not alone, Agent Vogel?"

"I'm with Hannah Marcus."

"She's with you now?"

They knew. She could hear it in his voice and he hadn't missed a beat. They had known all along that Hannah was alive.

She continued, "Also, I recovered a document, written in Farsi, from the pack one of the men was carrying. It looks like it was being delivered to the village."

There was a long pause on the other end of the line.

"Any sign of who it was going to or when or where the meeting was to take place?"

"Yes. There's no indication of when but there is a map pointing to a boarding house on the corner of two cross streets in the village—Boktar and Lutfi, the northwest corner."

"Do you know what's in the document?"

"I do now. Hannah Marcus reads Farsi and was able to translate."

"You know she doesn't have clearance."

Something wasn't right.

"I thought the potential importance of the document outweighed such considerations."

"You know the protocol and should have called for go-ahead."

Rennie didn't respond. She wondered if this was just bureaucratic bullshit administered at the worst possible time or if something else was going on.

"What's in the document?"

"A list of names. Of terrorists, most are connected to a London mosque, the Masjid Ibrahim."

"Anything notable?"

Rennie paused.

"One of the terrorists named is an American. A Jon Harrison."

There was a long moment before he responded.

"Okay."

Okay?

"Do you have the document in your possession now?"

Hannah was sitting uncomfortably against the rock, still intently reading the document. Feeling Rennie's attention on her, she glanced over at her, eyebrows raised. Rennie's intention of holding out her hand, stopping her from continuing, died before she lifted her arm. Something wasn't right.

"Yes."

"Good. Keep it safe. How long will it take you to reach the village?"

Rennie thought if everything went right, if they both stayed strong and pushed on with little to no rest, they could reach the village the following night. Two days.

"Three days. The woman is very weak."

"Fine. We'll send someone in to check out this boarding house. Maybe whoever is waiting on the document is still around. Regardless, the agent will stay in the village to accept the document from you when you arrive. Understood?"

"Yes."

"And check in every twelve hours."

"Understood."

Then there was nothing but silence. Rennie looked at the phone. Her supposed lifeline. Just a hunk of useless plastic. She wanted nothing more than to hurl it into the river. Her conversation with Ryder had frustrated her and left her with countless questions. Why wouldn't her team have been told that Hannah Marcus was still alive? Even if the government had no intention of rescuing her, the team should have been informed. But maybe she was making too many assumptions. What possible reason could they have for keeping this information from CT3? There were so many things he hadn't asked. How it was that Hannah Marcus was still alive? And was she healthy? And why had Rennie ignored nearly every protocol in the book? *Why had she?*

Rennie turned back to Hannah who sat shivering against the rock still looking at the document. It was almost fully light now, but the sun was obscured by clouds and it looked like it might rain.

"You can rest for a little while and then we'll have to get moving again."

Hannah gave Rennie a peculiar look that she couldn't read.

"What is it?"

Hannah cleared her throat. "There's something else here. I missed it the first time around. It's about this Jon Harrison. There's more background on him than I picked up in the first reading."

Hannah paused. Rennie wondered why she was hesitating. "Yes?"

She finally spoke. "His father is a case officer. For the CIA."

Rennie narrowed her eyes. *Martin Garrison.* Of course. And his son was Jon Garrison, not Harrison. Hannah had misread his name. Jonathan Garrison. Ryder had put it together, but for some reason had deliberately kept it from her.

"You know who he is?"

Rennie turned her attention again to Hannah.

"Yes. I've never met him, but I've heard of him."

Martin Garrison. Rennie didn't know too much about him other than he had been a spy under diplomatic cover in Saudi Arabia for years, at least since the Cold War ended. Before that, he'd made his career in Moscow. And had recently gone rogue when responsibility for a bombing at a government building in Philadelphia had pointed to his son. No one was killed but the FBI had gone after Jonathan Garrison aggressively. When they took a confrontational stance with Martin Garrison, he decided to go out on his own and try to bring his son in before the FBI found him and went in with guns blazing. An impossible situation made more impossible by the usual lack of interagency cooperation.

She knew more about the son. An only child whose anticapitalist pacifist leanings emerged in high school, Jonathan Garrison believed the interventionist policies of the United States were ruining the world. In college, when he finally understood that his father was a CIA operative, he broke from his family and disappeared. There had been no sign of him until forensic evidence connected him to the Philadelphia bombing. His pacifism had slipped away and he had adopted the philosophy of terrorists everywhere, that change will come through the barrel of a gun—or a homemade bomb or a mushroom cloud. When a homegrown militia group claimed responsibility for the bombing, it was thought he had hooked up with them, but there was always some suspicion that he might be working on his own and the militia group was just riding his wave. Regardless, the connection to the London mosque showed that he had indeed moved on.

Rennie took the document from Hannah and secured it in her pack. Armin had to be trading this information for something. But what? It wouldn't seem to be in his best interest to betray his colleagues. But what else could it be? Why pass on such information? Rennie didn't have the energy to think about it anymore. And it wasn't her responsibility. Her only responsibility right now was to get herself and Hannah to the village alive and deliver the document. Rennie sat down next to Hannah who was hugging her knees to her chest and shaking from the cold.

"Here," Rennie said, pulling off her T-shirt, her tank bloodied and damp underneath. "It might help a little."

"Thanks."

"I know this isn't ideal, but I want you to get some rest before we head out again."

"Long way to go?"

"Yeah."

Rennie settled in next to Hannah against the rock. She was exhausted too, but wouldn't sleep. They had come too far to risk any mistakes that could be avoided. She pulled her pack to her and opened the medical kit. There was a small pharmacy in one of the pockets. Pills for pain, antibiotics, antacids and a little white pill that would be her lifesaver over the next forty-eight hours. Rennie swallowed the pill with a big gulp of bad-tasting water.

"Are you hurting?"

"No. I'm okay. This will help keep me awake."

Special forces and other military had been taking Provigil since it was introduced a few years before. It would keep her awake and alert and allow her to forgo sleep.

"I don't even know if I can sleep. It's so cold."

Hannah was shivering violently and Rennie worried that she wasn't well.

"Here," she said, spreading her legs. "Lean against me and I'll try to keep you warm."

Hannah nodded and scooted into her, settling her thin body against Rennie's chest and thighs. Rennie, her sub-gun beside her where she could get to it fast, held Hannah close. Hannah's skin was cold but, with their bodies touching, quickly began to warm. Her exhaustion ceded to sleep in a moment and Rennie felt her chest rising and falling, her breath even and deep.

Rennie couldn't help but note the incongruity of the moment. This woman she hardly knew, sleeping in her arms. And it felt good. She had never spent an entire night with a woman. Had never slept, never let herself go, allowing consciousness to slip away. Her experiences had always been furtive, always afraid she would jeopardize her career. The closest she had come to a relationship was with Marta. And that was rotten at its core from the start. Two desperate women taking occasional solace in one another. Before that, a few women she had met in bars when she was so lonely she couldn't bear to go home to her empty apartment. But she always went to their place. And never stayed.

The hour she allowed Hannah to sleep passed quickly. Rennie's thoughts traveled through dangerous territory, entering places she never allowed herself to broach. Wrong time, wrong place to consider whether she had made the right choices, to ask herself if this life was the one she wanted.

Rennie hated to wake Hannah. She needed more sleep, but she knew that even an hour was incredibly restorative to the body.

"Hey," she whispered in Hannah's ear. "We need to get going."

Hannah woke slowly, swimming up from someplace very deep. Releasing her, Rennie gave her one of the little white pills to throw off her grogginess—she needed her alert.

A few moments later Rennie crested the bank carefully, scanning the woods for any sign that they had company. The sun still hadn't broken through the clouds and there was light fog swirling through the trees. It made the woods look otherworldly.

142

All seemed clear as far as she could see. She reached down and gave Hannah a hand up.

They would follow the river line until they were able to skirt the swampy area that had hampered her progress on the trip in. Rennie thought they could make better time this way. They set out at a good pace, moving through the fog.

CHAPTER FOURTEEN

CT3 Command Center
Quantico, Virginia

Brian Ryder drove out of the security checkpoint at the Quantico Marine Base with a wave to the guards and headed toward I-95. He was exhausted. He had pulled night duty for five days and counting and dreaded his morning drive home to Alexandria. The engine of his brand-new Corvette was itching to unwind, but it was a little after seven a.m. and traffic had already been crawling for an hour. He usually went into his office on the FBI Academy campus early and left late. A perfect time to drive with the lights of the interstate illuminating the dark road that cut through darker fields. Tearing north toward the glow of the city, keeping an eye out for troopers, he could never keep the smirk off his face. It felt too good. But since CT3 had headed out to Central Asia, he had been coming to work in the evening to attend the final daily briefing before settling down for a long night manning communications in the command center. It was a grueling schedule.

But it had paid off. Ryder was at his post when the call they had been waiting for came in and he loved nothing more than being in the middle of the action. It had been four days since CT3's GPS signal had gone dead, the blinking red light disappearing from the computer screen like a heartbeat flatlining. There had been a collective intake of breath in the command center and everyone knew it couldn't be good news. And then the wait began. Everyone suspected that something could have gone so awry that they were waiting in vain, that a call would never come.

Ryder had worked for years with the Hostage Rescue Team, as one of the many links between the team and the brass. But it was always reactive work, responding to crisis situations that could erupt at any time of day or night. He had jumped at the chance to continue his work with the new international team. International counterterrorism was where it was all going to happen and he was glad the FBI was finally on board in a more proactive way. The CIA shouldn't have all the fun. Ryder had been studying the subject for years, focusing on Islamic militant movements. This was where the real danger lay. No longer were nations the threat they once were. The U.S. was too powerful, the last big superpower, and no one was stupid enough to attack them openly. But the Islamists were another story. They had nothing to lose and didn't care who got hurt in the process of furthering their agenda.

Ryder's clearance for this assignment had been raised, but it only went so far. Once, in an early meeting, he asked why they had chosen to go after Armin who seemed little more than a small-time crackpot. After all, there were other groups who were better organized and had more of a network. His question was ignored and Ryder was savvy enough to not bring it up again. He supposed they had their reasons and it wasn't his job to question them. But he still knew more than the team. Keeping the team on a need-to-know basis might prove to have been their biggest mistake. The meeting of a few hours before, still fresh in his mind, only confirmed his suspicions.

Ryder had raised his hand the moment the call came in and the agent in charge of the mission, Will Jenkins, was at his side slipping on a headset before Vogel had even identified herself. After the call, they had taken the long walk down the dim hallway to the assistant director's office.

Tower Morgan, who at five-foot-nine never lived up to his mother's hopes, was on the phone with his wife when Ryder and Jenkins walked in. The assistant director's office, as usual, was suffused with the aroma of strong coffee. He motioned them to sit. They didn't.

"What's up?" he said, hanging up the phone and pinching the bridge of his nose, a gesture that indicated he was already stressed.

Jenkins took a deep breath and briefed him on the call from Tajikistan. When he concluded with the information about Hannah Marcus, Morgan pursed his lips and reached for his coffeepot.

"We fumbled this one."

Jenkins didn't respond. He stood staring at a map of Central Asia on the wall, rubbing his hand over his face.

"Do we know how Vogel discovered the woman was alive?" the director said.

"No." Jenkins looked at Ryder who confirmed with a shake of his head.

"The team should have been briefed that Marcus's status was unknown and that they weren't to concern themselves with her," Morgan said.

Jenkins nodded. Ryder could see that his boss was worried. This was a big mistake and had already made the Bureau look like a bunch of amateurs.

"The likelihood that she was still alive was slim to none," Jenkins began, ready to make an argument for his decision. Morgan waved him off. He had heard it all before.

"We'll have to bring CIA in on this. With the Garrison angle. We don't know enough to go forward on our own."

Ryder could see Jenkins cringe at the thought. The CT3 assignment was Jenkins's baby and Ryder knew he felt like a fool having to call in the spies. Morgan picked up the phone without another word, waving Ryder and Jenkins out of his office.

Ryder braked as traffic suddenly slowed and for the first time since the call had come in he thought of the team. He didn't know them well, hardly at all really. He had participated in a few background briefings with the entire team assembled. And he would see them every once in a while on the Academy campus, heading out or coming in from training. But mostly he knew them from their files. His world was the realm of data, always one step removed from the real thing. He knew everything he needed to know about them to do his job and a lot about their personal lives that didn't have any bearing on anything. And now they were dead. All but the woman. Ryder loved women, had faith in their abilities, but nevertheless firmly believed they had no place in combat. Yet Vogel had done something right. She was the only one still breathing.

With traffic finally moving, Ryder crossed the Fourteenth St. Bridge into the city instead of exiting into Alexandria. He was too pumped up from the events of the night to go home and go to bed. He felt like eating a greasy breakfast and knew the perfect place on Florida Avenue. Grits and scrapple and fried apples always made him feel like he was sitting in his mother's kitchen. After, he might take a little detour and let the 'Vette stretch her legs. He knew the car was tacky. Not the usual choice for an African-American Yale grad who employed the diction of an evening news anchor, knowing his natural southern rhythms could put him in a box, one he would never allow himself to be trapped in. But sometimes the man had to satisfy the whims of the boy.

Martin Garrison sat in the small Shuroabad Café reading a week old copy of *Le Monde* and drinking a cup of desperately strong coffee. It matched his mood. Armin's men had not arrived on time with their delivery and he was having second thoughts.

Something must have gone wrong. Armin was as anxious as Garrison to make the exchange.

Garrison had arrived in the Tajik capital, Dushanbe, two days earlier carrying the French passport of a man named Claude Raffarin. He'd plucked the document off a dead Soviet spy he'd found garrotted in a fetid Paris alley years before. Garrison never knew the man's real name, but he knew the quality of the document would not be questioned—you could count on the Russians for their thoroughness, especially when it came to espionage. Garrison had a box of such documents in a small compartment at the back of a wardrobe in his home in McLean, Virginia, just a few miles from CIA headquarters. The documents were his safety net, in case anything went wrong. And something had gone terribly wrong. Anyone who had been in as deep cover as Garrison knew there might come a time when he would need to get out. And he knew his employer would never find him, until he wanted to be found.

Garrison had taken a hired car to the little village of Shuroabad where he settled into a rented room. He had spent two days in the café waiting for Armin to send the promised information on his son.

Jonathan. A sensitive boy born of a sensitive woman. Garrison's wife had almost ruined his career with her trips in and out of psychiatric wards. But he'd loved her with an intensity he could never fully explain even to himself. She was his one point of weakness and when she died, finally, by her own hand, he promised himself never to come under the emotional sway of any human being again. But his son, so like her, seemed determined to bring him down. Jon had inherited his mother's instability and her passion for causes.

The café owner, a small grizzled man of about fifty, indicated to Garrison that he was closing up for the night. Garrison settled his tab and stepped into the street. It had rained most of the day, which had blessedly washed away some of the stench the neighborhood usually emitted.

Garrison decided to walk for a bit, taking the long way back to the boarding house. It was almost time for evening prayers and all the shops were closing for the night. He had never been drawn to religion or any form of organized philosophy. Except the CIA. As a young agent he had swallowed their message lock, stock and barrel. Time had tempered his enthusiasm. Once, Mormons had come to the door in their dark suits and name tags and bright white smiles and Jon seemed to swallow their entire dogma whole. For a few months he had gone twice a week to church and spoken of where he might be sent when he went on his mission. And then, just as fast, he was done with them. Their conservatism, well hidden under a mask of pseudotolerance, finally offended his democratic sensibilities. He was a good boy. Always siding with the underdog. That was the only way Garrison could explain this new fervor for Islamist causes. That and the touch of his mother's madness.

Garrison walked more quickly than he intended and found himself at the back door of his lodging house. Old habits made him prefer this less direct entrance. One could never be too careful. He hoped the next day would offer up Armin's men and the document that might save his son.

Hannah could barely lift her legs after walking all day with only short breaks. They had picked their way through the fog-blanketed woods all morning. The sun, emerging for a brief and blessed moment midday, had quickly given way to rain. The rain was welcome, washing away days of accumulated grime, but after the sun set, a chill sank into Hannah's bones. Her clothes were no longer dripping, but were damp, like a clammy second skin. She still wore Rennie's shirt, which left Rennie with just her tank top. Hannah wondered if she was cold too.

It had been nearly twenty-four hours since they had seen any sign of Armin's men and Hannah began to hope that they might have gotten away. Living for so long in the little stable, she'd had plenty of time to consider what it meant to be free. Not the grand idea Americans spoke of, a concept bundled with rights and protections. Instead it was the simple idea of physical autonomy. The freedom to walk out your front door and take yourself wherever you pleased.

Being detained by force had been a horror. Penned in, she'd shrunk into herself and for the first time realized that before she was taken, moving freely through the world, her notion of herself as a physical being extended beyond the boundaries of her own skin. She *was* her own familiar network of streets, the corner grocery, the park. How far did it extend, she wondered. The feeling that all is you. If you are safe, perhaps it is infinite. And there is a comfort in that. Once she was taken, bolted in and confined by four walls that seemed to get closer and closer as the days wore on, she knew that all she was, in her entirety, was her own flesh and blood and bone and nothing beyond and she had never felt more alone. It was like waking up and realizing you have been buried alive or that you're the last person on the face of the earth. But with time the horror had passed and with it the feeling that she had touched madness.

Here in the woods, she felt herself begin to expand once again, beginning that communion with her surroundings that she had always taken for granted. Her instinct was to fight against it, to struggle against her passage back into the world. It made her feel naked and raw.

"Let's stop for a bit." She heard Rennie speak, her voice seemed to be far away, and Hannah realized that her pace had slowed to a shuffle, her legs no longer cooperating.

"Beef stew tonight," Rennie said, ripping open the package. "Do you mind if we share?"

They must be low on food.

They ate together in silence, sitting against a tree, feeling the dampness of the ground seep into their pants and not caring because it felt so good just to rest. They sat shoulder to shoulder against the tree and Hannah thought of the morning, so long ago it seemed now, when she lay against Rennie, feeling her warmth. How long had it been since she felt the touch of another person? It had been divine, like slipping into a warm, enveloping bath. She had enjoyed it for only the briefest moment before sleep had taken her. This was unusual for her, physical closeness with a stranger. She was never the type of woman others would touch spontaneously. She always had a barrier she kept in place. She watched Rennie's hands as she ate. Strong hands with long, thin fingers. She felt safe with this woman and felt a sudden desire to slip her arms around her and rest her head on her shoulder. How strange.

Hannah shifted away slightly, creating a space between them. "Should we go?"

Rennie turned to her, surprised. They had finished eating. Hannah felt restored by the food. It built a warmth in her that fought against the dampness of her clothes.

They stood, Rennie adjusting the pack and Hannah shifting the strap on her AK-47 away from her collarbone where it was beginning to chafe. The pill Rennie had given her was doing the trick and she was alert. The outlines of the landscape were crisp and distinct and the sky was clear, finally free of clouds.

Hannah seemed stronger after their meal and the few moments of rest. Rennie was thankful for it. She worried that Hannah's strength might just give out. And then what? She couldn't carry her out of these woods. She would have to leave her, go and get help. Or call on the sat-phone and be told that she would have to manage on her own. To have survived in the camp for so long, Hannah had to have determination and she hoped it would carry her through to the end.

It was a still night without the slightest breath of movement. No breeze, no rain, even the animals seemed to have taken the night off. Rennie stretched out her arms as she walked, letting her MP5 hang at her side. She hadn't worked out in almost a week, but it seemed much longer. Her routine had been so structured for so long, it was her nature to thrive on such regimentation. It was only when she discovered structure and discipline that she had been able to accomplish anything. In that way, the FBI was perfect for her.

The weekend before they were to leave for their mission, the team had run through a three-day practice scenario. They hiked all day, camped at night and made a shoot on the third day. It had gone well. The day was hot, but they had plenty of water and were all running on adrenaline. She could still see Brad's smile as he turned to the team after a perfect head shot to the dummy that had been set up in the Virginia field. After months of regular workouts and course work, they felt they were ready to roll. They had spent the next few days doing light workouts and then were sent home for two days with instructions to do nothing but rest and let their bodies heal.

In her apartment again after so long, Rennie had fallen into a funk. She lay on her bed, feeling antsy, wanting nothing more than to slip on her New Balances and run. But she didn't. She accepted the hierarchy of the life she had chosen and took her orders seriously, like a good soldier. So, she spent the two days puttering around the apartment, shuffling from room to room like an old woman, not knowing what to do with herself.

Here in the woods, she certainly wasn't lacking for exercise, but it lacked the focus of her workouts. She remembered when she first discovered that she could transform her body. It was a revelation. She went from a slightly doughy girl to a woman she could hardly recognize. As the fat melted away, curves of muscle revealed themselves. Bone, too, seemed to be resurrected out of the mass of her flesh and she felt that she had the power to mold herself into whatever she wanted to be. As her body changed, so had her face. Cheekbones she never knew she had emerged along with a strong jawline. And women began to notice her. She enjoyed it at first, but the attention always seemed to be focused solely on the way she looked and she grew cautious.

Hannah was walking ahead of Rennie. She stopped and waited for her to catch up.

"How long do you think it will be before we're back in the States? After we get to the village."

"It's hard to say. It depends on whether they'll want to debrief you here. Or at home."

"How long will it take?"

Rennie shook her head. "Could take days." She smiled at Hannah. "You've been gone a long time."

And then there was the problem of Hannah's connection to Armin's assassination. Rennie guessed the FBI would press her to say she had made it out on her own in the confusion. It was an unlikely scenario but they would have to feed something to the press. And the press would eat it up. It was a great story. Now, more than twenty-four hours after Armin had fallen to the rough stage, his brain switched off by Rennie's bullet, she knew his death had already hit the papers and that some poor Iranian who'd made a deal with the U.S. to act as scapegoat had been picked up by international forces. His family would reap the benefits of his sacrifice in cash, a deal negotiated long before Rennie and her team set foot on the plane that carried them to their mission.

Rennie wondered how cooperative Hannah would be when asked to participate in this charade. She might balk, but the FBI knew how to apply pressure, suggesting that things would be made difficult for her if she didn't go along. The whole thing was already beginning to smell of rot.

It struck Rennie then that she would probably never see Hannah again after she delivered her to the authorities. Any connection between them would be impossible. She felt a sudden rush of anger at this life she led, made up of violence and deceit. She felt like a pawn in a sprawling game that would never resolve. But why was she thinking these things now? Similar doubts had bubbled up before but never with such force. Why did the idea of not seeing Hannah again, a woman she didn't even know, fill her with dread?

"What are you thinking about?" Hannah touched her lightly on the arm. "You look upset."

Rennie paused before answering. "I was just thinking about my own debriefing."

There was that. When she would have to explain herself. It wouldn't take place here. It was too big for that. It would be in that big, black, foreboding building on Ninth St. in the city. FBI headquarters. Agents called it The Black Hole and she wondered if she'd be able to find her way out of it or forever be caught up in its swirling red tape. Nevertheless, she looked forward to going home. For better or for worse. Whatever fate awaited her. It was nearly September, when the heat would finally begin to break, ceding to the first bite of fall. It was the time of year she liked best. But she had no idea what she would be going back to. If her actions in these woods would bring punitive measures. She was still too close to it to see it clearly.

Rennie tramped on in the darkness. It was inevitable that they would pass near the ambush site before too long. They were already on a path that Rennie thought she recognized. It might well lead them right to it. She wasn't sure how she felt about it. How long had it been? It was hard to think. She had been awake for so long the days ran together. More than forty-eight hours. Forty-eight hours in the heat and the rain. A finger of pain ran along her temple at the thought of seeing them. But she would. If she had the chance.

CHAPTER FIFTEEN

Kulyab, Tajikistan

The tall blond woman knocked on the cab driver's window just outside the airport terminal. It was late, she should have been there hours ago, but her plane had been delayed. The driver was dozing and didn't seem interested in interrupting his nap. She barked out her destination as she tossed her bag in the backseat, speaking the language badly. The driver glared at her in his rearview mirror.

Margot Day settled into the seat and fitted a scarf over her head to cover her hair, to make herself less noticeable. She hadn't had time to dye it. This entire venture had been unexpected. A call just as she was about to leave the office. She almost didn't answer it, had stared at the phone, considering whether it could possibly be important before she plucked it off the cradle on the fourth ring. She had already shut down her computer and was thinking about a glass of Glenfiddich at the bar around the corner from her apartment. She knew something was wrong as soon as she heard the voice. Working so many years at the CIA, she could detect the slightest trace of anxiety in the most monotone voice. And everyone at the CIA seemed to have a monotone voice. The voice told her she had to fly out of Dushanbe immediately and her first thought was of the sink full of dishes she had allowed to accumulate over the week and how vile they would be whenever she returned. The voice from Washington—a city she despised, a city that didn't even know what to call itself: Washington, D.C., the District of Columbia, D.C., the District, the Nation's Capital and her personal favorite, Warshington, courtesy of the locals—said that she was to fly into Kulyab and take a car to the little town of Shuroabad. From there she was to find Martin Garrison and detain him.

She had never been in this part of the country, this far south, so close to the Afghan border. She knew that the farther you were from the capital the more lawless the country became, the reason it was desirable to terrorists looking for a place to set up shop and not be bothered.

Margot rolled down the window of the car. It was humid from the rain and her face was damp with perspiration. And she was anxious. She had never met Garrison but she knew of his reputation. And her work in Tajikistan hadn't exactly honed her skills. But she was good at what she did, even if she never gave herself enough credit. She had been two years in Dushanbe under diplomatic cover. She spent her days at her desk, glued to her computer, and her nights at embassy cocktail parties sniffing around for anything her country might be interested in. It wasn't what she imagined for herself when she joined the CIA. But since the Soviet Union collapsed, the work of the spy was much less glamorous. She also knew that her time here was just a stepping stone. She did good work and eventually it would pay off. This assignment showed that her bosses were confident in her and if she pulled it off, a promotion was inevitable.

She caught a glimpse of herself reflected in the side mirror of the taxi, wide eyes peering out from the headscarf. Even with her hair hidden, she still looked impossibly American, with the pert good looks of a Midwestern beauty queen. She was very pretty and a bit vain about it. She still wore what she had worn to work, a dark suit with a subtle pinstripe. She hadn't had time to change before leaving, barely had time to rush home and throw a few things in an overnight bag. She fished a cigarette out of her purse and lit it, drawing in deeply on the smoke. She wished she'd had time for that drink before she got the call.

Okay, Margot, it's time to get it together. She felt her nerves begin to settle.

Margot had first heard of Martin Garrison right out of training when she was stationed in Moscow for her first gig. There were still a bunch of oldies but goodies moldering in the embassy who couldn't quite believe the Cold War was over. And Garrison was their hero, a celebrity in the world of espionage. Few agents worked with him since he spent so much time in deep cover, spending as much as a year underground—no wonder he had family problems. But his exploits were known and revered. And now she was supposed to detain him. She fingered the gun under her arm. *Detain him.* That was what they said, at first. But it quickly became clear that by "detain" they meant for her to shoot him on sight. The CIA had zero tolerance for agents who betrayed them. They knew too much and were too dangerous.

Margot knew she had to be careful. She couldn't afford to be spotted by Garrison—he was too good and could take her before she knew what hit her. But her talents lay in stealth and in firing a weapon with absolute certainty. The silencer was in the pocket of her jacket. Garrison would be waiting for a delivery that would never come. And she would be waiting for him. The voice on the phone had told her not to get near him, not to speak to him—just fire on sight. And then strip him of all ID, connect with the FBI agent, accept the document and get the hell out.

Margot thought of the 1976 ban on political assassination. It was laughable. It was what her government did when they ran out of options. Everyone in the business knew that. She flicked her cigarette out the window and reread the article on Ahmad Armin's death, printed off Lexis after she got the call. Her presence in the little village closest to Armin's camp was no coincidence and neither was Martin Garrison's. She didn't know exactly what was going on but she knew what she had to do.

Shadowy fields flitted past her in the darkness. She could see lights up ahead and knew she was near the village. She should have gotten some sleep on the plane but her nerves were jangling too loudly for that. She would check into a room, settle herself and then head to the building opposite Garrison's boarding house—CIA had no idea what it housed—and see if she could procure a place to watch.

Hannah walked alongside Rennie. It was late. Or early, depending on your perspective. Nearly four a.m. and they would soon begin to see the first signs of day. The night in the woods was the most difficult—the period from midnight until the first intimation of dawn seemed interminable, minutes crawling by in the unchanging dark. Rennie had said that this would be their last night in the woods, that tomorrow would bring the village. Hannah believed her. She had to. She couldn't last much longer. Rennie had given her another of the little white pills a few hours before and her mind was wide awake. But her body seemed disconnected from it, a sluggish mass her mind had to drag along after it. But they had kept up a challenging pace and were making good time. She would continue to push herself, anything that would get her closer to home. *Home.* She wasn't even sure what it meant—her country, her city, her apartment? Like Dorothy, she wanted to click her heels and just be there, no matter what it meant, someplace where she wasn't locked in or carrying a gun and looking over her shoulder.

Growing up she'd always felt out of place. She loved Baltimore in her own way, the way you love a scrappy, unruly dog who knows how to steal your heart the moment you're about to write him off. But she never felt truly at home there. She was always a traveler at heart and had stolen away the moment she'd had the chance. She wanted to perceive the world through eyes other than her own, eyes without the permanent cloud of someone else's history. Her work as a reporter brought her into contact with every form of human misery—hunger, strife, boundless grief, hopeless despair—and she found that seeing such things firsthand was the only thing that blunted her cynicism. But she always found it easier to extend her sympathy to strangers. She was much harder on the people in her life, the friends and family and lovers who were supposed to matter.

She remembered her first assignment overseas, in Tehran, during a demonstration against the country's oppressive theocratic government. It was the first time she had witnessed real chaos. Here were people desperate for change. Screaming, chanting, fists pumping in the air. Violence was the undercurrent, on the verge of erupting at any moment. Witnessing the expression of such raw, unconstrained emotion had made her want to weep. Until later when she learned that the demonstration wasn't what she thought it was, the spontaneous eruption of a people kept down for too long. The men in the street—brought in from the slums in the south of the city—had been paid a pittance to form a mob, feigning passion and allegiance to a burgeoning political faction that opposed the Ayatollah. She felt like a fool. She had forgotten the first lesson she should have learned from her parents—a mob can be manipulated to believe or they can willingly participate. *You can never truly trust anyone but your family.* So they had said. An evil thing to tell a child. But she seemed to have succeeded in following their advice, at the very least, in her relationships.

Hannah glanced at Rennie forging ahead through the woods. Rennie, who seemed so earnest. So earnest, perhaps she was a fool. Trusting her country enough to kill a man for it. Hannah wondered how that felt, to believe in something so completely to be able to kill for it. It struck her as fanatical, as unreasonable as the Islamist terrorists they condemned. But maybe she was making assumptions. Nevertheless, Hannah found herself powerfully drawn to Rennie. She questioned where the attraction was coming from. Maybe it was as simple as that she owed Rennie

159

her life.

She now knew her own government never intended to bring her home, even though they knew they would be within a few hundred yards of her cell. In a world where some strive for power, a few struggle to hold on to it and the rest only hope to avoid getting caught in the crossfire, violence and deception are the oil that makes the engine run. It was the way of the world. Hannah didn't dispute this or feel any need to lament it. She just hated the hypocrisy. But Rennie had done the right thing, even if her government hadn't, and in the process risked her life and her career, too, Hannah imagined, to bring her out of the hell she'd thought she'd never escape. Now, she wanted nothing more than to go home and be done with it all. And she didn't know if she'd ever leave home again.

The night was warm and, aside from the fatigue of her body, Hannah felt better than she had in days. Her clothes were finally dry and the chill she had taken into her bones by the river was nearly gone. Walking was easier, the ground even and the trees less dense. She was continually surprised by the different aspects the woods manifested—one moment seeming grand and protective and the next ominous and foreboding. Rennie walked more slowly now and seemed to be scrutinizing every rock and tree. Her energy must be flagging too.

But something was wrong. Rennie seemed on edge, keyed up in a way Hannah hadn't seen before. Then Rennie stopped and turned to Hannah, exhaling forcefully.

"This is where it happened."

The ambush.

"I need a moment," she said quietly, indicating to Hannah to stay where she was.

Rennie walked away from her, slowly through the trees towering above her. It was the farthest they had been from one another since the rescue and Hannah felt strangely alone, leaning against a tree, the bark rough against her back. Watching Rennie from a distance, she seemed so much smaller, a slim silhouette in the faint moonlight. Hannah saw her stop and stand before the bodies. She could smell them from where she stood, an unholy stench that wormed its way into her brain, imprinting an indelible memory, and making her stomach leap to her throat.

She was never able to think of death with any kind of clarity. Her parents had seen hundreds of naked, emaciated bodies that never made it into the ground or to the synagogue to have the rabbi speak over them. She'd grown up with those images rendered in black and white. It was an introduction to a subject most American children only encountered in the safety and artificiality of the funeral parlor—a loved one made up in their Sunday best, laid out for the eternal sleep. She hated having those photos, that history, always in her mind. It seemed like it was her reference point for everything. Every experience filtered through that one monumental event.

Rennie knelt on one knee, her head in her hand. Watching her, Hannah saw that here was a woman bound by duty and loyalty first and foremost. Hannah wanted to go to her and offer comfort. But she knew that this was Rennie's last opportunity to make whatever kind of peace she could and Hannah let her be.

She recalled those archetypal stories of war, of soldiers risking their lives to rescue the bodies of their dead comrades. Before, she believed it to be rooted in a kind of militaristic machismo antithetical to practicality. Men whose blood still beat in their veins risking their lives in order to bring home rotting flesh to be put in the ground. It seemed wasteful. To honor the living, that was what mattered. But now, with these men before her on the ground, the black-and-white pictures seemed to blur and fade. There was nothing like the real thing in front of you. Even in the dark she could imagine the vivid color—the red of spent life, the green of rot—and the stink of death soaking into every pore.

Rennie stood slowly and turned away from the dead men. She knelt again a little off to the side where a heap of packs lay. She finally turned and walked back to Hannah. Hannah could see that her face was set, pain written all over it. In her hands were a stack of magazines, a few MREs and clothing. An automatic pistol was stuck in the waistband of her pants. She tossed the load

161

next to their pack.

"Okay." The word only a whisper, she could barely speak.

She bent to arrange the pack, but Hannah stopped her, pulling her close, slipping her arms around her waist. Rennie stood against her, stiff and unyielding, but then Hannah felt her muscles relax and Rennie leaned into her. Hannah held her tighter and then Rennie's arms were around her, holding her so hard Hannah thought she might break. Rennie didn't utter a sound and her breathing remained even. They stood together for a long time. Finally, Rennie released her hold on Hannah and, looking into her eyes for a long moment, she laid her hand along her cheek.

For hours they walked, without a word. As the night wore on, the woods became thick and pitchy with darkness, but as dawn broke, the sky was streaked with curtains of pink and purple. It became a bright clear morning.

Rennie's body carried her forward, but she hardly knew where she was. Her legs continued to move and she was aware that she was alert, watching for any sign of danger, but her mind was operating on some animal level, concerned only with survival. Since leaving the site of the ambush, something in her prevented any coherent thought to form but now she began to return to herself. How could it be that she was the only one to survive? It seemed like a cruel joke. The irony was that as the only woman she would be blamed for everything that went wrong instead of being recognized for making it to the end. But what was the end, she wondered.

They should stop soon. Hannah must surely be hungry. But Rennie couldn't think of food, of sustaining her body, and didn't know if she ever could again. She didn't know if the smell of them in her nostrils would ever leave. *Say their names, Goddammit!*— *Goode, Smythe, Levin, Baldwin.* Like a prayer, she recited their names in her mind. *Goode, Smythe, Levin, Baldwin.* Reduced to almost nothing. A horror of putrid flesh, an oozing fetid mass. She could hardly tell where one ended and the other began. To be reduced to such a condition so quickly, what a thin thread life was strung upon, always only a step away from dissolution.

What if she had been alone? Kneeling before them, childhood terrors rearing up in the dark? Thank God for Hannah. A good Catholic, religion returned to her in times of stress. All those dead saints. They were surely mad, God speaking to them in the dead of night. Would it have been the same for her? If she had been alone. Her mind becoming unhinged. Did she owe them that?

How could things have gone so badly? She mourned for all of them. Even Smythe. But it was Brad that made her hurt, ache from the loss of him. Her friend. She had loved him. He was absolutely good, at his core, where it mattered most.

Her mind was growing weary. And her body craved rest. She knew the trauma of the early morning hours was dissipating as she became aware of her own needs. Hannah strode beside her, holding her AK-47, like a good soldier.

"Let's take a break. I need to change the dressing on my arm."

Hannah looked relieved to stop. "I can do it."

Hannah pulled the medical kit from the pack and spread it open on the ground. Rennie sat staring at the twisted roots running along either side of her from the tree she sat against. She ripped the bandage off her arm, wincing at the pain. Her wound looked good. No infection.

Hannah approached her with the antiseptic. "You ready? This might sting."

It did sting, sending an arc of pain through to her bone and radiating down her arm. Hannah finished with gauze and tape.

"You were lucky," Hannah said softly.

"Yes."

"And I was lucky."

"You think?"

"Yes."

Rennie ripped open an MRE and they sat in silence, sharing their meal.

"Are you all right?" Hannah said without looking at her.

"I'll be fine."

"I know you will." Hannah laid her hand on Rennie's thigh, kneading it with her fingers.

"I guess you have no idea what you'll be going home to." Rennie laid her hand on top of Hannah's, hesitantly at first. Then Hannah turned her hand, taking Rennie's and intertwining their fingers. "I know you're not married. Is there a boyfriend?"

"No." She took a deep breath. "I just hope my parents are okay."

Rennie could hear Hannah's voice tightening as she continued. "I spent most of my life trying to get away from them. From the weight of what they went through in Ravensbrück. Now, all I can think of is whether I'll ever see them again."

"How old are they?"

"Old." She tossed her head, throwing off the emotion. "And they don't take care of themselves. Can't seem to get away from that Old Country diet. Sausages, meatballs, butter, cheese. If it's bad, it's on the menu."

Rennie was only aware of Hannah's hand. Their hands together.

They would reach the village before the next day passed. She could feel it, knew that step by step they would get there before midnight. It would become night, but they wouldn't have to endure the small hours, when the dark felt like death. When even the moon seemed to fail them, turning in on itself.

CHAPTER SIXTEEN

London, England

After finishing his morning prayers, Mukhtaar Abdullah stood in the middle of his one-room flat lost in indecision. He wasn't well and these periods when he was unable to formulate a thought were coming more frequently. He was very weak. He ate little more than a crust of bread and an egg every day, convinced that living the existence of an ascetic would make him fit for the important work he had to do. He didn't have much choice, anyway. He had no money and lived off the charity of his brothers at the mosque. His beloved mosque. Thank Allah he had found it. It was his salvation. And his room, a dirty hovel in Hackney, a slummy East End neighborhood, was only about two miles from the mosque. His thin legs carried him there every day even when he thought he couldn't take another step.

Mukhtaar sat down carefully on the threadbare, spindly

couch. The room had come furnished or he'd be sitting and sleeping on the floor. Not that he would mind. He didn't mind anything. Except that he felt his body was failing him and he feared he wouldn't be much use to his mentor, Abdul-Haafiz al-Katib, who had great plans for him. He lifted his T-shirt and looked at his ribs, prominent against his thin skin. He seemed to be wasting away. It wasn't always like this. When he first came to London, he was strong and never had the lapses of memory or concentration he had now. What was wrong with him? He was finally living the life he knew to be good and true. Maybe he just needed to take better care of himself.

He went to the cooler by the door where he kept his food. He would need to get ice soon. Two eggs, his last, had slipped out of their carton and floated, bobbing, in the icy water. He fished one out and broke it in a dish. While the pan heated he inspected the egg for any sign of disease. He was very careful not to break the yolk. He spotted a cloudy area and, before he began dry heaving, he slipped the offending egg down the drain, running hot water so that every trace of it was washed away. He had better luck with the second, his last egg. Frying it without oil—he had none—it blackened quickly in the heavy pan. He ate it standing at the stove, mopping up the yolk with a quarter of a slice of bread. His mind began to clear.

He had always been troubled by food, resorting to precise weights and measures whenever something worried him. Like a woman, his father had said. It started again after he added Abdullah to his name. When he converted to Islam, he had taken the name of Mukhtaar, the Chosen, never to use Jonathan again, never to *be* Jonathan again. Jonathan was a non-person, someone who was never meant to exist. But after leaving the States he knew he had to rid himself of Garrison, too. Nothing could tie him to his former life. Abdullah it had been. The ultimate renunciation. He had once read of the Malaysian custom of giving the surname Abdullah to Muslim children born out of wedlock, when no claim could be made to the name of the father. He was a bastard child now, no son of his father's. Allah was his only father now. His true father. And always had been, only Mukhtaar hadn't known it when he was living the life of lies at home.

He would eat more. Brother Abdul-Haafiz had begged him to take better care of himself, had pressed money into his hand at every turn, but Mukhtaar would always drop it in the collection box as he left the mosque. He searched his mind trying to discover anything else that might be bothering him, that would bring back the issue with the food. He couldn't imagine. He was happier than he had ever been. It must be the thing with the name. It was like him to take the blame for things he shouldn't. Like his mother.

His mother had taken him to see her shrink in D.C. when he first began to get weird about his food. It was the time when he had begun to be obsessed with his father's guns. He had always been horrified by violence of any sort, but suddenly the knowledge that a gun was present in the house fixed in his mind and he could focus on nothing else. He had known for years that there were guns in his father's life. He had walked in on him once as he was dressing, standing before the wardrobe and bending to reach into the bottom drawer, the one that was always kept locked. The boy had seen not just one gun, but many. It was years before he understood why and that lack of understanding made it all the worse. He would ask his mother: *Why do we need guns? We have a security system. We live in a nice neighborhood. Nothing ever happens here.* That was before he had been able to see the value of weapons.

As the protein continued its restorative work on his body, Mukhtaar thought of things he fought to keep hidden from himself. Things that made him doubt what he was doing in London. He knew Brother Abdul-Haafiz didn't truly care for him. Mukhtaar was valuable to him only as an American who would rouse no suspicion in anyone. An American who was willing to betray his country. Soon he would shave his beard and don his American clothes again. And then fly home and begin the revolution.

Mukhtaar finished cleaning his pan and went to the window.

He peered through a small tear in the blind. Something wasn't right. His mind was clear now. He went to his trunk and got the gun. The door to his flat was cheaply made and hollow. A jagged hole, the size of a medium-sized London mouse, was about a foot from the floor a few inches from the hinge. He had made another hole, just large enough to see through, a half-foot above it on the inside of the door and a larger one in the outside panel. He crouched to it now. Peering through, the barrel of his gun in the lower opening, he saw nothing unusual but his view of the hall was limited.

They were coming for him. He could feel it. He knew he wouldn't hear them, but there was only one way to his apartment door—up the stairs and straight down the hall. He could see the landing of the stairwell from his spot.

Then he saw legs, black booted. Mukhtaar fired, hitting the lead man in the thigh before the rest scattered.

He left his position and went to the narrow iron bed next to the window. He was glad he had eaten the egg. A thick knotted rope was tied around the joint of the bed. He didn't have much time and this was his only chance. He peered around the blind again. No sign of anything out of the ordinary, just the usual street traffic and junkies on every corner, but that didn't mean anything.

He lifted the blind, tossed the rope over the window ledge and leapt over, shimmying down the side of the building, the toes of his tennis shoes scraping against the brick. His feet had just hit the sidewalk when he heard the splintering sound of his door being ripped from its hinges. They would see the rope in a moment. An alley ran along the side of his building, but he needed to blend with the street traffic as much as possible. They couldn't fire on him if he was surrounded by pedestrians.

Out of habit he turned in the direction of the mosque, jogging down the pavement. So far, so good. He might just make it. He kept close to the storefronts along the street to avoid being seen from his window. He was almost at the corner. He would turn there and cross the street and then dart into an alley midblock. Running, his cheap tennis shoes slapping the concrete, he clipped a massive leather-clad man with his shoulder.

"Watch yourself, wanker!" The man grabbed him by the collar of his shirt pulling him close and breathing hot, oniony breath into his face before shoving him away and staggering down the street.

Mukhtaar was nearly at the corner. He turned and looked back at his building expecting to see a black-suited figure leaning out of his window with a scope trained on him. Nothing. He turned the corner and exhaled in relief. Then an arm shot out of a recessed doorway and grabbed him by the arm.

"Going somewhere, Jonathan?"

The bearded man, who wore a sport jacket and looked like any average Londoner, swung Mukhtaar roughly against the wall and cuffed his arms behind his back before he could think to struggle. A useless thought anyway. The egg could only do so much.

Martin Garrison had the features and complexion that could pass for almost any ethnicity. Today he was a Frenchman. It had been years since he had played the role. Not too much of a stretch. A lot of it was in the expression, especially the set of the mouth. Though he changed his hair and beard only slightly, anyone who knew him would be hard-pressed to recognize him. Sometimes when he slept deeply, which was rare, the names of all the men he had been ran together in a kaleidoscopic whirl, twirling through his sleeping brain. He would wake and for a moment have no idea who he was. Fortunately it only happened when he was safe in his own bed in Virginia, never in the field, and the familiar setting of his own bedroom quickly brought him back to himself. The histories of the men he had been ran through his veins, were stitched into his musculature, instantly accessible, each detail catalogued in his mind.

Deep cover wasn't something everyone could handle. Most agents burned out in a few years. It takes a particular personality to be able to completely subsume your own identity. It had been early in his career when the Agency discovered Martin Garrison's aptitude for transformation and dissembling, the two talents most required for an undercover agent. That and a kind of fearlessness that can't be taught.

Garrison was sitting in the café again, his legs crossed at the knee, reading the same copy of *Le Monde* he had taken from the plane out of Paris. He had read every inch of it and now resorted to the classifieds. He hoped Armin's men would turn up before he resorted to the advertisements. They would be in perfect French, of course. The French government's stranglehold on the language and its purity always struck Garrison as autocratic, a long hidden tendency in the French breast. He wondered when it would emerge and in what form. Garrison motioned for the café proprietor to order breakfast. He was achingly hungry.

If Armin's men didn't show up today, he might scout around for a newspaper in his native tongue before going back to his boarding house. Surely some shop in the village must carry a *New York Times* or a *Guardian*. Even a more recent edition of *Le Monde* would satisfy his need for news at this point. He was already thinking of what he might do next if Armin didn't come through for him. He would have to resurrect some of his old contacts, sketchy characters he preferred to have no dealings with and who the CIA might already be watching, anticipating his next move. But he would do whatever he had to do to find Jon.

He blamed himself for Jon's conversion to Islam a few months after his mother's suicide. On assignment at the time in Berlin, he had known nothing of it until he returned. By then it was too late. Jon was already attending a mosque in nearby Falls Church and had grown a patchy beard. He was still taking classes at George Mason, but only sporadically. Garrison had hoped it was just another phase, that it would wither before taking root. But he'd been home only a few weeks before he had to go back out and was focused on his next assignment. He should have taken a leave of absence, taken the boy in hand and shaken some sense into him. But he'd left, as he always had, and by the time he was home again, Jon was gone. He could be anywhere now.

Garrison had a friend look into the Falls Church mosque. It had a handful of extremists, militant figures who raised the spectre of jihad on the quiet to those who were sympathetic and who had connections all over the world. Jon could be in Paris, Hamburg, Syria, Palestine, London or, God forbid, Afghanistan. Or countless other places where fanatical Muslims sowed their hatred of America and the West, distorting their religion for political purposes. So, Martin Garrison had played the easiest card in his hand. Ahmad Armin.

Garrison reached into his suit jacket and touched the envelope, secure in his inside pocket. The photographs. The incontrovertible proof that Ahmad Armin's outrageous claims that the CIA had murdered his brother, Nasser, were absolutely true. By stealing them Garrison had betrayed his country and committed an act of treason that would put him in prison for the rest of his life. If he got caught. But he would do anything for his son. He was a little late coming to the game, but it was time to make up for the past.

He had contacted Armin a week before and made him the offer. Armin was suspicious at first but Garrison explained his situation and finally convinced him that it wasn't a ploy to capture him. It was a nasty business, the story with Nasser Armin, and Garrison was glad he hadn't been involved. Just one more misstep in a long line of mistakes the CIA had made with Iran.

The café proprietor's teenage son, a handsome boy with black eyes, served Garrison his breakfast. Garrison nodded his thanks and whispered a prayer that today would bring the document with Jon's whereabouts. And then he ate.

Hannah took another of the little white pills that Rennie handed her and thought it was too bad she didn't have them in grad school. Her mind was active and alert on a level she hadn't felt in years. It was like she was finally waking after a long and torturous nightmare. Light in her stall at the camp had always been muted, weak rays slipping through the dirty pane high on the wall of the stable. She knew now that the absence of sunlight had had its effect, causing her mind to enter a place of near hibernation. She had slept a lot. What else was there to do? To make the days pass and avoid thoughts of the future and all that was lost.

Now, finally, she was beginning to see things, as if nature's palette had been restored after a long monochrome dream. Summer was coming to a close and the woods were still lush and full and verdant. Her eye took in everything—veins of leaves set in relief, patterns and varying shades of gray and white in the rocks speaking of their long history, soft beds of moss at the base of a tree, the shocking reds and yellows of wildflowers. The woods, with the sunlight filtering through the trees, were so fine it made her ache to think how long it had been since she had taken in beauty.

Hannah always yearned for beauty but had never tried to attain it in such an undiluted form as nature. She was thoroughly urban and natural beauty had seemed to her too benign, too banal and prosaic, as if it had slipped into a hackneyed stereotype. Such thoughts seemed absurd to her now. She had always sought man-made beauty. Pigment on canvas gripping her like a panic. But no romantic landscapes or impressionist confections for her. She had discovered a young artist whose work spoke to her like no other. Paintings bright and light using the colors of summer but the addition of raw flesh tones, rendered ambiguously—meant to be living or dead?—cast a darkness of mood over the work. So it always was with Hannah—everything good tempered with dark. But here in the woods, those old conceptions retreated in the face of summer in full bloom. She was alive and free and, for the moment, no taint was able to sneak into her vision.

Rennie, too, loomed larger than ever before her. She was finally struck by the awareness that here was a woman she felt drawn to in a way she had never experienced. With anyone. Something was being forged between them, had been in the process of being forged ever since she had come back to herself as they ran down the hillside from the camp. Something she didn't want to name and couldn't if she tried. Whatever it was, it was entirely new.

She remembered birthdays as a child. Her parents always waited to give her her gift after dinner just before she went to bed. She would finish brushing her teeth and crawl into her pajamas. Sitting cross-legged on the worn living room rug, she was unable to sit still with excitement, wagging her knees and wriggling her shoulders. She would have an hour with her new toy before bedtime. The magic hour. Finally tucked snug in her narrow bed, she would lie grinning, suffused with absolute happiness. The next morning when she woke and remembered the gift, she wouldn't rush to it, but lay warm in her bed turning it over in her mind. This was when the magnificence of the toy reached its zenith, never to be had again. Her joy over its novelty imbued it with qualities it almost certainly didn't have. In her sleepy imagination, it was perfect, becoming almost cinematic in her mind, taking on a luster that real life never had. She had never had this experience with people, only things, and not since she was small. Until now. She felt foolish, realizing that Rennie had taken on that indescribable hue. Glancing at her, Hannah wondered if it was the drug. And she wondered if, like the toy, it would pass as quickly.

"You okay?" Rennie said, noticing her look.

Hannah nodded. "Yeah. I'm good." She smiled. "Really good."

Hannah looked at Rennie, taking her in fully. She was tall and angular and intensely beautiful. Hannah felt foolish, responding to beauty in such a simple form. Sharp bone met muscle in a way not often seen in a woman. Her muscle curled over her body like a snake, rising and dipping over her frame as if she had shed every ounce that wasn't necessary to maintain herself. Hannah wondered briefly if it was something akin to masculinity that she was drawn to. *No.* That wasn't it and she swore to herself at that moment that she would never again mistake something for what it wasn't, no matter how much it made her afraid. She wanted something pure and unadulterated, something devoid of her

173

past. No more false connections built upon a foundation riven with hollows of rot. Whatever this was she would approach it with an open heart.

"What are you thinking about?"

"I was thinking how absurd it is that I'm actually enjoying this moment. Walking through these woods. With you. On a gorgeous sunny day."

"And carrying a high-powered weapon."

"There is that," Hannah said, lifting the AK-47.

"It works for you," Rennie said with a trace of irony in her eyes.

"You think?"

"Yeah." Rennie paused. "You're doing great, you know? I know this hasn't been easy."

Hannah stared at the ground before casting her eyes back to Rennie. "Thanks."

They continued picking their way through the forest in silence, Hannah walking next to Rennie but slightly behind, watching her. Rennie never wavered. Every moment she was scanning the woods for danger. Keeping them safe. Hannah knew without a doubt that she owed Rennie her life. And she knew that even in the absence of that monumental fact, she was still drawn to her.

Rennie broke into her reverie again. "We're going to make it, you know?" she said, looking back at Hannah.

"I know."

It hit her then. She knew it was true and knew it was all Rennie. She could have shot Armin and gone on her way, as was surely her mandate. But she had risked her life to bring Hannah home.

Hannah reached out and took Rennie by the arm, stopping her.

Rennie looked concerned. "Everything all right?"

"Yes." Hannah let go of her rifle, letting it dangle from its strap and slipped her arms around Rennie.

"Yes," she said again. Rennie was nearly half a foot taller and

174

Hannah stood, her face buried in the hollow of Rennie's neck just above her collarbone, taking in her scent. Their bodies still close, she pulled her head away and looked into her eyes.

"Thank you."

Rennie shook her head. "It's okay."

Hannah reached up and kissed her lightly on the cheek, her hand on the back of Rennie's neck. "Yes. It's okay."

CHAPTER SEVENTEEN

Shuroabad, Tajikistan

Sitting on an old bench, the stuffing peeking out of the upholstery, Margot Day yawned as she stared through the crack in the soiled drapery, peering out at the door of Martin Garrison's boarding house. At least she hoped it was Garrison's boarding house. She had yet to receive any confirmation of the intelligence from the FBI. She had seen every variety of shady character come and go from the door that fronted directly onto the street, but none of them, she was sure, was Garrison. For all she knew he may have found another link to his son and her efforts were for naught.

She hated surveillance. She hadn't done it in years. She had to constantly fight against the tedium that led to fatigue. Exhaustion tugged at the edges of her consciousness and her mind wandered without her permission. She couldn't help but think of Andy

176

Rivera, the new case officer in the Tajikistan embassy. They held similar roles and worked together often. And their attraction to one another had emerged soon after his arrival. She had resisted it so far, knowing the Agency frowned on such relationships. She wasn't looking for a boyfriend, just wanted to let off a little steam. Which didn't really count as a relationship, she justified. All the same she wasn't willing to risk her career for a few nights of pleasure.

Just then, the door of the boarding house swung open and a man emerged. Margot raised her field glasses to her face and the man leapt into view. He was short and stocky and very dark. Not Martin Garrison. She lowered the field glasses, took a deep a breath and glanced around the room.

The family that lived in the house she'd commandeered for her surveillance was not happy with her presence. But crisp Tajik currency had turned their heads and so she was now ensconced in the workroom of the lady of the residence. Often, during the day, they were there together, as they were now, the woman seated on the floor by the other window, embroidering colorful skullcaps in rich shades of purple, green and pink and eyeing Margot with suspicion. The floor was layered in carpets, locally produced. They were beautiful—not as beautiful as those Margot lusted over in Iran—she always took a few small samples home as gifts for her friends. But the color that permeated the textiles in Tajikistan broke the monotony of the drab architecture. Margot had an eye for fashion and sometimes lamented the clothes she was compelled to wear for her work. Clothing in Tajikistan was a riot of color and she loved color, always tending toward reds and oranges and purples in her private life. Anytime she was outside of her own room in the village, Margot dressed as a traditional Tajik in a long multicolored dress with loose striped trousers underneath. On her head she wore a hat, the same type the woman was making, covered by a headscarf. But here, in the house, she abandoned the headscarf as was customary. The two women sat at their work, one dark, one blonde and fair.

The woman addressed Margot in Tajik. "Your husband's a

bad man?"

Margot shifted her position so she could keep an eye on the door of the boarding house and appear to give a sliver of her attention to the woman.

"Yes. It's very sad." This was the role Margot had taken on in order to gain entry to the house—spurned wife.

"Who is the woman?"

"Just a common slut."

The woman nodded in understanding. "My first husband, for a long time he went with another woman, like the woman your husband is with."

"Oh?"

"But I accepted it. That and everything else." She paused, reaching into her basket for a different color, holding the needle to the light to snake the thread through the eye. "Where did you meet him, your husband?"

"He worked for a time in America."

"You should have stayed there," she said, not raising her eyes from her work.

Tell me about it. The woman was a distraction and she wished she would just concentrate on her sewing, but at least her chatter helped keep Margot awake. She glanced down the street. There was never much foot traffic and only the occasional car or bike. She suspected Garrison was coming and going through the back door of the boarding house that exited into an alley. But she had no vantage point from which to watch it. And she could hardly loiter in the alley until he came along. If he didn't turn up soon, she would have to go out and canvass the streets for him, an almost pointless and possibly dangerous endeavor.

She felt the vibration of her cell phone and hunting through the folds of her dress, plucked it from the waistband of her trousers. The woman cut her eyes toward her. The conversation only took a moment and when she hung up, the ever-deepening line between Margot's eyebrows had relaxed a little. The CIA had Jonathan Garrison and would soon be boarding a plane with him for Tajikistan. Her orders had changed. Now that they had some leverage, they were going to try to bring in Martin Garrison without violence. Margot felt like doing a dance, feeling Garrison's reprieve as deeply as if it were her own. Now she just had to keep an eye on him and make sure he didn't go anywhere. But first she had to find out if Garrison was even in the village.

"I need to go. But I may be back."

The woman didn't understand. She turned her dark eyes on Margot and nodded. Margot wondered if the woman enjoyed her company on some level, a distraction from her deadbeat husband who, though he didn't cheat on her, spent his days slumbering in an opium-induced stupor, his addiction funded by his wife's hard work.

In a moment, Margot was out the door and down the steps, taking two at a time. She usually wore a suit at work and it was a strange feeling—all this material flowing around her, the shoulder holster of her automatic snug under arm, directly against her skin. On the street, she adjusted her headscarf, making certain her hair was hidden. It was blazing hot with every inch of her covered. Without a glance at the boarding house, she headed for the corner. It seemed hopeless. Randomly walking the streets, looking for Garrison. But what else could she do? Jonathan Garrison, the little bastard, would be en route any moment. If she found no sign of Garrison in the village, she would have to take the precarious step of entering his boarding house to see if she could find any trace of him.

Jonathan Garrison returned the stare of the agent sitting across from him. Jonathan was in custody on a military transport speeding toward Tajikistan. The engine of the plane they had taken out of Heathrow was loud, its vibrations coursing through his body and setting him on edge, the long flight giving him plenty of time to think. The agent near him was tall and dark with a close-cut beard, sitting with his long legs outstretched, his hands behind his head. He had removed Jon's cuffs once they were in the air, knowing he was no threat.

It's over, Jonathan thought.

His adolescent rebellion had taken a dangerous turn and for the first time he could see it all with perfect clarity. He had envisioned the end countless times before. But he always imagined it as a martyrdom, a face-off where he would acquit himself admirably, and die a hero for his cause. But the actual event was a slap in the face. He hadn't fought, but run like a scared rabbit. And when the CIA agent grabbed his arm, he was like a man waking from a dream. His madness slipped away like a silk sheet and he became docile and cooperative. In that moment Mukhtaar Abdullah disappeared as if he had never existed.

The CIA had taken Jonathan to their London office where self-preservation soon kicked in and he thought of what would happen when all of this was over. He would not fare well in prison. But who knows, with a good lawyer, maybe he wouldn't be in too long. He had made a few threats and, with Al-Katib, had planned much worse, but the Feds didn't know that and he had no intention of telling them.

The plane hit a rough patch of turbulence and Jon squeezed his eyes shut. He hated flying. He whispered a prayer in Arabic out of habit, the first words that came into his mind, and recalled his early days in the mosque in Virginia when he first discovered the beauty of Islam. Before his mind had been seduced by dreams of jihad, Islam spoke to him and he felt accepted. He was happy and for the first time had friends, young men his own age who liked him. Or so he thought. Eventually the young men spoke of what Jon could do for Islam and he was filled with dreams of himself as a savior. Now he could see himself for what he was—a lonely boy in search of some kind of connection, in search of acceptance.

He caught a glimpse of his reflection in the small window of the plane. Anatomy is destiny. In his case, the blond, boyish looks he had inherited from his mother had kept him a boy for too long, given him an excuse to sink into his weaknesses, to realize their ultimate potential. But it had been a choice—he knew that now—child's play gone horribly awry. He could have taken his medicine and struggled against his mental quirks.

Instead he romanticized them, took them as a sign that he was special, gifted with a sensitivity and openness that others lacked. Without the chemicals to smooth out the rough edges, he was prone to superstition and felt compelled to perform rituals. Like now, he sat tense in his seat, feet flat on the floor, his hands curled around the armrests maintaining a distinct separation between each finger. And what would happen if he allowed his fingers to touch, the heel or toe of his shoe to lift off the floor? The plane might teeter in the air, become unbalanced and plummet. He knew it wasn't true, but something in him wouldn't allow reason to be the victor.

Enough.

He crossed his legs and relaxed his grip on the armrests, covering his face with his hands. A vein rose on his forehead, pulsing with pain as a tiny panic rose up at this small rebellion.

The plane will be fine. Unless you're sitting in the cockpit, your actions have no control over it. That much is true.

A lump formed in his throat and his anxiety rose as he refused to give in to the mania in his brain, an inherent reluctance to partake in what is perhaps God's greatest gift to man—logic. His father had said that to him once, speaking of God one night on the deck of their Virginia home after too many glasses of bourbon. Martin Garrison valued logic over all else and it was perhaps the only instance Jonathan had ever heard his father speak of God. He knew it would take time to puzzle everything out. To separate the truth from the fictions his mind spun. He knew just one thing for certain—it was time to become a man.

Now they were taking him to his father who was in as much trouble as he was. Jon would never have guessed that the old man had it in him, to break from the organization that was his lifeblood. Jon would go with the Feds and hope they could find his father before he did something that would irrevocably cement his fate. Then Jonathan Garrison would make amends to his father and his country.

Rennie felt herself failing and knew she should have taken

the pill miles back when she first felt her vision begin to swim. But there were only two left and they still had hours to go before they reached the village. She should have thought to collect more when they were at the ambush site when she retrieved food and ammunition and clothes from the packs of her teammates. And she should have taken her gun with her when she stepped away from their campsite that first night. So many mistakes that couldn't be undone. She hadn't thought herself capable of such failure. It stung and burned to the very quick. As a young agent she had received year after year of commendations. And then she became the first woman on a special operations team. Everything fell into place. Until now, when the whole world seemed to be disintegrating around her.

Still walking, her panic rising, she slipped her pack off her shoulders and swung it around to her front before going down on one knee and unzipping the first pocket she saw. Then Hannah was by her, her hands on her shoulders.

"Are you all right?"

Fatigue coursed through her body. She could feel her heartbeat thumping everywhere, her body pushed to its limit, as she stared dumbly at the pack. In her state, she realized she had no idea where the medical kit was stored.

"The pill."

She unzipped another pocket. It was the wrong one, but in it was the satellite phone. And it was blinking. The signal for her to call in. She pulled the phone out of the pocket and sat down on her haunches, covering her face with her hand.

Hannah was kneeling next to her now.

"What is it?"

Rennie looked up into her face. Was it fear or concern playing out over her features? Rennie's perceptions were too muddled to be able to tell. But she knew she couldn't fail Hannah, too. That would be too much.

She tried not to sound desperate. "It's okay. Do you know where the medical kit is?" she said, squinting at her.

Hannah nodded, wide-eyed, and reached for the pocket on

the opposite side of the bag. She pulled out the kit and handed Rennie the pill.

Rennie stared at it for a long moment before popping it into her mouth and swallowing it with a gulp of foul, warm water. It would take effect quickly and just knowing it was in her, working its magic, brought her around.

"Thanks," she said, taking Hannah's proffered hand up. "Stay here and rest for a moment. I need to call in."

Hannah nodded and Rennie dialed the number as she walked.

As before, the call was answered on the first ring. This time she was certain it was Brian Ryder. "Yes. We're secure," he said.

"This is Vogel."

"Where are you?"

Rennie paused. "Maybe five or six hours from the village." They were hours ahead of her earlier estimate.

"We believe Martin Garrison is in the village waiting for delivery of the document. CIA is there already and will pick him up."

That's a huge assumption.

"Call in as soon as you're established in the village. More CIA is in transport with Jonathan Garrison, but won't arrive until after 0200 hours. You will turn over the document to them."

Jonathan Garrison had been captured as a result of her intel. At least something beneficial had come out of the ambush.

"Is that all?"

"Let's hope so," the agent said after a beat.

Rennie slipped the phone into her pocket and ran her fingers through her hair. *Let's hope so.* What was that supposed to mean? She shook her head. The FBI needed to hire handlers who weren't so ambiguous.

She turned back toward Hannah who was sitting against a tree with her head resting on her knees. The drug was already worming its way through Rennie's veins, evening her out, and quashing unwanted emotions on the verge of bursting to the surface. Kneeling to Hannah, she put her hand on the back of her neck, which was damp and slick with perspiration.

"Let's go. We'll stop and have a real rest in a couple of hours."

Martin Garrison paid his bill and left the café. He stopped on the sidewalk and scanned the street in what now seemed the futile hope that Armin's men might turn up in this last moment before he left their meeting point for the final time. Tomorrow he would board a plane, leave Tajikistan, and fly to Berlin where he had a contact he had put off using, knowing it would solidify his betrayal to his country in a way that was irreversible.

He walked in a direction away from his boarding house. After sitting for so many days, he needed to stretch his legs. The afternoon sun was strong but milky, casting hazy shadows on the street. It was busier than usual as people hurried to the shops and markets before they closed. He walked several blocks, thinking of Jon. Time was running out. He had to get to Jon before the CIA found him. Turning a corner, he found himself in front of a bookshop. Local newspapers were stacked outside the door, weighted down by pieces of broken masonry. His need for current news drew him inside. The shop was dark and close, dust motes floating in the still air. Paperbacks were stuffed into every conceivable nook and in stacks on the floor. They emitted that pungent, sour smell of books printed in developing countries. Garrison stood just inside the door, allowing his eyes to adjust to the darkness. He didn't pretend to browse.

There was no counter. The clerk sat on a low stool drinking tea and arguing in a quiet voice with a customer. Garrison spotted more newspapers in the back of the store and went directly to them. Copies of *Tajikistan* and the *Times of Central Asia* were slumped against the back wall. There was no *Le Monde*—he was almost thankful for that—but, amazingly, a single two-day old *Guardian*. Garrison snatched it off the floor glancing at the headlines above the fold—the usual Israeli-Palestinian deadlock, an article on the psychological benefits of exercise and not much else. He folded the paper, paid the clerk—who eyed him warily and put his money in a box on the floor—and went back out onto the street. At least he would have fairly recent news to get him through the evening in his smelly room.

Garrison had developed finicky habits over the years and tried to hide them, knowing they weren't masculine, were perhaps even un-American. They had developed, not through upbringing, but through philosophy, or so he thought, unwilling to believe that they might reflect his own true nature. Humanity was steeped in mediocrity and the detritus of human leavings filled him with disgust. In such moments of clarity, he wondered if his son's quirks weren't solely the responsibility of his mother.

Garrison walked for awhile, circling past his boarding house before turning back. The sun was lower as he crossed his street a block east, heading toward the alley that led to the back door of his residence. It was a short block and he could see a woman entering the front door of his house. The battered entrance fronted directly onto the street, no sidewalk, no steps. Even from his distance he could tell that the woman wasn't Tajik. She wore a headscarf and traditional Tajik female attire but he could see by her coloring that she was probably blond. And there weren't too many blond Tajiks. His body shifted gears as his instinct told him she was an American, something about the way she held herself.

They had found him. It must have been through Armin. Or more likely, Armin's men. He had learned long ago that sometimes the most militant-seeming extremists will abandon their cause in a moment if they believe that they have a chance of a life in a free country. Armin's men may have cut a deal with the CIA. Garrison stopped at the corner before turning into the alley. He had everything he needed to jump into a car and run to the airport. He had no reason to go back to his room. But he had to know what this woman knew.

Garrison rounded the corner of the alley with caution. Where there was one there could be many. He walked quickly, his hand inside his jacket within reach of the 9mm Browning snug under his arm—the only reason he was wearing a jacket in such a climate. The alley—too narrow for a car—reeked of urine.

He could see the proprietor of the boarding house sitting in the open door, smoking a hand-rolled cigarette. He was probably only thirty but looked much older, with deep lines crossing his forehead. He nodded as Garrison approached.

"A woman just entered the house from the front." Garrison spoke to him quietly in Russian. "Did you see her?"

The man breathed acrid smoke through his nostrils and shrugged. Garrison wanted to gut him on the spot for his apathy, his blind acceptance of his wretched circumstances.

Control.

Instead, Garrison stepped past him and moved down the narrow hallway to the staircase. The building had sprung up, probably overnight, during the time when Moscow still held the reins over most of Central Asia. The house had been erected without care for its longevity and now it was crumbling. Climbing the darkened stairway silently, careful to avoid the creaks in the old, badly fitted wooden boards, Garrison reminded himself that he would have to be restrained. This woman was likely an American. She was only doing her job. He had no ill will for her. How long had it been since he'd killed a man? Or a woman for that matter? He never relished it but it did come with a certain satisfaction.

The air in the hallway was close and stale. The proprietor seemed to think he could keep his lodging fresher by leaving the windows closed and keeping out the stink of the street, a miscalculation in Garrison's mind. His room was at the end of a narrow hallway on the third floor, a nasty little garret that made him think of Raskolnikov. His mind often went to the Russians as a point of reference, an inheritance from learning his trade as the Cold War wrapped up.

Garrison moved down the hallway as silently as a cat, dim light barely emitting from a naked, flickering bulb badly attached to the low ceiling. Reaching his door, he could see that someone had entered his room—the mark he always left was disturbed. He moved past the door and stood in the shadows, his ear against the wall.

He could hear movement in the room through the thin wall. He knew it was the woman he saw entering from the front and he wondered what he would do with her. His instincts, sorely won through countless horrific events, would have to guide him now. He slipped the Browning from the shoulder holster and tucked the *Guardian* into the back of his pants.

He stepped closer to the door and could hear drawers being opened and closed. She wouldn't find anything of interest, nothing to incriminate him or give any hint of who lived there. He put his hand on the knob of the door and inched it open—he had oiled the hinges himself when he checked in.

The woman stood at the wardrobe at the back of the room checking the pockets of his suitcase. He couldn't help but smile a little. This would be too easy. Silently, he stepped into the room and closed the door behind him. He stood for a moment watching her. He could see the butt of her weapon under her arm through her unlikely clothing. Then she froze, sensing him.

"Not a movement. Not a breath. You mustn't try anything foolish."

The woman raised her hands and turned slowly to face him.

CHAPTER EIGHTEEN

Rennie walked fast, keeping her pace. They were so close now. The entire ordeal would be over soon. But she knew it would also bring an end to her time with Hannah. She didn't know how to think about that and kept it pressed down deep. *Control.* She had always maintained control in her emotions with women. Never show too much. She never opened herself up completely. Never felt whatever it was that would allow that to happen. No woman had touched that place in her. But now, she could feel herself stirring. Something new was opening up inside her. And she wanted to take Hannah in, deep inside, where no one had ever been. It terrified her. To go there was dangerous. It meant making herself vulnerable, open to a kind of pain she had never felt before—and, yes, perhaps with it the potential for happiness. She didn't know if it was worth the risk.

She had been alone for so long. In D.C., when emptiness cut away at her until it reached her very core, she would go to a club, some trashy place in a sketchy part of the city where the boys cruised each other every night of the week. There were girls there, too. Always a few, at least on the weekends. Paying her cover at the door, she would feel the thumping bass rousing her senses. She'd move into the room, a mass of undulating flesh, slowly, striding fluidly and deliberately into the mix. The space throbbing, pulsing, lights flashing, she would press herself into the twisted knot of bodies, moving to the never-ending thump. She always wore something dark and tight, showing off her arms and the perfect chisel of her abdomen. She moved in a sultry half-cadence to the tribal beat permeating the room, drawing energy from the sea of sweating, shirtless men. Each time was like the others. Eventually and inevitably, a woman appeared out of the crush, behind her, moving against her. This was what she came for. A moment's connection in the dark, chaos rearing up on all sides. She moved against her, feeling the contour of her body, a phantom woman still, creating and reshaping her as the music insinuated itself into the very rhythms of her brain. This was the moment, before she knew who moved against her, where an instant of pleasure meant more than anything in the world. Then the knowledge that the moment had passed, and it was all a farce, crawled, scrabbling like an animal into her consciousness. Finally, she turned and their bodies, hers and the phantom woman's, would meet, face to face. Social convention kept her there an instant more and then she went alone into the night. She never went home with a woman from a club, only from bars. The club was a sacred, desperate, unholy place that she returned to like a junkie.

But here in the woods, that world seemed a million miles away and the desire for that transitory passion felt utterly meaningless. Rennie could hardly believe she had ever wanted it. This was real—she and Hannah fighting for their lives, discovering what they were made of in the worst possible conditions. Rennie's arm was tense under the weight of her weapon. She saw the shape of the muscle as it embraced the bone. Her body was strong. She could feel its strength and rely on it. She wondered about the rest of her. What else was there? Did she have anything to offer another person? Someone who wasn't just a moment in the dark. She glanced over at Hannah, who looked ragged.

"Can we stop and rest? Just for an hour?" Hannah's voice broke with fatigue.

It was time. It was a good spot. Hannah must have been keeping an eye out for a suitable place. Rennie shelved her thoughts to attend to the moment.

"Yes," she said as she threw down her pack and sat upon the soft earth. She spread her legs and Hannah settled in between them. They didn't speak. They both knew the drill by now. It wasn't very cold but Rennie slipped her arms around Hannah. Hannah curled her own around Rennie's. Their bodies warmed to one another quickly. They sat in silence, feeling the indescribable pleasure of not moving. They both understood the comfort of the moment, the closeness of their bodies. Hannah leaned further into Rennie and dropped her head back onto her shoulder.

"What did you leave behind?" Hannah spoke quietly, turning her head slightly so that she could speak just under Rennie's ear. Rennie's body began to respond, to the intimacy of the moment, Hannah's breath on her neck, her voice velvety smooth. "Before you came here, to shoot bad men in the woods?"

Rennie found herself unable to speak. A sound emerged from her throat, but it wasn't language. It came from somewhere deep, from that place that hadn't ever been touched. The touch stung and she felt the pain of it mixed with something else so perfect she couldn't name it if she tried.

"Nothing."

It was true. No close family or friends, no pets. Her one close friend had made the journey with her, but wouldn't be returning home. What was there to go back to? She had put so much into her career that there was never anything left over for the things in life that she knew really mattered. Maybe she had planned it that way.

Hannah trailed her fingers lightly along Rennie's arm. "No lover?"

There was Marta. But they weren't that to one another. Everyone she had ever been with had been a convenience and nothing more.

"No. No lover."

They sat in silence again.

"This was our first mission together. My team. Me. Most of us were new to special forces."

Hannah drew Rennie's arms more tightly to her body. She hesitated before she spoke, seeming to choose her words carefully. "Do you think it's unusual to send a newly formed team on such a mission?"

Rennie thought of Smythe and what he had said to her in their briefing meeting. It seemed so long ago, another lifetime. *Had* they been set up to fail? A young team sent on a mission beyond their capabilities?

When she finally responded, Rennie spoke with more honesty than she intended. "It *is* unusual. But I don't think any of us could allow ourselves to think that. Yes. It is very unusual."

Rennie moved her cheek against Hannah's, banishing all thought. And then, her mouth open, she moved her lips along Hannah's neck, taking in her scent, so close to a kiss, so close. Hannah leaned into her and Rennie could feel her breathing deepen.

She had to stop. This wasn't the time. She wondered if it would ever come.

"Sleep now, sleep. While you have the chance."

Hannah paused for a long moment and then drew Rennie's hand to her lips, turning it, and kissed her palm lightly.

"Okay, okay."

Then she shifted slightly, laying her head on Rennie's chest, and slept.

Margot Day heard the voice and felt a cold sweat rise to the surface of her skin. She turned slowly, her hands raised in

191

supplication. Martin Garrison stood just inside the door holding a silenced automatic. She said nothing, there was no use. She knew he would never take her for a local thief.

"Put your hands against the wall and kneel." He spoke softly. His voice seemed to hum.

Margot followed his instructions, hearing him move behind her. She could feel his nearness. He reached under the folds of her dress and plucked her pistol from beneath her arm. Then, he put his hand on her head resting it there gently for a moment before he delicately peeled off her headscarf. She felt the silk of the scarf slip slowly, almost sensuously, from her neck and then replacing it was the hard butt of the silencer at the base of her skull.

God. No. It can't end like this.

Margot felt sorrow wash over her for everything she had left undone and waited for the motion of Garrison's finger on the trigger. At least it would be over quick. When it didn't come, she began to tremble. It began as a shiver creeping up her spine until it met the gun against her head. Her muscles began to twitch, in waves. As if she were giving birth, the waves came more frequently as her panic rose until she was shaking so hard the silencer was tapping against her skull, politely knocking. She felt her eyes begin to well.

Don't cry. Goddammit, don't cry. At least die with dignity.

Then Garrison laid his hand on Margot's shoulder, his thumb along the back of her neck just under the gun. Her trembling ceased under his touch and she tried to think. She had to think if she was going to save herself.

What were his options? He now knew the CIA had his location. He obviously had no intention of turning himself in and was willing to add to his crimes by detaining a fellow agent at gunpoint. Did he have anything to lose by killing her? Absolutely. He would be a fool to draw more agents after him. Okay. So maybe she could assume he wouldn't kill her unless she forced his hand. Hopefully. Then what was the point of this? Why wasn't he saying anything? He had slipped into the room unnoticed. He could have just as easily closed the door and run. Like any good agent he would have his documents on him—he could have abandoned the clothes, the toiletries and the dog-eared copy of Gogol's *Dead Souls*, and escaped the country while he had a chance. But he hadn't. He had to know how much she knew and maybe most importantly, if she had any information about his son. That's why he was wearing her down by waiting her out.

Garrison still had his hand on Margot's neck and began to stroke her lightly with his thumb.

Bastard. If only she could get a read on his state of mind. If she could sense any instability, a vulnerability, she might be able to turn the tables.

She felt the pressure on her shoulder increase and heard the bedsprings give as he sat down. He laid something on the bed. Then he was by her ear.

"Short-staffed, were they?" His voice was low and insinuating.

Margot said nothing. She recalled her training on interrogation techniques and knew he was working her, but she couldn't help but bristle at the remark.

"I imagine someone more experienced is en route right now. Hmm? But that will take time. And we'll use that time productively, don't you think?"

He was so close to her face Margot could smell the stale coffee on his breath. Her mind raced. She needed to deflect him from the line he was taking before she just shut down.

"Let's make this simple, what do you say? You tell me what brought you here to me and we'll be done with it."

Margot stared at a long, jagged crack on the wall she faced. CIA had Jonathan. She could use this. And then she suddenly felt so tired she just wanted to lean her head against the wall and close her eyes.

"Hmm. The quiet type, huh? I can relate to that. I don't think I've said two words to anyone in weeks. But it's a lonely business, right? We knew that going in. I can tell you, though, you'll be glad to be out of it. Yes. This is your day. You should feel fortunate. Knowledge is what we all want, isn't it? And now you know. You know the day. The hour, I might even say—but we'll have to see. I'm a little rusty."

Margot swallowed hard. She could feel the hair standing up on the back of her neck and knew Garrison could sense her terror. He was playing her. And it was working.

"I know, it's a little scary at first. But I think you'll come to see how lucky you are. Just think, you'll never have to experience the slow, grinding decay of your own body and believe me, I'm older than you, it's not much fun." He chuckled lightly as if he were letting her in on a private joke. "Yes. Today is your day. And the question is, how will you spend these last moments? In comfort? Or not."

He was bluffing. He must be. He knew what resources would be put into his capture if he killed an agent. He wouldn't risk it. *Right?*

Margot's mind began to wander. An image floated before her on the wall. The ace of hearts. She had a card to play. But all she could do was move her finger along its imaginary edge. She thought of her brother, Mark. Her parents had died when she was young and Mark had raised her. He was so proud of her. She had never known a man as tender, as caring as Mark. It made her hurt to think of him, imagining him seeing her like this. She felt herself crumbling. All that she needed to remember, that the CIA had Garrison's son, that she could use it as leverage, and that it would surely work, it all dissolved, blending and disappearing into her fear which overwhelmed any possibility of rational thought.

Garrison reached over and switched off the bedside lamp. Darkness. She heard the snap of the safety on the pistol and flinched, but he held her firm by the shoulder.

He won't do it. He won't do it.

She had no ability to save herself.

She heard him snap the safety again. Back and forth. Each time she expected the next inevitable motion of his finger on the trigger. She squeezed her eyes shut and then forced them open again and tried to focus on the crack on the wall, barely visible in the dark. Then she realized with finality that she was mourning herself. She had accepted the end. She kept very still and thought of nothing.

Hannah woke in darkness as Rennie shifted her body behind her. She hadn't intended to sleep. Their mouths had been so close. Even though Rennie drew away and told her to sleep she hadn't wanted the moment to end, not then, but she succumbed. Now she knew it was time for them to walk but she didn't want to move, not yet, and drew Rennie's arms tighter around her. She felt perfectly safe. Absurd, considering she could hardly be in more danger with Armin's men hunting them, thirsting for revenge.

What would her parents think? Falling for a girl, *a girl, a woman*—and worse, *the horror*, a girl with a German name. *Vogel*. How inappropriate. How less like a bird could this woman be? She laughed light and low, her voice muddied with sleep.

"You okay?"

She felt Rennie's arms tighten around her chest. Hannah stretched, feeling Rennie's soft breasts and hard abdomen against her back. She was so ready. She raised her head and moved her cheek along Rennie's, soft and smooth against her own. She felt Rennie respond, moving against her, her hands moving down Hannah's sides to her hips, on to her thighs and then back. Hannah shifted her hips, moving closer into her. Rennie made a low sound and then spoke.

"We really need to go."

"Yes." Hannah rested her hands on Rennie's, following her motion along her body.

"We really should go, now."

"Yes."

Rennie stopped the movement of her hands, suddenly, and Hannah opened her eyes. Rennie was looking at her, their mouths almost touching. She looked serious and sad in the shadows, her face flushed with desire.

195

Hannah cleared her throat. "When?" She wanted her now.

"Soon."

"How?"

"I don't know." Rennie leaned closer. She seemed ready to take her in, stopping just before their lips met. "I'll find a way."

Hannah could barely breathe. "Promise me."

Rennie nodded. "Count on it."

Hannah stood, slowly, and offered Rennie a hand, pulling her up and into an embrace. They stood like that for a long moment, Hannah's face in the curve above Rennie's collarbone.

"Let's go. It won't be long now and then we can truly rest."

They walked, as they had walked for so long. It seemed to Hannah that she had spent a lifetime in these woods. The night was dark and Rennie led. Then the ground leveled and the walking was easier. Hannah's nerves ate at her. They were so close now she felt that disaster must surely strike at any moment. It was her nature. A pessimism born of her past. All that's good can be wrested from you even before you realize what is happening, before you realize your life is over. But she had already been through this. In her cell, she had believed her life was over, that she would never get out. She just didn't have the courage to end it on her own terms. She remembered discovering a tear along the edge of her blanket. They had given it to her that first day, when she was still dazed from the drugs. It was dirty but amazingly hadn't rotted. She had pulled on the tear, had seen that it would rip straight and if she persisted she would have a three-inch wide strip of strong material that would wrap snugly around the beam above her cot.

For weeks she obsessed on that tear, fingering it, tempted to continue it. The blanket was pale blue, a roughly woven cotton that made her think of bawling babies, of life just beginning as she fantasized about ending her own. She wondered how they might have acquired it—a fund drive at the mosque? Little old ladies rooting through their drawers to find something they no longer wanted, to donate to a good cause? When she would lie awake at night, the blanket drawn up to her chin, she'd tuck the ends tight around her throat, relishing the sensation of what was possible, an end to everything, a comfort. One night, lying in the darkness, she decided she would do it as soon as the sky began to lighten. Then she slept, more deeply than she had since she'd been taken. When she woke, it was late, she had slept far past dawn. Her stall had warmed and she had kicked the blanket off her body during the night. But the ends were still tight around her neck. She was soaked with sweat from the complete absence of circulation in the stall and the rough, damp fabric pressing against her throat felt like an attack. She clutched at it as if it would strangle her, and tore it from her neck. She put her legs on the floor, sat up on the edge of the light cot, careful not to tip it. Her face in her hands, she squeezed her eyes tightly shut, knowing she would never do it and knowing the tears wouldn't come.

Hannah took a deep breath. Recalling that time always filled her with dread. But here in the woods, moving toward freedom, she could feel its power recede. She drew a finger along her neck. Her bones were still intact. She could still feel the ghost of Rennie's breath.

CHAPTER NINETEEN

Rennie felt her adrenaline begin to surge like a racehorse at the gate, and it was all she could do to hold herself back from breaking into a run. They were that close.

All the horrors of the past week began to shimmer and fade in the face of this. She knew the terrors would return, perhaps in the night, rising up in the dark, but now all she could think was— reach the village, drop the documents with the CIA contact, go home. Every other concern slipped into a distant second place.

As she walked, she realized she had been imagining time for the promise she had made to Hannah. In a boarding house. On the plane home. Foolish adolescent fantasies. As soon as they left the country, the FBI would want them as far away from one another as possible. They couldn't risk any connection between Rennie and Armin's death. She shouldn't be thinking about this now. It was completely beyond her control. And she despised surrendering control over her own life.

Rennie pressed the button to illuminate her watch face. 2300 hours. 11:00 PM. Then her eye caught the change in the light up ahead as the woods ceded to the field where days before she had floated down in the blackest of nights. A shiver rippled up her spine. She felt the tension in her forehead smooth. She closed her eyes for just a moment.

Thank you.

She turned to Hannah and watched her face change as she took in the sight.

"Is this it?" she said quietly.

Rennie nodded.

Their shared instinct may have been to break into a run, but they both seemed to feel the weight of the moment and slowed their pace. Each had been transformed through their experiences—Hannah in ways Rennie could only imagine. She wanted to take her in and wipe it all away, but knew nothing was that simple. For herself, Rennie wondered how she would be changed by all that had happened. Would she be the same or did she even want to be the same woman who'd jumped from the plane a week before? A woman who took no chances, who kept herself safe, at least in regard to her heart. Her career might be over when she got home. She vowed to open herself, to surrender to something that might be real. So much had happened in these woods. Death and terror. And a connection was wrought between her and Hannah. She couldn't know whether it would survive reentry into the world.

Beyond the field was the road and from there it was only a short walk to the village. Rennie felt her mind settle. Thoughts of the future and of the past would have to wait. It was time to finish this thing, finish it as cleanly as she could.

"We need to change into fresh clothes before we get to the village. The locals don't appreciate Western women in pants, let alone Western women covered in blood and dirt."

Rennie dropped her pack to the ground. She pulled the shirts and pants from the pocket where they were compactly stored. Hannah turned her back as she changed. She wore no bra and her ribs seemed even more defined in the moonlight. Rennie stripped quickly, dressed, and bent to pick up the satellite phone and clip it onto her waist. The moment it was in her hand the call-in signal light began to glow.

Now what?

She raised a finger to Hannah indicating for her to wait and squatted, punching the numbers on the phone, expecting the worst.

"We're secure. Vogel?"

"Yes."

"Location?" Rennie thought she could hear tension in Ryder's voice.

"We're almost out of the woods. We'll be on the road in minutes."

"Good. There's been a change of plans."

Rennie put her hand on the stock of her sub-gun.

Ryder continued, "CIA has lost contact with their agent in the village. Garrison may have her."

Brilliant.

"Orders?"

He paused. "I have CIA on the line who will brief you."

"Agent Vogel?" Rennie heard a woman's voice.

"I can hear you. Go ahead."

"We've lost contact with our case officer, Margot Day, and think she may have gotten into some trouble." Her voice hardened before she spoke again. "As you are the only U.S. personnel on the scene, we would appreciate any help you can give us."

I bet.

The woman gave Rennie the location of the boarding house, which they were only aware of because of her document. She also gave her Margot Day's address in the village. Garrison's son would arrive in a couple of hours, probably too late to use as bait.

"You need to move, Vogel. Garrison won't take much time

with her. He'll take what he can get and move on."

"Understood."

"And be careful." The tone of her voice sounded as if this advice was pointless.

Rennie keyed off the phone and pulled on her pack. Hannah was looking at her expectantly.

Rennie shook her head. "There's something else we have to do." She told Hannah about the call.

"Sometimes I feel like this is never going to end."

Rennie laid her hand gently on Hannah's shoulder. "It will. I promise."

They crossed the threshold, where woods became a sea of grass without fanfare, wading into the long tendrils. She could hear sheep in the distance. Rennie glanced over at Hannah. She was fully alert now, the transition having shaken off her fatigue. Her features seemed almost electric with awareness as she took each careful step. The field was vast and Rennie thought of the farmer who cared for the land and wondered if he ever paused as he worked the field and thought of what lay beyond the woods. Rennie knew next to nothing about agriculture. The landscape of her youth was defined by a few city blocks.

They made their way through the field, apprehension replacing excitement. Before they stepped onto the road, Rennie looked back one last time at the woods, looming dark and gothic, like a great beast.

Martin Garrison was tired. Exhausted to his very core and had been for a long time. Before this business with Jonathan came up, he'd been thinking of stepping back and settling into the inevitable desk job. He knew he would never leave the CIA, move on to politics or any of the other natural transitions. No, the Agency was so tightly knit into the fibers of his consciousness, he knew he would be lost without it. Even the idea of retirement caused him to feel himself instantly diminished, shrinking before the thought of day after day of nothing.

And now. His final "mission." Terrorizing a colleague. His

heart wasn't in it and he knew he was unwilling to do what was necessary to extract the information he needed from her. If she even knew anything. And he was running out of time.

Garrison reached over and snapped on the light. The woman had begun to shake again. The two of them had been sitting in darkness for over an hour. He wasn't going to get anything from her unless he stepped up the pressure. And that meant hurting her or making her believe that he would.

He couldn't do it. Not even for his son. But he *would* scare her.

"Stand up."

She stood slowly, bracing herself against the wall, weak from the stress of the moment. Still holding the gun against her, he ran his free hand over the length of her body, hidden under the soft folds of her dress. He pulled a cell phone off her waist and lay it on the bed next to the newspaper he had slipped from the back of his pants. He hadn't looked at it yet except for the cursory glance at the headlines above the fold when he bought it in the bookshop. But now, the *Guardian* lay so that the paper was exposed below the fold and his eye lit upon the headline, *Iranian Terrorist Ahmad Armin Assassinated*. He squeezed his eyes shut.

"Kneel. Hands against the wall."

Garrison kept the silencer trained on the woman and picked up the paper and laid it on his knees. He quickly scanned the article. Armin had been shot and killed during some sort of celebration, by an Iranian countryman who had subsequently been captured and had confessed.

Unlikely.

Garrison figured an American special forces unit was responsible for the shooting and had picked up Armin's messengers and the document containing Garrison's location and the information on his son's whereabouts.

Christ.

That meant that more agents were on the way, knowing this was their best chance to capture him. He had to move.

Garrison lay the paper back on the bed and scrolled through

the menus of the woman's cell phone until he found her incoming calls. The phone was set to silent and had rung three minutes earlier. A London exchange. No message.

London. Jonathan.

It seemed a likely place for him to be and if they had the document from Armin's couriers, they knew where Jonathan was. But had they captured him yet?

"Stay. Hands against the wall. Don't move a centimeter."

Garrison stood and brought the wooden armchair from the other side of the bed and positioned it in the corner. He slipped his knife from the sheath strapped to his calf under his pants. He threw back the stained bedcover, pulled the sheet from the mattress and cut it into strips.

"Stand. Slowly. And sit in the chair."

He bound the woman's arms and legs tightly to the chair, stuffing a strip of the sheet into her mouth and securing it with another strip around her head. She looked into his eyes, trying to maintain her composure. She was attractive. Blond. Her age laying lightly across her features. He wondered if she was regretting her career choice.

Garrison turned and showed her the knife, holding it delicately between his thumb and middle finger as if he were offering it up for auction. He detected the motion of the agent's windpipe as she swallowed hard. Garrison had chosen the knife for its effect. It was a narrow, tapered, double-edged boot knife that came to a very wicked point. The contoured handle was made from Grenadille, a beautiful African blackwood. He always enjoyed the reaction it produced. He smiled and shook his head. He had the ability to find amusement in almost any situation—it sickened him.

Garrison moved aside the large scarf that was draped around the woman's shoulders. Underneath she wore the traditional sleeveless shirt, cut a little lower than usual. Her breasts rose and fell beneath the delicate fabric as her breathing increased. He lifted the knife and drew the tip lightly along the outline of the shirt. She controlled her breathing. Short breaths through the nose. No chest motion. Then he took the knife up along her breastbone until the sharp point rested under her chin. Her composure failed. Her mouth tensed, her nostrils flared, her brow crumpled. Always interesting, Garrison thought.

"Where is my son?"

Her eyebrows drew together in anger. Garrison knew his tactics weren't going to work. It would take too much time. But one last try wouldn't hurt.

Garrison brought the knife down again to the outline of the shirt at the point where her cleavage rose. Again, he ran the point of the knife along the line, then he turned his wrist and the blade broke the skin. The cut wasn't deep and the blood only beaded in a broken line. Garrison watched her face. Anger looked as if it might cede to rage. This would definitely take too much time. When Garrison was a young agent he believed women to be unsuited for the life of a spy. Long experience had proven him wrong. He drew a handkerchief out of his pocket and absorbed the blood before it dripped, applying pressure to the slight wound.

"Okay."

He tucked the edge of his handkerchief into her shirt. He closed and fastened his suitcase, the *Guardian* safe inside, leaving the agent's gun on the bed, slipping her cell phone into his pocket. Before he opened the door he laid the knife, wiped clean of his fingerprints, on the floor next to it.

"Best of luck."

He opened the door and stepped into the dim hallway.

Hannah knew the walk along the road would be mercifully brief, though a part of her wished it would never end. She worried what they would find in the village. This was what she got for allowing herself to feel safe. She always fought against fatalism, that particular strain of neurosis carried down from a people who never seemed to catch a break. But Hannah trusted Rennie. Trusted in a way she never had before. She had to believe they would get through this last snag.

Snag.

She laughed to herself. Another habit she inherited from her parents. Exaggeration and understatement. An inability to express things just as they were. Fortunately, most people thought it was funny. Except when they thought it was cruel. It all depended on the tone. But whenever Hannah heard it emerging from her mouth without forethought, she questioned, *What are you running from?*

She looked up, pulling herself away from thoughts that seemed to form in the contours of the deeply rutted road. She could see the dark low shapes of buildings just ahead. Rennie had broken down her weapon and stowed it in the pack before they crossed onto the road, though she kept her pistol tucked in the waistband under her shirt. They'd abandoned Hannah's AK-47 in the field since they couldn't hide it. Hannah had carried it for so long she missed the pull of the strap on her shoulder, its deadly comfort.

"It won't be far to the boarding house once we pass into the village."

"Then what?"

"We'll have to see." She paused. "I'll keep you safe, you know?"

"I know," Hannah said. "You, too, I hope."

"Yes."

They passed the final few hundred yards quietly. They came to a house sitting alone, like a sentinel, before the village proper began. It was a rough low house made of stone and mud with a half-hearted attempt at style. There was a niche in the house wall, three or four feet deep, an abandoned entrance to the house, an old door, now sealed with mud and straw and rock. Rennie turned to Hannah with a strange look, a mixture of intensity and ambivalence. She took Hannah's hand and pulled her into the doorway, pressing her into the corner. Hannah felt the stone rough against her back. There were no preliminaries. Rennie leaned in, moving her body along the length of Hannah's, and kissed her, long and hard. Their tongues met and lingered, just for a moment, and then Rennie pulled away, looking intently into Hannah's eyes.

"Soon."

"Yes."

Hannah, finding strength in her weary limbs, drew Rennie in again and their lips met for the second time and for a moment she wasn't standing in the doorway of a crumbling house in a Third World country, a loaded automatic pressing against her hipbone—she was in a city, after a fine dinner and an even finer bottle of Chilean wine, standing in the darkened doorway of a boutique kissing Rennie, and it was absolute perfection—then the moment was broken as Rennie pulled away again.

"We have a few more things to do."

Hannah nodded taking Rennie's hand, strong and sure, as she led her back to the path.

Soon the dirt path became gravel and then something approximating pavement. Houses and shops rose up around them. They walked in silence, keeping close to the structures on the right of the street. There were signs in Russian. They walked several blocks until Rennie stopped at a corner. The entire town seemed to be in slumber.

"This is it, but I want to approach it from another direction."

They doubled back and took the first left down a narrow street where houses fronted directly onto the pavement. They turned again at the next corner and Rennie slowed her pace.

"It's just ahead. We'll go directly in if it's unlocked and find a place for you to hide while I check things out."

Hannah was afraid and it showed. Rennie took her by the shoulders.

"Everything will be fine. But just in case. Take this."

Rennie handed her the satellite phone, having her commit to memory the direct line to her FBI handler. They crossed the street heading for the doorway of the house on the corner. Rennie tried the latch and the door opened silently. The boarding house was stifling. A few feet ahead of Hannah, Rennie turned and put a finger to her lips, motioning her to stay.

The entryway was narrow and Hannah could see the proprietor asleep in a room no larger than a closet. He was snoring low and unevenly, several days growth of beard covering his cheeks and neck. Rennie crept to the doorway and peeked in, craning to see around the corner. She reached in and silently lifted a key off a board on the wall and then motioned Hannah to follow her. The key to Room 15, the room indicated on the map, wasn't on its hook.

They moved up the stairs, a few steps emitting a creak that seemed to scream out in the silence. At the first landing, Hannah followed Rennie down the hall until she stopped in front of Room 3. She fitted the key in the lock and they were in. Rennie switched on the light and set her pack on the narrow bed.

"Okay. Garrison's key wasn't on the board, so he may still be here."

Rennie checked her automatic and took two extra clips from the pack. Hannah wanted to say something, she wasn't sure what, but Rennie already had a hand on the doorknob.

"Lock the door and don't open it for anyone but me." She laid her hand on Hannah's cheek. "Hopefully I won't be long."

At the top of the stairs, Rennie pulled the automatic from her waistband and switched off the safety. She inched down the darkened hallway, thinking she heard voices and wondering if it was her imagination. There was a thin light creeping under the door of Room 15. She passed the door and stood on the opposite side. She pressed her ear to the wall, trying to pick up any sound from the room. She could hear movement. He was in there. She moved farther back, into the dark corner, pressing her body against the wall, bracing herself for whatever might come. She knew she was exhausted, but her fatigue was unable to penetrate the ever-thickening shell of her adrenaline. Realizing she was gripping the automatic so tightly her hand was becoming numb, she switched it to her left hand, and was shaking out her right when the light from under the door suddenly evaporated.

She heard the sound of the doorknob turning slowly. She readied her weapon, her body tense with anticipation. Her eyes were still adjusting to the darkness when the door edged open. Martin Garrison stepped into the hallway, ghostlike, seemingly insubstantial. Form emerged out of shadow and she could see that he was carrying a slim suitcase. His head turned, he glanced toward the corner. She stopped breathing. Not seeing her, his eyes still filled with the light from the room, he turned away. For the moment she had the advantage.

"FBI. Set down the case and put your hands on your head."

Garrison froze, turning only his head toward her as she stepped out of the shadows.

"Do it. Or you're a dead man."

"FBI? Hmm. That's interesting."

Garrison began to turn toward her. Rennie wondered how accessible his weapon was—she knew it would be close.

"Stop. Set down the case and put your hands on your head. Cooperate and you'll live to see your son," she said, using the only leverage she had.

"Yes, ma'am." His voice was light and beguiling, as if Rennie were only a minor inconvenience, but she heard a thread of tension beneath it.

Then he moved, lightning fast, turning and swinging the suitcase in a wide arc. It seemed to materialize out of the darkness in slow motion. Rennie ducked, feeling a disturbance in the air as it passed overhead. Her instinct was to fire her weapon. Double squeeze and then again. She could hear the retort in her mind, see his body crumple and fall. But she didn't want to shoot this man. Death had pervaded everything for so long and she didn't want any more of it. As the suitcase crashed against the wall, Rennie kicked out hard, catching Garrison in the ribs. She felt them give and his body arched wildly backward from the impact. She moved to slam the butt of her pistol into the back of his head, but he somehow recovered, doubling over and ducking as she made her swing at him and then coming at her with all his weight.

He crashed into her, lifting her off her feet. And then they both went down, Rennie slamming hard onto the floor. She felt her breath rush out of her with the impact and all she knew was that she couldn't breathe. She heard herself wheeze, desperate for air.

Calm, calm, calm. Do not panic, it will be the end of you. This will only last a moment.

Rennie became aware of a sharp pain in her hand. Garrison had her by the wrist and was slamming her hand against the floor to loosen her grip on her gun. Finally her lungs filled as the gun popped from her hand, unable to withstand the assault any longer. It clattered across the floor. In a moment he would have his weapon or hers in hand and she would be done for. He was heavy on top of her and she felt his beard rough against her cheek. He wouldn't be able to get to his gun without letting go of her. And then he made his move, pushing off her and reaching under his arm as he still straddled her. Rennie brought her leg up quickly and caught him between his legs. Garrison doubled up in pain as Rennie leapt up and her fist connected with his head at the temple. He flew backward and she followed him, taking him down. Grabbing him by the beard and the hair, she slammed his head against the floor. Again and again until she felt his body slacken under her. Quickly, she rolled him over, pulling the cuffs—her only pair—from her pocket. In a second his left wrist was shackled to his right ankle.

Rennie sat back on her heels, breathing heavily. Garrison lay motionless in his contorted position. She leaned over and laid her hand along his neck. His pulse was strong. She reached into his jacket and removed his gun. She completed a pass over his body and found no other weapons, only an empty sheath at his calf.

Thank God. It's done, it's done. Let this be the end.

"Are you okay?"

Rennie jumped at the sound, raising Garrison's weapon. She could barely see Hannah standing tentatively at the end of the hall. How long had she been standing there?

"You shouldn't be here," she said, lowering the pistol.

"I'm sorry." She edged slowly down the hall. "I was worried. I heard banging." She stood as still as an animal caught by a bright and sudden light. "I was worried," she said again.

"Stay there. Don't move."

"Okay."

"You should have stayed in the room."

Rennie could see her taking in the scene. Rennie looking beaten, a man still and twisted before her. Rennie felt like she had been caught at something sordid. And maybe she had. She was so tired she wanted to just lie down next to Garrison and sleep. She looked again at Hannah, her expression unreadable in the darkened hallway.

Rennie retrieved her automatic from the corner where it had flown and stood with difficulty. Never had she felt more like an old woman, her muscles stiff, drawn tight against the bone with exhaustion. Garrison began to stir, a low groan emitting from his throat.

Rennie eased open the door to his room and switched on the light. A knife lay on the floor just inside the door and a gun was on the stripped bed. A blond woman dressed as a Tajik sat in the corner of the room, gagged and bound to a chair. A bloodied handkerchief was stuffed into the fabric of the dress above her breasts.

Margot Day.

"Are you okay?"

The woman nodded, her eyes wide.

"Rennie Vogel. FBI."

The woman nodded again and seemed on the verge of becoming emotional.

"We need to set up shop here."

Rennie stepped back into the hallway and called for Hannah, instructing her to free Margot Day. As Hannah worked on the agent's bindings, Rennie dragged Garrison into the room and closed the door. She retrieved his small suitcase from the hall. It was caved in on one side where it had smashed into the wall and she had to force it open. Dumping the contents on the bed, she found nothing out of the ordinary. She opened every seam in the lining but found nothing. Then she turned to Garrison. Whatever he had for Armin must be on him. He was still lying on his stomach and she had to roll him to his side to check his front. She found the envelope in the inner pocket of his suit jacket. She was about to raise the flap when Hannah removed the gag from Day's mouth.

"Wait."

Rennie turned to her. Margot Day was regaining her composure fast.

"What?"

"You don't have clearance."

Rennie's fingers were still on the flap. This could be her only chance to know what Garrison had that Armin wanted. Day's hands were free now. Rennie exhaled in frustration and laid the envelope on her lap. It was time to call in.

"Hannah, I need the phone."

Hannah had finished releasing Margot Day's binds. It was strange to be with Hannah around other people and Rennie realized it was the first time she had used her name.

Is it all finally over?

Hannah handed Rennie the satellite phone and sat on the bed, exhausted. For so long, time had crept along without meaning. Suddenly the world seemed to be spinning wildly on its axis. Hannah looked at Garrison lying on the floor. He was awake now. They stared at one another for a long moment before Hannah turned and lay on the rumpled bed. She heard Rennie's voice and the voice of the other agent but she couldn't take it in. Was her future being determined? Once again beyond her control?

She thought about the Baltimore apartment building where she and her parents had lived. There had been one Gentile family on their floor. They had a dog, that's what she remembered most, and a little girl her age who she played with one summer and never saw again. The dog, who always had a lint-covered

211

joint from the butcher, would approach its bone warily, unsure what to do with it. The poor animal seemed torn between two natures. Was he a creature of the wild? Or one whose instincts had been transformed into something wholly unnatural? Hannah never quite trusted the animal, never having been around dogs, unaware of their ability to adapt their nature, like people, to the ever changing world. Hannah, too, had adapted her nature, but in the opposite direction and now she had to fight her way back.

Living in D.C., she regularly went to the National Gallery. On the lower level was a room, not particularly large, with a famous Pollock. There, too, was a Rothko, vast and deep, and this was what she came to see. A field of orange and yellow ceding to an ambiguous black border. Standing before it she'd often heard the remark, *Well, anybody could do that.* In those moments, Hannah, who was a cynic, felt for all of mankind, for those who could see the Rothko and want to drown in it and for those who couldn't.

Closing her eyes, she thought of the orange and the yellow, its vibrancy and fecundity, and of the monochrome fields of black and gray that Rothko produced before his suicide. How long had she lived with the black and the gray, keeping that glorious burst of color her heart's secret?

When she returned to life, she would bring in the orange and the yellow and maybe even red. *Yes, red.* She would place a beautifully cut red sofa in the midst of her monochrome world. As a reminder of what she had learned and must never forget.

CHAPTER TWENTY

Martin Garrison had lived his life walking the precarious line of simultaneously adhering to the rule of law and flouting it at every turn. At home, he'd done what was expected of him—attended meetings on time, applied the social graces appropriately and climbed the Agency ladder, skipping a rung here or there but never climbing over anyone. But when he was on assignment, on foreign soil, and tasked with undermining the existing power structure, all bets were off. There was only one priority, one rule—allegiance to your own country. Aside from that one restriction, he was a free man, with leave to maim and kill, lie like a sociopath and illegally obtain whatever he required for his mission. Many agents crossed the line, drunk on a kind of autonomy most people who were fortunate enough to live in civilized society never had a chance to taste. Garrison had crossed the line before, but never so far that he couldn't cross back. Until now. He had betrayed his country in an attempt to repair the nearly rotten fabric of his relationship with his son.

Garrison shifted uncomfortably in his seat on the military transport. He had no knowledge of where he would be taken. His colleagues, the CIA agents Rennie Vogel had handed him to, weren't telling him anything. He heard the engines of the plane rumble to life, a deep, almost comforting vibration beneath his shackled feet. His hands were shackled as well—the metal cuffs tight, biting into his skin. It was a familiar sensation—he had gotten himself into scrapes all over the world—but never had it felt so permanent. A small tornado formed in his brain as the knowledge that he was no longer free, and would likely never be free again, gripped him like a vise.

Rennie Vogel. FBI. He bristled at that. His capture should have been effected by his own agency. She was obviously a part of their new counterterrorism special operations group. He wondered why she was alone and if she had carried out the assassination on Armin. Women in special forces. He'd never thought he would see it, never thought it possible. She was incredibly strong for a woman not more than five-eight. Her body, compact, almost elegant, belied her strength. But Garrison knew that strength could come from anatomy or it could come from desire. And when he'd encountered her, felt her react as he tried to take her down, he saw her will overcome any limitations her sex imposed on her. He thought again of the great Russian novelists and how literature, the great literature of the past, had failed to consider woman in all her many and varied permutations.

Garrison heard the distinctive clank of heavy boots on the corrugated metal steps of the plane. A close-cropped bearded head came into view followed by more footsteps on the stairs— these much lighter—and then the pale blue eyes of his only child met his own.

His breath nearly escaping him, he stood quickly until the hand of the burly agent next to him clapped his shoulder forcing him back into his seat. Garrison turned to the man—they hadn't exchanged a word since he was escorted aboard the plane.

"Please."

The man nodded. "Just keep yourself in check."

Garrison rose slowly, taking in the vision of his son—was it an illusion?—as he walked toward him. It had been almost a year. He was still blond as the sun and slight as a girl. How could this frail creature be any son of his? So like his mother.

Jon was cuffed as well, at the wrist and the ankle, and as they made their way toward each other, slow and sure, the links of their chains rang out in the silence of their cabin. They stood, almost chest to chest, staring into each other's eyes—what was there to say, after all?—until finally their heads dipped onto each other's shoulders, as close to an embrace as they had ever shared.

CHAPTER TWENTY-ONE

Dushanbe, Tajikistan

Rennie sat on the lumpy, standard floral-patterned sofa in her suite at the Best Eastern Tajikistan Hotel. She was clean and wearing fresh clothes. Somehow they'd found her a pair of loose cotton pants and a T-shirt. She warranted a suite because her government wanted to keep her at arm's length—nowhere near the embassy or the intelligence offices—and they needed enough room for her preliminary debrief. There weren't many decent places to stay in Dushanbe and the Best Eastern was the best of the lot, which wasn't saying much.

Sitting across from her, on what she imagined was an equally lumpy sofa, patterned the same, sat three representatives from the FBI, looking uncomfortable in such a casual setting. Too bad they couldn't order a cocktail—it would likely benefit them all. The CIA had already come and gone—somehow they had finagled first dibs at her—and she was tired, having slept only a few hours on the flight from the village.

Rennie was tense, the weight of all that had happened in the last week pressing hard on her. They had already covered the details of her ordeal—just the facts, ma'am—and here came the hard part. She could feel the shift in the way the men held their bodies as they geared up for her interrogation.

Agent Randolph, seated in the center of the sofa, his suit slightly shiny at the knees, spoke first. "Agent Vogel, I know the ambush of the team was an intensely traumatic experience, but tell me why you didn't call in after it occurred."

Rennie could have given an excuse, had thought she would when this moment came, but she was too soul-weary to attempt to salvage her career. They would have to take it for what it was. She began to speak but her voice caught. Covering her mouth with her hand, she cleared her throat.

"I knew that if I called in I would be instructed to turn back. I thought I owed it to the team, after the sacrifice they made, to continue."

The agent to his left, Abrahms, the most senior of the group, narrowed his eyes at her. "You must have recognized what little chance you had of success. While I respect your sentiment for your team, I think it was woefully misguided. On your own you were at high risk for failure and capture. Caught with a sniper rifle, you would have put the United States in a very bad position."

"But I wasn't caught," Rennie said, meeting his eyes. But she knew they were right.

"Such risks are unacceptable, Agent Vogel. We're not mercenaries. You know we don't operate that way."

Rennie didn't respond. What would her assent imply? His tone was that of an accusation but she didn't think they would charge her with anything—anything so public would only serve to draw attention to their own misconduct. They weren't even recording her debrief. No, whatever punishment was meted out to her would be on the quiet.

"Do you agree?"

"Yes."

"Good. I'm sure you understand that your decision-making on this issue will be further questioned once we return to the States."

And there it was. She probably wouldn't be fired but she was unlikely to ever have any input into her choice of assignment again. Here was reality. She could win the day and still go home looking like a failure.

They all sat in silence as Abrahms made notes on his pad. Then he glanced at Agent Gerard at the opposite end of the sofa. Gerard was small but strong, his physique apparent under his well-cut gray suit. Sitting with his ankle on his knee, he leaned forward and took a surprisingly delicate sip from the glass of water on the coffee table between them.

"Renée Vogel." He spoke her given name, which he knew she never used, dispensing with her title as if he were personally stripping it from her. "I want to talk about Hannah Marcus."

Rennie met his hard look without wavering. On this one point she was absolutely confident in her actions.

"After making it through the woods, securing a position from where you could make your shot, you discovered Hannah Marcus alive."

"Yes."

"Then, with only minutes before you would lose your opportunity to successfully hit Armin, you left the woods, slit the throat of Fareed Reza, brought Hannah Marcus back with you to your position and situated the M2 explosive under the armory to make a disturbance." He paused as if he couldn't accept the next fundamental point. "*Then*, you made the shot."

"That's accurate." And it was. Her week from hell distilled to a paragraph.

Gerard chuckled and shook his head. "I have to hand it to you, Vogel, well done. You got a lot done in those few minutes." His demeanor changed. "Of course, you broke protocol at every step."

Rennie accepted his challenge. "You're suggesting I should

have made the shot and left Hannah Marcus?"

"I'm not suggesting it, I'm telling you that. You were lucky and your mission was not designed to factor in luck. Sometimes we have to make hard decisions for the good of something larger than ourselves."

Rennie sat forward. She said evenly, "She was right there in front of me. I could see the expression on her face through the scope. An American hostage who no one was going to rescue. Our policy and the economic constraints of her parents guaranteed that. It was a miracle she was still alive. And I knew that even though I would risk exposure by leaving my position, doing so would also allow me to create the diversion with the bomb, which may be the only thing that saved us. The design of our mission was never flawless. Risks were built into it. My actions, though against protocol, only made it more certain of success."

Rennie paused. "Tell me, Agent Gerard, would you have left her there?"

Gerard returned her stare but didn't answer.

For the next twenty minutes they returned to particulars. Had she noticed anyone else in the camp who looked like they might have a position of importance? How would she characterize Armin's men? Rennie knew these were questions designed to corroborate Hannah's account.

"Okay then. That will do it for now."

As they were gathering their things, she stood and spoke. "I understand that my fate in the Bureau is yet to be determined. Standards or no standards, the FBI will see what they want to see. You know as well as I do that I got this job done under impossible circumstances and rescued an American thought lost along the way."

Abrahms closed his briefcase and stood. "That will be kept in mind, Agent Vogel."

Rennie suddenly felt directionless. "What happens when I get back?"

"I can't speak to that. Because of the particular sensitivity surrounding this incident, it will likely be dealt with outside of the usual framework."

"Will I see active service again?"

Abrahms glanced at Gerard, his lips tight against one another. "I wouldn't bet on it."

CHAPTER TWENTY-TWO

When they were gone, Rennie stripped off her clothes and stepped into the shower a second time. In a way she felt that she would never be clean. She knew now that the CIA had, indeed, murdered Nasser Armin. They had shown her the photographs Margot Day hadn't allowed her to see. Shown her, and emphasized that the truth could never be revealed. She understood the impact it could have on national security and how it would undermine the credibility of the United States. But how much had the FBI known? She had to question if CT3 had been used to silence Ahmad Armin who was determined to embarrass the United States by proving their culpability in Nasser's death. She might never know if they had just cause to assassinate Armin but fully realized that she couldn't consider such things now.

She knew the agents were there as a faction of the organization that had wanted her to fail. And they would write the report that way, no matter what the facts. The administration would accept it and that would be it. And she would be the scapegoat. The FBI's experiment with women in special forces would likely continue. There was no turning back from that now. But what her role would be was uncertain.

Would there be a place for her? She could never tolerate staring at a computer screen all day. Even after everything she'd been through. She wouldn't go back to that. If active service was no longer possible she'd have to rethink the FBI. She'd have to make her way somewhere else.

As the steaming water ran over her aching muscles, Rennie thought instead of Hannah in the next room. Was this thing, wrought between them in the most unlikely circumstances, what mattered most in the end? Was their connection born of something real? Or merely a product of two people cleaving together in a desperate situation? How could she know until she tested the water—something so potentially inhospitable to the safekeeping of her soul that she might drown before she surfaced?

Here they were so close, the government saving expense by keeping them in adjacent rooms to necessitate only one guard in the hall. They weren't meant to see one another ever again. As they told her, national security was at stake. But here was something she wanted.

You can't always get what you want.

But she had never believed that. It was her birthright as an American to believe that everything she wanted was there for the taking. You only had to want it enough. And be willing to do what it took to get it. That was what had gotten her so far in the FBI.

Rennie felt her mind clear and her muscles relax in the heat. She cut off the shower and reached for a towel.

Hannah Marcus lay in bed in her room. It felt like heaven. She had bathed and eaten and slept. All of the things that formed that first step in her return to humanity. Now all she needed was

222

a cup of coffee and the *New York Times*. And a smoke.

After being gently grilled by what seemed like every conceivable agency of her government, she was finally left to herself. So concerned were they for her, she had to wonder if they were worried she might sue them. A year and a half of her life lost. Gone. Disappeared. Life taken as payment for the sins of her government. Had they been negligent? And how much was that worth? Anything at all? Confinement had caused her to take stock. Day in and day out she'd had to ask if she was worth saving. But whenever she asked herself what made a life worthwhile, she was unable to come up with a satisfactory answer. Or maybe she was just unwilling to confront how selfish she had been.

Now, relishing the sensation of her naked limbs under the cool, rough sheet, she doubted anything would be different when she got home. How could it be? Could a woman change her nature? And did she even want to, becoming some self-sacrificing bleeding heart? She couldn't contemplate the mysteries of her life, could only delve into sensation, so long lost. Before her confinement she had always slept nude. She didn't feel quite comfortable doing so now, but she needed something familiar.

Tension tweaked at her consciousness. Thoughts of Rennie kept intruding. She tried to keep them out, knowing she had no power to get what she wanted. She wondered if Rennie was even still in the country. Her promise in the woods returned to her and she kept an ear tuned to any movement at her door. But she knew it was only the FBI guard shifting his position in the hallway, probably dying of boredom.

It was hot in the room, almost unbearably so. She threw off the sheet and climbed out of bed. She threw back the curtain and opened the door to her balcony. Fresh air streamed into the room. She found it strange how free she felt, standing nude at the open door in the darkness looking out over the city. The moon was massive, low and shining so much light that she covered her eyes with her hand and stepped back into the room for fear she might be seen. She knew she should sleep—she was to fly home early the next morning—but this first taste of autonomy was too delectable to let pass.

She slipped on the thin robe hanging on the back of the bathroom door and peered through the peephole into the hall. She could see the middle-aged agent who looked like he was fighting to keep himself awake leaning against the opposite wall, chewing on the cuticle of his thumb. She eased open the door.

"Hi. I was just wondering, do you think there is any way you could have someone get me a couple of beers?" The agent just stared. "Listen, I'm having trouble sleeping and I thought it might help me relax."

The agent looked annoyed under his nearly inscrutable expression. "I'll see what I can do."

"Thanks," Hannah said as sweetly as she could and closed the door, locking it. She could hear the agent talking faintly and was already dreaming of a cold bottle and the feel of the alcohol seeping into her tired limbs. She lay down again on the bed, the moonlight streaming over her body. She didn't know how much time had passed when there was a light tapping at the door. For a moment she entirely forgot about her request and rushed to the door fully expecting to see Rennie standing before her. The agent held two brown bottles, a smirk on his face.

"I'm a miracle worker. They're even cold."

The door barely closed, Hannah twisted off the cap of the bottle with a corner of her robe. She took a long pull on the beer, a light and crisp Russian lager. Too perfect. She let the robe slide from her body to the floor, enjoying the heat and the light breeze through the open door of the balcony.

She stood again at the moonlit door, careless now of being seen, her arms wide as if to bring everything before her into a deep embrace. An old Van Morrison tune strayed into her head and she moved in time to the gentle rhythm her mind was thrumming to, passing in and out of the moonlight.

Rennie leaned against the rail on her balcony. She wore a pair of khaki shorts and a tight white V-neck T-shirt. She knew what she was going to do. Only four or five feet from her balcony was

Hannah's. So close. She could see that Hannah's balcony door was open. They were on the seventh floor. A good number if you believed in that kind of thing. Rennie didn't, but inexplicably her hand rose to the St. Catherine medal at her throat.

She peered at the busy street far below. A long way down. Cars, lights red and white, clogged at a stoplight. She could have been anywhere, any city. After everything she had been through, this would be easy, right? She wouldn't allow the thought that this was madness reach the part of her brain that kept her safe.

Rennie took a deep breath and climbed over the railing, her heels on the narrow ledge, facing Hannah's balcony. One chance. She leaned forward, her heels still on the ledge, her fingers tightly curled around the railing, her body arced over the gap, now seemingly vast. Rennie felt a moment of indecision and pulled herself back in. Hannah was probably asleep, long ago succumbed to exhaustion.

No.

Rennie had said she would find a way and she could feel Hannah's pull, strong and deep, like a lodestone. She leaned forward again, reaching out with one hand for the opposite railing, deeply aware of the void just beyond her toes. She bent her knees, feeling the strength in her legs, sure of it, and leapt.

The space between the balconies seemed endless, a gaping chasm she felt she was being pulled into, when her left hand finally smacked the top of the railing and grasped it. Her other hand followed and grabbed a vertical rail. Her body swung down fast and slammed hard against the concrete of the balcony. Before her weight settled and stilled, she swung one leg up and caught her foot on the ledge. Pulling herself up, she became aware of the almost blinding moonlight. She wondered why she hadn't noticed it before. Her body pulsating with the exhilaration of the jump, she climbed over the railing and onto Hannah's balcony.

Peering through her door, Rennie saw Hannah, naked, her body awash in the moonlight, swaying to some phantom rhythm. Rennie unbuttoned her shorts, letting them drop to the balcony floor, and slipped off her T-shirt. She stepped into the room.

Hannah, her back to her, was still moving in a slow, languorous dance. Then she turned and opened her eyes.

Hannah stopped. Rennie moved in close. They stood, just inches apart, for a long, seemingly endless moment.

An image flashed into Rennie's mind. The two of them sitting side by side at a table on a sidewalk, suffused with deep red wine, the sound of the surf in the distance. Just as quick, the image was gone and she moved into her, her hipbones above Hannah's. They both kept their hands at their sides, their bodies barely touching. Rennie dipped her head to Hannah's neck and they both began to move, light and slow, the slightest sway. Finally, Rennie reached out to her and placed a hand on her ribs. So thin.

They continued moving and Hannah raised her face to Rennie's. Their lips met. Rennie took Hannah's mouth, full and open, with her own. At first slowly. A long, lazy kiss. And then their tongues came together and they began to gulp at one another. In the moonlight they stood, breast to breast, all mouth and hands and skin.

Hannah moved to the bed and lay down, pulling Rennie with her. Rennie eased down on top of her slowly, wanting the moment to last, to take in the feeling of every inch of their bodies meeting, flesh clamoring for flesh. They met then, hip to hip, and a sound escaped from their throats at the same moment, such a simple, basic human need, raised to the level of the sacrosanct. It had never been this way for Rennie, so right. Every nerve ending felt glutted with sensation. They kissed again, this time close and tight, their lips alternating above and below, their lips fitting, their bodies fitting exquisitely. Rennie lay to her side and trailed her hand between Hannah's breasts.

"Don't wait. I need you now."

Rennie touched her then. Hannah was ready. As ready as she could ever be.

They moved together. Climbing, climbing, slow and fine and smooth and deep, taking their time. Until Hannah pulled Rennie close and held her so tight their muscles seemed to meld. Rennie found herself drowning in the moment and buried her face into Hannah's neck, tasting her sweat. They held each other for a long time, Rennie draped across Hannah, until their breathing evened.

Rennie could feel the soft thump, thump, thump beneath Hannah's ribcage, in time with the beat she felt against her hand. She hated for the thump to subside. She didn't want to move. Wanted to stay inside her forever. Hot ceding to warm.

Hannah shifted and she was turning, slipping from under her and Rennie felt herself opening, laying back, her limbs slack and taut at the same time, offering herself. She felt Hannah's open mouth at her neck, her hand moving slow and sure, along her thigh, across the sharp bone of her hip. And then that desperate perfect curve, past bone where all grew soft.

The control that always made her feel so strong, that nothing could take her down, relaxed and her muscles softened and she allowed Hannah to touch her. From far away she could hear a small thin sound. It was almost a whimpering, a creature newly born and using its lungs for the first time. And then the small voice became more insistent, stronger, and Rennie recognized it as her own.

Hannah held her, sure and strong, until her body's tremors subsided. After a time, Hannah raised her face from where it rested in the cleft between Rennie's breasts. Her eyes were filled with fire, her body again tense.

"Don't tell me this will be the only time."

Rennie felt captured by her look and then her mind began to function again. How could she give any assurances knowing that the heavy-handed grasp of their government would do everything it could to smother this thing between them? But so much that had seemed impossible had shown itself to crumble under unrelenting effort.

"It won't." Rennie smiled. "It won't be the last time."

"I have to believe you."

They lay together for hours, limbs entwined. Hannah slept deeply as Rennie dozed. It was the first time she had truly rested.

227

At first, she was afraid to close her eyes. Afraid of the images that might rise up and ruin the moment. Her mind, for once, offered her a reprieve and as she held Hannah, fighting against sleep, she slipped away to a place so deep it was beyond dreams, a place of peace she had never visited. Hannah, even in her slumber, held her close until, finally, Rennie drew away from her before daylight. She kissed her lightly on the forehead, taking in her scent.

She dressed on the balcony, shivering, the heat of the night finally broken. Just inside the balcony door, she looked at Hannah one more time as she lay sleeping. Then she turned and buoyed herself for the leap back.

Publications from
Bella Books, Inc.
The best in contemporary lesbian fiction

P.O. Box 10543, Tallahassee, FL 32302
Phone: 800-729-4992
www.bellabooks.com

WARMING TREND by Karin Kallmaker. Everybody was convinced she had committed a shocking academic theft, so Anidyr Bycall ran a long, long way. Going back to her beloved Alaskan home, and the coldness in Eve Cambra's eyes isn't going to be easy. $14.95

WRONG TURNS by Jackie Calhoun. Callie Callahan's latest wrong turn turns out well. She meets Vicki Brownwell. Sparks would fly if only Meg Klein would leave them alone! $14.95

SMALL PACKAGES by KG MacGregor. With Lily away from home, Anna Kaklis is alone with her worst nightmare: a toddler. Book Three of the Shaken Series. $14.95

FAMILY AFFAIR by Saxon Bennett. An oops at the gynecologist has Chase Banter finally trying to grow up. She has nine whole months to pull it off. $14.95

DELUSIONAL by Terri Breneman. In her search for a killer, Toni Barston discovers that sometimes everything is exactly the way it seems, and then it gets worse. $14.95

COMFORTABLE DISTANCE by Kenna White. Summer on Puget Sound ought to be relaxing for Dana Robbins, but Dr. Jamie Hughes is far too close for comfort. $14.95

ROOT OF PASSION by Ann Roberts. Grace Owens knows a fake when she sees it, and the potion her best friend promises will fix her love life is a fake. But what if she wishes it weren't? $14.95

KEILE'S CHANCE by Dillon Watson. A routine day in the park turns into the chance of a lifetime, if Keile Griffen can find the courage to risk it all for a pair of big brown eyes. $14.95

SEA LEGS by KG MacGregor. Kelly is happy to help Natalie make Didi jealous, sure, it's all pretend. Maybe. Even the captain doesn't know where this comic cruse will end. $14.95

TOASTED by Josie Gordon. Mayhem erupts when a culinary road show stops in tiny Middelburg, and for some reason everyone thinks Lonnie Squires ought to fix it. Follow-up to Lammy mystery winner *Whacked*. $14.95

NO RULES OF ENGAGEMENT by Tracey Richardson. A war zone attraction is of no use to Major Logan Sharp. She can't wait for Jillian Knight to go back to the other side of the world. $14.95

A SMALL SACRIFICE by Ellen Hart. A harmless reunion of friends is anything but, and Cordelia Thorn calls friend Jane Lawless with a desperate plea for help. Lammy winner for Best Mystery. Number 5 in this award-winning series. $14.95

FAINT PRAISE by Ellen Hart. When a famous TV personality leaps to his death, Jane Lawless agrees to help a friend with inquiries, drawing the attention of a ruthless killer. Number 6 in this award-winning series. $14.95

STEPPING STONE by Karin Kallmaker. Selena Ryan's heart was shredded by an actress, and she swears she will never, ever be involved with one again. $14.95

THE SCORPION by Gerri Hill. Cold cases are what make reporter Marty Edwards tick. When her latest proves to be far from cold, she still doesn't want Detective Kristen Bailey babysitting her, not even when she has to run for her life. $14.95

YOURS FOR THE ASKING by Kenna White. Lauren Roberts is tired of being the steady, reliable one. When Gaylin Hart blows into her life, she decides to act, only to find once again that her younger sister wants the same woman. $14.95

SONGS WITHOUT WORDS by Robbi McCoy. Harper Sheridan's runaway niece turns up in the one place least expected and Harper confronts the woman from the summer that has shaped her entire life since. $14.95

PHOTOGRAPHS OF CLAUDIA by KG MacGregor. To photographer Leo Westcott models are light and shadow realized on film. Until Claudia. $14.95

MILES TO GO by Amy Dawson Robertson. Agent Rennie Vogel has finally earned a spot at CT3. All too soon she finds herself abandoned behind enemy lines, miles from safety and forced to do the one thing she never has before: trust another woman. $14.95

TWO WEEKS IN AUGUST by Nat Burns. Her return to Chincoteague Island is a delight to Nina Christie until she gets her dose of Hazy Duncan's renowned ill-humor. She's not going to let it bother her, though. $14.95

Bella Books

The best in contemporary lesbian fiction

P.O. Box 10543, Tallahassee, FL 32302
Phone: 800-729-4992

www.bellabooks.com